CW01336780

elmos konis

MAGNETTE

A CYPRUS ODYSSEY

Magnette - a cyprus odyssey

Published by Armida Publications 2010

Printed and bound by
Kailas Printers and Lithographers Ltd, Nicosia, Cyprus

ISBN 978-9963-620-74-6

Armida Publications
P.O.Box 27717, 2432, Engomi, Nicosia, Cyprus

www.armidapublications.com

elmos konis

MAGNETTE

A CYPRUS ODYSSEY

armida | 2010

CHAPTERS

to my son Kris

Prologue

Perhaps only once in a lifetime for most of us, if we are lucky, we get to meet somebody who profoundly affects our lives, the way we think and the way we behave.

The following is an account of such an encounter. I have tried to keep it as close to the facts as I recall them. Because sometimes real life and real people are larger than fiction.

I hope I have done it justice.

"I tell you, someone will remember us,
even in another time."

Sappho (c. 630 BCE)

He was in a deep slumber when it hazily made its way first through his subconscious and then his conscious mind. He opened his eyes and remained very still.

There! He heard it again. A rasping sound… Like some kind of a scratching noise. He wondered what it was. Where it was coming from. Probably a damned rat, munching onto something down in the basement. Maybe making its merry way through a book, he thought with mild dismay. He did not abhor rodents as much as most other people did. Of course he did not exactly like them either. Nobody did. But he could tolerate their existence. At least till tomorrow morning. He made a mental note to do something about this problem first thing. With that thought he was about to slide into deep sleep once more.

But then he heard something again. A louder sound this time. Now he snapped fully awake. This was different. More rhythmic. He tried to locate its source. Much harder to do this with the lights out…

It was coming from the door. The front door. Like a tap, exaggerated by the darkness and the silence of the night. He waited, again, for what seemed like minutes. Nothing.

"Just my imagination," he concluded, relieved.

Still, he decided to go check the door anyway. As he got up he stumbled onto something on the floor. He switched on a dim bedside light. It was the book he had been reading the night before. A big old thick Bible. He picked it up to put it on the small table. He glanced at the open page at the last line he had been reading before he dozed off:

"Repent, for the kingdom of heaven is at hand!" (*Matthew 3:2*)

He shuddered and closed it. He carefully made his way to the front door. He looked through the peep hole. It seemed unusually quiet out there, even for this time of the night. Then he wondered what time it actually was. Instinctively he glanced toward the grandfather clock in the corner, but it was too dark to make out the dials.

"Nobody out there," he mumbled to himself, but he kept looking anyway. It disturbed him a little that it was so quiet.

Suddenly, a big eye appeared right in front of him. Somebody outside was looking at him, magnified through the peep hole. He jumped back, shocked. Now there was a knock on the door, loud and clear. Followed by another.

"Who is it?" he asked in panic, not daring to look through the hole again.

No reply, just another couple of knocks, persistent.

He felt really sad. Of course he knew who it was. Who was he fooling? He made his decision. He reached out to turn the key to unlock the door. Then he slowly, resignedly turned the door knob to the left to open the door. He expected the worst but still he continued.

The door swung open. His eyes were stung by the bright light.

He sat up in his bed. He looked around him, sweating, perplexed. What was he doing in his bed? He sat there motionless, thinking, for a full thirty seconds. It took him that long to figure out that it had all been a dream. The morning sun rays were shining right onto his face, through the half open curtains.

I must have driven past that place hundreds of times. And he probably sat there all those times, except when it was raining or too cold to be on the front porch of his aging house. Although he fit the general picture so well that one hardly noticed him, the house itself, when you did look its way, seemed to rest uncomfortably among the tall modern buildings around it. Yet, maybe, a long time ago, perhaps fifty years or so, it was the best in the neighbourhood.

It was my customary route to work. A shortcut I had discovered only a few weeks after getting the job at the local college. I had first tried the main avenues, a straightforward trip which literally included just three turns, but, given the heavy traffic and my propensity to leave things until the last minute, this had resulted in a few close calls with a class full of students patiently waiting for the arrival of yours truly. So I began trying various other roads, some of them to catastrophic effect, with me arriving in class drenched in sweat, looking as if I had just run a marathon. Finally I was able, through trial and error, by twisting and turning and by progressively avoiding the various traffic jams along the way, to carve out the ideal itinerary, shaving, Schumacher-like, a full six minutes off my original record.

Still, there remained one bottleneck I could not get around. Others from my area heading the same way must have gone through the same motions as I had, because this was the one busy part of the shortcut. It included a narrow street which led to a difficult turn on a main avenue which was constantly busy with traffic. Half way along this side street, on the left, sat the old house and the old man. I think no one really noticed him because of his exceptional chameleon-like camouflage. His earth grey colours, both in clothes and complexion, blended perfectly with the fading and fume-polluted paint of the aging house. But it was not only that. The house sat back, out of the way, as it was old-fashionably graced, fifties style, with a relatively large front yard. There were two tall trees, pines, and no flowers, just a few tough looking low dusty green bushes, which had possibly found their own water supply and were resigned to taking care of themselves.

The old man did not seem to have the energy to be the gardener type. The main reason so many drivers failed to notice him was his statuesque immobility. He just sat on an old wooden chair and hardly moved. I was almost surprised to see him for the first time. But after that, given the minute or so that I routinely had the house in sight I realised that he was there at exactly the same spot almost every day of the year.

So many busy people passing by and all of us focused on where we were going rather than on what was around us, a blur of buildings, cars and billboards. One morning, as I again casually glanced toward his direction to absentmindedly confirm that he was in his place, I thought I spotted the slightest of nods toward my direction. Surprised and ashamed, I turned my head away instead of doing the obvious, nodding back.

The next day I was prepared. As soon as I caught sight of the old man I performed the biggest Japanese bow I could muster, almost injuring myself on the steering wheel. But he must not have noticed, or worse, he was upset that I had ignored his greeting the previous day. We got it right at the third try. He solemnly but clearly nodded to me and I nodded back. I was glad that little misunderstanding (?) had been brought to rest.

During the following days we routinely greeted each other as my car stalled in the traffic in front of his house. In fact it got to be more exaggerated as we eventually actually waved at each other, the old man showing more spark and mobility than I thought he had in him. One day when the traffic was really slow, I happened to get stuck right in front of his house. We had already exchanged our customary greeting, so I looked back ahead. But I felt that his eyes were still fixed upon me. I turned back towards him only to see that I had been right.

How can one tell? Or is it just a logical assumption that one only thinks is some kind of sixth sense? In any case, as our eyes locked, I smiled, nodded again and opened my window without thinking much about it. The old man was a good forty feet away from the car but in Cyprus many people still do not think twice about carrying entire complicated conversations at that distance. The habit comes from the old days in villages when phones were very scarce and there were more open spaces. People would 'chat' to each other, quite loudly, for a few minutes from large distances and then go on their way. Moreover, if a third person happened to pass by and caught onto this not too private discussion, and if his vocal cords were up to it, then he too could chime in.

I noticed he had a book in his lap. So, I shouted the first three words that came to my mind:

"Sitting and reading?"

I had just committed that most irritating of conversational blunders that all of us do almost daily in our lives: stating the blatantly obvious. A colleague sees me as I am about to enter a class and asks,

"Going to class?"

Then during break as I drink my coffee another asks,

"Drinking coffee?"

And, when I am about to step into my car at the end of another day, someone at the parking lot asks,

"Leaving?"

The very next day, the old man was again at his post. I waved hello, he waved back with his right hand while he turned his left hand round and round in a circular motion, as if turning the handle of a car window. So I opened the window again for the second time in two days.

"Driving?" he asked, not too loudly but clearly enough, and then he smiled full heartedly, a smile that instantly knocked a good ten years off his face. I nodded yes and smiled back.

Say something

I have always been fascinated by anything from the past. The further back the better. I teach business administration but if I were to choose a career again, I would probably be an archaeologist or a palaeontologist.

I love going to junkyards and garage sales, not necessarily to buy stuff, but mainly, to look and touch. Objects, just like people, hold untold stories within them. If you look at, say, an old iron, you are looking at much more than a heavy piece of metal. Let your imagination do some walking and you can almost see a glimpse of its history unravel right in front of you. There is its first owner, a young lady, dressed in traditional Cypriot clothing, preparing the hot coals to place in the iron. Open the lid of the iron. Can you see the remains of those ashes, still there from a last action taken so long ago? The very next day the family had replaced this iron with an electrical one. When was that? Can you guess? Would you like to know? Once you make this much out, then maybe you can look around and see more: The coarse clothes that were about to be ironed, in a pile. The 1900's kitchen with its old stove and old-fashioned tiles, the copper pots and pans, the porcelain dishes, the blackened cutlery. Perhaps there are other people around too. The husband, sitting on a wooden chair, drinking Turkish coffee, smoking a cigarette and reading a paper, all at a leisurely pace which is long long gone.

I only buy an old item if it 'talks' to me. If it has a story to tell I'll take it. I am not an antiques expert. My criterion is never an item's value, not even its appearance. Does it have a story to tell me? I am sold. I have collected all sorts of things this way, some of them from around the world. I have a couple of two-thousand year old Roman coins. A few years ago I picked up a more modern '5 centesimi, 1861' Italian coin with the bust of a King Vittorio Emanuelle II on the heads side. I found that one in a decrepit antique shop in Rome, run by an old lady. I paid one whole euro for it. Later I looked up the coin's year of production. Modern Italy was created that very year. Venice was not yet even part of the country at the time. I have many other coins as well. For example, there is one from the Soviet Union depicting Stalin, another from Germany, a Swastika on the tails side. Coins, having passed through a lot of hands, had busy lives and have a lot of things to say. I also possess old pocket watches, so out of place now, hidden in my desk-drawers. A long time ago they snuggled proudly in gentlemen's waistcoat pockets.

If you open those same drawers you can see a disorganised assortment. Fragments of ancient painted pottery, silver matchboxes, old chocolate tins, and so on. I have a small worthless fragment of a dinosaur tooth. I found that one on the shore of Lake Mary at Glacier Park in Montana, back when I was studying at the local university. Touch it and you can almost hear the terrible roar of the great Tyrannosaurus Rex. Feel it, cold, right there in your palm.

It is a fact. Objects, just like people, hold untold stories within them. Finding them out can be interesting or fun or even a cause for regret.

The old man probably had a sense for suspense, because he proceeded with the unveiling at a snail's pace, as if he had all the time in the world.

I had not even noticed that there was a garage to the left of the house. In fact, it was not much of a garage. Just four rotting, thick, wooden posts and a flimsy tin roof, only barely sufficient to keep the rain out. There was a car under there, no doubt, but it was concealed by an old rugged, weather-worn canvas cover.

By now there was no doubt that this old, lonely man looked forward to seeing and greeting me on a daily basis. Did he live alone? It seemed that way, for I never saw anyone else around. Could he take care of himself? I hoped so.

Although I never happened to see him get out of his chair, he, or someone else, or perhaps just the wind, moved the canvas cover off the car, a little at a time. But I suspect it was the old man himself, because he turned his head toward the car the first couple of times immediately after we had exchanged our daily greeting. He wanted me to look that way.

I could tell it was not a new car even before I saw any of its body. I could tell by the hump of the canvas that the design was not a modern sleek one. I could not discern an immediately recognizable outline, like that of the VW Beetle. It seemed slightly shorter than that and a touch longer. When I eventually got to see the front bumper and the bottom half of its grille, I still could not guess its brand. Certainly it was no Bentley. Was it a Morris Minor, so common on the Cyprus streets about fifty years ago? It couldn't be, this one was surely much longer. Then I thought maybe it had the old Volvo cut, its dimensions and even the headlights seemed to fit that model. Or was it a Mercedes? A Singer? Like I said I am no expert.

The old man had won. I was curious. I looked at my watch. I had some time to spare, for once. I parked off the road and got out of my car. He was sitting where he was supposed to be, in his wooden chair on the veranda.

"Good morning," I called out as I approached.

"And a good morning to you sir," he replied, with a broad smile, seemingly not one bit surprised that I had been defeated by curiosity. So, I immediately got onto the subject.

"Is that your car under there?" He nodded yes and all but jumped out of his chair, displaying an athleticism I could not have fathomed.

"Do you want to see it?" he asked.

So we strode to the garage together.

On first glance, it seemed a typical fifties car. The car industry had finally managed to rid itself of its prototype ancestor, the horse and carriage. So, cars at this time looked less and less like the coaches of the twenties and up to the forties. But it still was, one could say, an awkward time for car design, with many hits and as many misses. What was this particular car? Perhaps something in-between. Nothing special. Except it had a large Rolls Royce-style grille, almost added as an afterthought to the otherwise conventional body. And, of course, that octagonal badge.

"An MG, eh?"

"Yes, do you know the model?" he asked.

"No, I can't say I do. It doesn't really look much like an MG. You know, endearing tiny cars, open top, two-seaters."

"You're probably thinking of the Midget or the MGA. This one's fourteen feet long. Not bad for the time. Of course, this car is a post-war model. Can you guess when it was made?"

"Early fifties maybe?" I ventured.

"Not a bad guess. Can you be more specific?"

How could I possibly. I was not even alive back then. As I pretended to contemplate, he said,

"How about a little bet? If you guess the year of production, I'll give you the car."

What? That surprised me. Was he serious?

And, anyway, I could not take advantage of a dear old man.

Or could I?

"You weren't even alive in the fifties, were you," he said. "You are right about the fifties, of course, so that narrows it down to just ten years… One in ten chance, even if you have no idea."

"You aren't serious… are you?" I looked at him, closely, for the first time.

He looked back at me straight in the eyes, his face grave. He nodded solemnly. Okay. That was that. I had to put an end to this charade right now. I took on a solemn expression.

"Sir, you don't even know me. Why would you make such a … bet? And anyway, a wager means that both sides can win something. You say if I get the year right you'll give me your car, just like that. All right then, what if I lose the bet? What do you get?"

He took his time to answer. Still, something tells me that he had already anticipated this conversation. He had probably gone through it a dozen times sitting there on his wooden chair. I momentarily wondered if he had specifically targeted me. When he finally did give his answer he did not hesitate further.

"You are right. A bet isn't a bet if one can't also lose. If you get the date right, you drive away with the car, simple. Like I said. No questions asked, as they say. Now, if you lose, you'll be my chauffeur, so to speak. Don't worry," he added hurriedly, searching my face. "I don't mean full time. I can tell you must be a busy man and a professional something. I wouldn't expect that from you. Just once a week, you will drive me around for an hour or so. Then you park the car, drop me off, and go on your way."

"Surely you can drive yourself around?" I blurted, meaning no offence. I remembered how he had just sprung out of his chair to show me the car.

"You are damn right I can," he replied with passion. "But, the bastards took my licence away. The judge threatened that he'd put me in jail if I was caught driving again. See that little scratch on the bumper?" he pointed. "Yeah, that. Well the motorbike fared much worse, I am sorry to say. The owner sued. It was his fault, cut in on me, but who listens to an old man? My bad luck; it was my second accident in a week. Doesn't everyone have a bad week?"

I empathised.

"I know what you mean. I had such a week about five years ago. Bumped into the front car at some traffic lights, fixed my car, had it painted all nice, and then crashed it again the exact same way the very next day. I'd never had an accident before that and haven't had one since."

He nodded understandingly. Then he said, "You're now probably thinking that this bet is not such a fair deal after all, what with a 90% chance that you lose. And no firm expiry date should you lose." He waited for a response, but I had none. I was still too confused. So he continued.

"So I want to make it easier for you. I'll give you some hints. I'll tell you some other things that happened that year, apart from the production of this car. You are an educated man, perhaps you will know when some of these events happened."

Why did I not stop this, right there and then? What kind

of person would even attempt to cheat an old man out of his possessions? That car must have been worth at least five thousand pounds, and that was just guessing. Perhaps more, given its near immaculate condition.

Yet, there was another perspective.

This is how I reasoned the situation: the old man was right. The odds of winning this bet were overwhelmingly against me. But, on reflection, it was not even like that. I wanted to lose that bet. If I won I would walk away, simple. I thought, what did he really want from me? Some company, someone to take him around for a little while, someone to talk to. And that was just for an hour or so, a few minutes per week. He was not asking for much. I remembered that I had never seen a single soul near the old man all those times I drove by, not even a cleaning lady. I assumed he had no one in this world. I really had no choice but to accept his bet, and to lose it too. Now, the odds were stacked 'in my favor'. Nine in ten that I got it wrong, which was my goal in any case.

"Okay, you're on," I said. We shook hands. He took a deep breath.

"All right, here's the bonus information. This car right here is the MG ZB Magnette. It replaced the MG ZA. More powerful, sixty-eight horsepower, this baby can fly. It takes a while to pick it up, almost twenty seconds to get to sixty. But it can eventually reach ninety miles per hour." He looked at me. "I presume all this doesn't mean anything to you?"

"No, you didn't help me all that much," I replied with a smile.

"Then, here's what else happened that year. You like Elvis Presley? Well, that was his year. He burst on to the scene, so to speak, even on these forgotten shores, with that hit of his that I'm sure you have heard, despite your young age: 'Heartbreak

Hotel'. Still no? Let me give you more then. You know the film, 'The King and I'?

"Sure I do. Etcetera, etcetera, etcetera," I said with my best Yul Brynner accent.

"And how about 'Around the World in 80 Days'"?

"Let me think: What's his name, Paspartu or something?"

"Of course. And here's an easy hint for you, the clincher," he added with a smile. "This was the first year of the Eurovision song contest!"

How did he know all this stuff? Did he actually remember it or had he looked it up in order to play this little game with the first sucker who fell for it? At any rate, I was still just as much in the dark. I lifted my shoulders and smiled, signalling that I recognised the momentous events he had just described, but still had no idea of a date.

"Hmm. Perhaps you're not an 'entertainment' type man then. All right. Let me think… I'll tell you what was happening in politics back then. Nikita Khrushchev was in the news a lot, as he was having an 'annus horriblis', what with the reaction to his surprise condemnation of the Russians' idolatrous adoration of Joseph Stalin, calling it a 'cult of personality' and, on top of that, having to deal with a bloody Hungarian uprising. Here in Cyprus it was pretty hectic too. Archbishop Makarios was exiled to beautiful Seychelles by the Brits… The whole world was in a bit of a mess. Not surprisingly, no one got to win a Nobel peace prize that year… Now that I think of it that should happen more often these days too."

He seemed to have more, but he stopped there, perhaps to let me reflect. In fact, he had helped. Surely, Elvis had 'burst on the scene', as he had put it, in the late 50's? And, I knew that the Cypriot uprising against the rule of the British Empire had occurred between 1955 and 1959. We all learned that in school. That is when the island's religious and spiritual leader was kicked out, was it not? If I was right, there were only five possible years remaining.

Yes, I was trying to get it right by that moment, not for the car, but because a pure competitive instinct had kicked in.

Reasoning further, he had said 'post-war' hadn't he? The late fifties would surely not really be considered as such. So, the most likely alternatives were '55 and '56. My gut told me to choose the former. And psychology books tell you that your first choice is most probably the correct one. That is what I tell my students to do when they are contemplating multiple-choice questions.

"Is it a 1955?" I asked.

"Is this your final decision?" he asked, like a game show host. There I stood, playing 'The Price (Date) is Right' as if my life depended on it.

"Yes, 1955 is my final answer," I replied, too gravely.

"Pheeew", he audibly exhaled, with the biggest grin. "This baby was actually made in 1956. (*So much for the psychologists*). That was the first year of manufacture of the ZB," he continued, matter of fact. "They went on to produce almost 20,000 of them. Far as I know, it's the only one in Cyprus. I wonder how many of them are still around. Probably no more than a couple of hundred, I'd say."

After a moment's pause he added, somewhat hesitantly, but still with a winner's glee in his eyes, "How about Wednesday?"

And that is how I got this chauffeur job.

I could not make it on Wednesdays, but Thursdays were all right. So we had shaken on it. A longish shake. His grip was firm and warm at the same time. I think it said, 'this is more than a business deal, I want to be your friend as well', or something to that effect.

Thank God I was on time, because when I got to the house, there were two Turkish coffees, along with two glasses of cold water, patiently sitting on a beat up but gleaming silver-tinted tray on a wooden chair which was similar to the one the old man himself was sitting on. He was dressed in his usual grey suit which had seen better days,his black shoes gleaming in the sun, his thick white hair neatly parted and combed.

"Hello," he said with a wide, warm grin. "Have a seat," he added motioning to the empty chair next to the coffees. "I hope you prefer your coffee *sketto* (plain, no sugar), that's how I brewed them both."

"You know, last week we forgot to introduce each other, what with the excitement of our little bet. I think I should at least know my employer's name," I added with a smile.

"Please don't say that," he said, feigning anger but smiling at the same time. "In my excitement I also forgot to tell you that there really was an expiry date for our bet, and it's not when I get to go visit Hades. Anytime you or I say so, it's over. Really. I do understand that you are a busy man, are you not?"

Instead of answering that I told him my name.

"Nice to meet you Alexis," he replied with a smile. "My name is Aris," he added.

"Aris, eh? Like the God of war?"*

"Actually my full name is Aristotle. Like the philosopher… So we meet again!" he answered on reflection. I am not sure what he meant but I think he was referring to philosopher Aristotle being the teacher and mentor of Alexander the Great back when the famous warrior king was growing up at Pella, Macedonia. Not quite the same reunion but whatever.

"Perhaps the philosopher is less glamorous, but he is still as important," I consoled him.

"You bet he is. Anyway I like to think I got a little of both," he added with a sly smile, referring now to the God of War and the philosopher.

I changed the subject.

"Ready for a ride?"

"I hope it starts," he answered, looking toward the old car.

But I knew it would. The MG was uncovered and very clean, sitting in anticipation in the garage, raring to go. Perhaps mysteriously, its nickel fenders and dark green coat ('English racing green' or something fancy like that) gleamed dully in the afternoon sunshine.

He did not sit in the back like one would for a taxi ride. He propped himself up next to me, his hand dusting an invisible speck on the dashboard. Still, I sensed that Mr. Aris felt just a little bit awkward sitting next to me in his car. It was obvious that his natural place was behind the wheel but he accepted his fate with dignity. I drove slowly onto the busy narrow side street. The ride was surprisingly smooth. All the 'antique' cars I had driven up to that time had been beat up old bangers and this must definitely have been a bit of a class act at its time. I liked the feel of the big old steering wheel. It seemed to say, 'trust me'.

---

* Ares is the Greek equivalent of Roman War God Mars.

"Where to sir?" I asked, trying to sound like a professional driver. He gave me a quick look, like to check if I was serious.

"Let's just see where the road will take us," he replied.

So we drove aimlessly around. We exchanged just a few niceties, which was a bit surprising, given the fact that he apparently wanted me for the company. Perhaps he expected me to speak up first. Maybe he was just enjoying the ride and he did not want to interrupt it with aimless conversation. Or he felt just as comfortable in silence. So, being the chauffeur, I decided to leave it to the boss.

In any case, I love driving. And this was more than just driving. It was like sitting in a time capsule. While everything outside was new, glancing at the dashboard and the well-preserved interior was like stepping back in time. The steering wheel, of course, boasted the big octagonal MG sign. The car's horn was a big shiny metal ring going half way round the wheel. And the speed dial was just perfect! An octagon, cut in half. This vehicle reminded me of my feelings when rummaging through my drawer full of old goodies, only even more so. Everything I saw and touched, even the faintly smoky dusty and leathery smell, oozed history. This effect cannot be replicated. I recently rode in a new American car, done up by the manufacturer as if it was an old model. Everything looked just right. Old fashioned round dials, 'period' buttons to push, all a true reproduction. But it still left me cold. Both the car and I knew that this was but a fancy dress party. This MG, well, it was the real thing.

As Mr. Aris did not suggest any particular direction to take throughout our ride, I just drove in the centre of Nicosia, around the city's ancient Venetian Walls. These particular streets were probably already in existence at the time this Magnette made its first appearance in Cyprus. They were acquainted with each other. Laboriously, the designated hour had passed. I drove around a little more, so as to show I was not skimping on my first day at work. I parked the car in the old garage, and both Mr. Aris and I got out.

"Next Thursday okay?" he asked with perhaps a touch of nervousness in his voice.

"No problem," I replied. I think he felt the same way I did. I was unsure about how it had gone. We had not talked much at all. I was actually concerned that we had not clicked. Maybe I had not tried enough, or had tried too much. Hell, this is how a teenager felt after a first date, not after sharing a car ride with an old man! I was a bit upset with my feelings. I was taking this too seriously.

Born to be wild

Get your motor runnin'
Head out on the highway
Lookin' for adventure
And whatever comes our way

(Steppenwolf)

The coffee was still hot when we exchanged greetings and sat down on the old porch the following Thursday. Proof that I was exactly on time.

"Where to today Mr. Aris?" I asked.

"Why don't we try the highway, give ourselves and the MG a chance to breathe a little?" he replied.

So we took to the Nicosia-Limassol highway. It was almost the end of another beautiful June day. This year Cyprus was living up to the 'sunshine-for-300-days-a-year' promise one could read on tourist brochures. Of course, to us locals such years were torture as this meant sweltering heat and drought and drying crops. But the view of the Mesaoria plains from the car was magnificent in the twilight. Mesaoria literally means 'between two mountains' in Greek: Troodos and Pentadaktylos* protectively looked down on us on either side of the car. The scorching sun was much kinder to the surroundings and the eyes by this time, transforming the day's blinding yellow-white colours to a more pleasing shade of pure gold.

Surprisingly, given the time, there were just a few cars on the road, most of them speeding past us. Of course, the car had no air conditioning but despite the heat the drive was quite pleasant with all the windows rolled down. It was generally much noisier travelling that way and our hair was blowing all over the place. But I had forgotten this 'open air' experience and I was enjoying it. That is how we all used to travel a couple of decades back, before the advent of car

* Pentadaktylos means five fingers, aptly named for the range's most interesting peak.

'climate control'. Only 'luxurious' taxis would display highly visible large stickers proclaiming in awkward but clearly comprehensible English, *full air condition*. People would be impressed. No further advertisement was needed. Each taxi door also had small stickers ordering passengers: *Don't slam the doors*, in this way merely providing further evidence to the vehicle's class. Our own private cars would require a right old swing for the doors to close firmly.

"I wonder if she can still make the speed limit," Mr. Aris questioned out loud.

"I am sure of it," I replied. "I am only pressing the pedal half way." I pressed down a little harder to demonstrate my point.

"How much are we doing?" he asked, leaning toward me and glancing toward the dashboard. We were doing about 55 mph. Soon we were holding our own on the road, reaching the speed limit, which is 60 mph* in Cyprus.

"Try to push it to 70," Mr. Aris suggested. "The cops don't book you for ten miles over."

He was right. I would often set my own car's cruise control to that speed and I had never been stopped. So I slowly pushed the MG to 70. The old car was shaking and heaving quite a bit by now, but she seemed to be enjoying the release as much as we were.

"Can you believe that there's still room for more?" I said, loudly, so he could hear me.

"Hit 80 and then slow her down," he shouted.

I hesitated. I searched up ahead as far as I could see. No police in sight. What the hell, I thought. Let's please the boss. So

---

* Speed in Cyprus is measured in kilometers/hour these days. Of course, the dials on the MG indicated mph. Drivers, especially older ones, know that 60 mph is roughly equivalent to 100 kph, the local highway speed limit.

I pressed the pedal down some more. The speed dial was still definitely, if hesitantly, climbing. By now everything on the whole car was rattling and shaking. It felt like pieces would start to fly off. The car seemed to be bouncing more than rolling on the road surface. But we made it to 80. I almost released the pedal when Mr. Aris prodded me on.

"Check if the old lady can still do what the MG manufacturer claims," he yelled, his voice barely audible in the chorus of the other noises. I sensed that by now the pedal was almost floored. Just a little more, I thought, and pressed a little harder. I felt the pedal reach its limit, but the dial was still climbing, agonizingly slowly. 85, 86, 87.

I almost did not hear the siren. But I saw the flashing lights behind me, a blur on the shuddering mirror. It took a couple of seconds to register. The exhilaration and the adrenalin momentarily refused to let go, but logic suddenly sank in, and I quickly slowed down and parked on the side of the highway. The sole policeman stopped right behind me. He marched toward us.

"Do you know how fast you were going sir?" he asked me, looking at the car with what seemed like a mixture of admiration and disdain. Before I could say anything he showed me the red numbers on his hand-held radar. It said 90!* I could not help but inwardly smile. We had hit the manufacturer's proclaimed maximum speed.

"You've got yourself an accomplice Mr. Aris?" the cop inquired, now ignoring me and looking beyond me at my copassenger. That is when I realised I had been suckered into breaking the law.

* That's 144 kilometers per hour.

Alone later, I tried to be angry but I could not. Even on reflection, the hefty fine was almost worth the excitement. The old man, myself and, yes, the Magnette, had permitted ourselves a few moments of reckless youthful abandonment and I felt that the experience had somehow bonded all three of us in a strange but palpable way. As for the car, it had convincingly proven that, despite appearances, it could still proudly adorn the octagonal badge of the once great MG.

After we had driven slowly away from the scene of the crime we were both silent for a few minutes. I was fuming. I had given Mr. Aris a stern teacher-like reproachful look and he had looked back at me with the guilty eyes of a child caught cheating in a test. A few miles further down the highway and he could not help himself. When I glanced in his direction I saw that he was smiling as discreetly as he could. What was so funny? Yet, his behaviour was childishly infectious. Before we knew it we were both snorting at first, and then laughing hysterically, tears streaming down our cheeks. It occurred to me that I had never heard an old man laughing so wholeheartedly and uncontrollably like that. For that matter, I could not remember the last time I had laughed that way. Were completely abandoned laughter and age two opposite experiences?

As I have mentioned earlier I have always been fascinated with old things. Now, I was preoccupied with two 'vintage' cases: The car and its owner. Mr. Aris was proving to be quite enigmatic. He had initially seemed almost incapacitated with age. This was obviously not true. Then, he had risked a car he clearly adored on a frivolous bet. And, at least one policeman was aware of his not so spotless driving record. No wonder they had taken his licence. Beware: public danger! Octogenarian hot rodder!

Sitting in my office at the college, I typed 'Magnette' on the search engine of my computer. There it appeared, in all its glory*. Owners from around the world had proudly posted pictures of their cars. Red ones, white ones and olive green, exactly like the one of Mr. Aris. And two-tone samples, apparently more luxurious and called Varitone. I had thought that that was a type of opera singer.

I also found out that we had apparently actually marginally beaten the manufacturer's claimed maximum speed. Perhaps Mr. Aris had knowingly exaggerated a little at the time of the bet? In any case, he had been right. His particular car could do 90. I had the certificate-ticket to prove it, on my desk right in front of me.

The MG's creator, Cecil Kimber, had this principle in mind: He said that a car must look fast even when standing still. I liked that.

I unearthed excellent old advertisements as well. I printed them out in colour and pinned them on the wall. One displayed the car's '*roomy luggage compartment*', full of quaint baroque bags of various sizes. Below, the then apparently famous campaign slogan: the words *safety* and *fast* printed right over the manufacturer's logo (*I wonder how many airbags it's got*). And here was the mouth-watering prospect of ownership: '*A superlative Luxury Car in everything but its price tag. The clean and uncluttered body lines of the Magnette are matched by its luxuriously appointed interior... deep comfortable seats upholstered in supple English leather. The instrument panel and door trim are in rich, beautifully grained polished walnut. Floors*

* Try www.magnette.org for some interesting information.

are thickly carpeted with finest...' I was sold. Imagine seeing a shiny unused version of this car, sitting in it, feasting on the untouched beautiful interior and smelling the walnut and leather. I hoped that the manufacturer or someone else had been prudent enough to save at least one Magnette that way, for eternity.

But really this was just silly sentimentality. Actually, the manufacturer could not even save its own hide, never mind an old Magnette. MG had recently closed its doors, seemingly permanently. A humiliating last gasp hope to be bought off by a Chinese conglomerate had fallen through, so it was truly all over*. One more rusty nail in the coffin of Britain's once proud automobile industry. In 2005, nobody wanted to adopt a tired 83-year-old 'child' anymore. MG had tried and tried to stay young and vivacious, but age had finally caught up with it. It should have grown up, but its 'parents' never let it, or perhaps it had not wanted to. It seemed to me that after the war poor MG had gone from one rich foster parent company to another. Few of these firms really understood what their child was about with perhaps the exception of its original dad, Morris Garages (hence the MG name). As a result, they often ended up embarrassing MG by dressing it up with funny clothes that did not suit it.

I was disappointed to find that our Magnette (Freudian slip) was considered by many MG enthusiasts to be one of the original instigators of the downfall. British Leyland, the then 'inconsiderate parent', had committed the ultimate crime of 'badge swapping'. This is like dressing up both your kids in the same clothes: another car in this company's stable, the decidedly pedestrian Wolseley had shared, almost entirely, the body and the chassis of the Magnette. How can you proudly drive

* Hopes have been rekindled again since writing this. Apparently, a Chinese conglomerate has brought back to life one MG model. Not the Magnette, however!

an MG that looks just like a Wolseley, for crying out loud? It is like your neighbour owning a Skoda that looks exactly the same as your Ferrari. This heinous crime was later committed with other boring half brothers such as the Metro and the Maestro.

On the next Thursday I telephoned Mr. Aris to inform him that unfortunately I could not make our weekly meeting. I had just remembered, I told him, that I had been invited to a colleague's presentation in Larnaca, a neighbouring city, and had already promised to attend. I felt a little bad because I had completely forgotten about this other commitment and here I was now letting Mr. Aris know just a couple of hours before our scheduled drive.

"Sorry I left it so late to let you know," I said. "I was going to call you yesterday, then I forgot and just now I was reminded again about this speech and it's an obligation I really cannot avoid. It must be difficult for you to make other plans for today now."

I should not have made that last comment. It sounded pretentious to both of us. What other plans could he possibly have? We both knew that if he had a diary it would contain only one weekly entry: our meetings.

He did his best to make it sound like it was no big thing.

The phone rang: a rather shaken Mr. Aris on the other end of the line. This was the first time he was using the phone number I had given him. I quickly glanced at my diary: Monday. Why was he calling?

"The car won't start," he said, desperation creeping in his voice. Like a relative was sick or something. What was the deal? Was he concerned for the state of health of the old MG, or was it trepidation that I would use this as an excuse to skip my weekly commitment once again?

A few hours later the Magnette was in my mechanic's garage, raised high above our heads. Mr. Aris had stayed at home, feeling a bit under the weather himself. The mechanic and I were standing underneath the MG surveying I don't know what.

"It's in good condition, given its age. It wouldn't start because of the battery, which I have changed. Still I wouldn't do 90 again in this tin can if I were you Mr. Thomas*," he added with a half smile while raising his eyebrows. His expression told me he did not quite believe my story. I wished I had brought the speeding ticket with me.

I took the car to my home. I gave it the full valet service, cleaning and waxing it and shining the ample chrome bumpers. I treated the leather interior with an outrageously expensive 'special cream' I had just bought (it smelled just like that cheap supermarket Nivea cream) and I polished the walnut dashboard. Working in such detail and proximity, I noticed for the first time the scars of time and use. Scratches here and

* Thomas is my family name.

there, the leathering cracked beyond repair in certain places. But it was true what my mechanic had said. This car had aged well. It was a youthful looking fifty-plus year old.

I then removed the back seats. Under them I found two items. A man's old comb, which made me smile. Back then, no self-respecting man would leave home without one of these accessories in his back pocket. I wondered who had dropped it when. I imagined his momentary panic when he had realised he had lost it. Tragedy! The other item I enjoyed even more: a two-shilling coin, now obsolete, the infamous chiftes*, as it was called. I was glad to say the word out loud. To 'dig it up' after it was buried in a dusty corner somewhere in the back of my mind in a drawer labelled 'obsolete words you once used very often - but will never use again'. This particular word was in so much common daily use only a few years back. Now even old people had forgotten it. They, especially, had clung on to the traditional names for money as long as they could, but they too had eventually succumbed and learned to talk sense in cents. Now the denominations for money had changed once more, from Cyprus pounds to Euros, and the elderly were struggling to cope once more.

I next got a screwdriver and proceeded with tightening any loose screws. In fact, they were all loose, in various degrees. Perhaps our little death-defying ride had contributed further to this. When I was done, I noticed that there was one screw on the carpet in front of the passenger's seat. Where had it fallen from? I could not find its place. Just when I was about to give up and throw it away, I noticed a small square metal sheet, at the lower end of the dashboard on the passenger's

---

* It was a heavy, bulky coin so to us kids it just felt valuable. Why infamous? Because people would occasionally threaten to throw it at each other when arguing or joking around, as it could perceivably cause serious damage (I never actually saw anyone carry out this threat). The word is derived from Turkish, meaning 'two'.

side. There were three screws on; one corner was missing its screw. I almost started screwing it back in its place. But then I wondered what was behind that cover. Why had the manufacturer put it there? Perhaps it was the fuse box. Or, maybe it provided easy access to some internal workings of the engine on the other side. No harm checking.

After I removed the cover, I looked to see what was there. It was at an awkward angle, I could not see a thing. I went inside the house and brought back my flashlight, shone it in. There seemed to be nothing there. Just a black back-panel. I touched it. Sure enough, that is all it was. I was about to seal the gap again when a thought occurred to me. I put my fingers back in the aperture, this time searching around the opening. I felt something at the bottom. I grabbed its edge using two fingers and slowly pulled it out. It was a small brown envelope, very dusty but intact.

In fact, it turned out to be two envelopes. With time they had stuck to each other. I carefully took them apart. Nothing was written on the outside, but I could feel that the envelopes were not empty. I took them to the kitchen where there would be better lighting.

I opened them. Each contained a single yellowing but well-preserved small piece of paper. I carefully unfolded them and laid them next to one another on the kitchen table. What was this? Hieroglyphics? I could not make head or tail of either. Both sheets were filled with strange squiggles. This is what I saw:

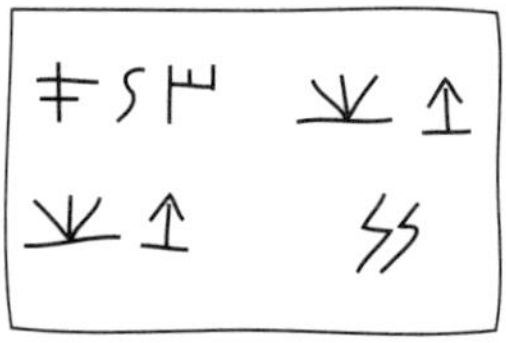

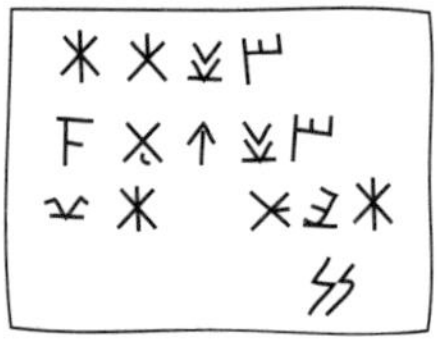

I had never seen such symbols before, or anything like them. To my untrained eyes, it all looked vaguely Chinese but, if so, shouldn't there be little 'houses' here and there?

Was it just a case of random doodling? It did not appear to be that way. There seemed to be some kind of method here. These characters were too carefully printed. And, on closer inspection, certain symbols seemed to repeat themselves, just like letters of the alphabet do in words and sentences. No, these pieces of paper each contained some kind of coded message...

I tried to make out patterns: should I be 'reading' them

from left to right, right to left or downwards? There were spaces between some signs. Did these partitions indicate separate words? And, in the first piece, the second and third words, if that is what they were, repeated themselves. In the second piece, the first two words ended with the same symbol. This same symbol was at the end of a 'word' on the other paper as well. Was that a coded way of referring to the letter 'S' with which so many Greek words end?

If that was the case, what were the other letters? No matter how hard I tried I could go no further. I gave up. I could not decipher them. Also, threateningly, I did not like the look of those 'SS' Nazi-like symbols at the end of each document. I felt a chill run down my back. I shook it off, reflexively.

"What have we got here, Mr. Aris?" I asked out loud.

Still, by now I was beginning to feel a little guilty, as if I was prying into Mr. Aris' private business, which I was, and somehow breaking his trusting the car with me. So, I folded the papers as I had found them and carefully placed them back in the brown envelopes. I resolvedly walked outside toward the MG.

As I opened the passenger door of the car, curiosity got the better of me. I reopened the envelopes and took out the sheets. I photocopied them using my home 'all-in-one' and then put them back where I found them.

It occurred to me that I truly knew nothing of Mr. Aris, except his name and his infamous old driving habits. I tried to imagine him as a younger man. He probably had been quite the lady killer: on the bony side, taller than average, sharp features (perhaps blunted now but still visibly retained) and those friendly, welcoming eyes. Yet, I had also seen those same eyes appearing distant and aloof, like the deep blue sea, gazing, at those instances, into another world and not the one right in front of them. Although the rest of him generally fitted the typical Mediterranean features, his eyes seemed out of place; just like that big old grille of the Magnette did not quite sit comfortably with the rest of the MG.

What had those eyes, still so intelligent and alive, seen and recorded since they first saw the light of day probably in the late 1920's? What mysteries, pain and happiness did they hide? Just who was this old man? Who had he been?

I determined to find out the next time I saw him. No better way to decipher a riddle than go to the source itself, I thought. Next time I saw him I would simply ask.

"And here I thought you were living up to your grand name," he replied when I did get around to asking as we sat on the veranda drinking our Turkish coffee.

"What do you mean by that?" I wondered out loud.

"You know: 'A-lex-andros': The letter 'A', meaning 'no'; 'lexi', ('word') and 'andras' ('man'): 'No-word-man', or, probably more correctly, 'A man of few words'"*.

* Not everyone would agree with Mr. Aris' interpretation. In fact most purport that the

Incredible. I had lived with and carried my nominal identity for all of forty five years and it had never occurred to me to break down my own name.

Then he turned philosophical on me.

"Does anyone really know who he is Alexis? Do you know who you really are? Where you came from? You call yourself a Cypriot do you not?"

"Well, yes… a Greek Cypriot."*

"Huh!!" he responded, uncharacteristic contempt and venom in his voice and face. Momentarily, I saw something I had not noticed before in his blue eyes: menace. It took me aback. This did not seem to be in character.

"What with your 'Great' name, you must be Greek, right?"

"Wow, hold on a minute! On this, I will agree with you Mr. Aris: we Cypriots are probably a mixture of all the neighbouring ancient tribes," I replied defensively.

Previously, when I said 'Greek Cypriot, I had only reflexively responded the way most people do: the old Greek versus Turk roots thing. The dispute, started centuries ago (or more, if you consider Troy!), continues to this day. And Cyprus is a common battle ground, given the proximity of the two sides. In general, the locals, mainly of Greek and Turkish origin, have lived together in peace in the same villages, sharing work and coffee, even friendship. But, perhaps crucially, rarely intermarrying.

"You know, this Greeks against Turks thing has to end

---

name is derived from 'aleko' and 'andras', meaning one who deflects men, or perhaps, one who protects men. But Mr. Aris may be right, the idea may be approximately the same. Leaving someone speechless, with no words to say in reply to a good point, may also imply deflecting or defeating him.

* Cypriots still distinguish themselves according to perceived ancestral roots: e.g. Greek Cypriots and Turkish Cypriots.

sometime!" he seethed, as if I had not agreed. "It's turning into a world joke. We here in Cyprus are the original melting pot, the original citizens of the world. So many ancient and modern peoples have literally passed over us, do you understand? Greeks and Turks yes, but also the Persians, the Egyptians, the Franks, the Latinos, the Brits, the Phoenicians and so on and so on. This blood that flows through our veins isn't red or blue*. It's rainbow... nothing wrong with that, you hear?"

"I won't dispute with you on all this Mr. Aris," I said, honestly in accord and also realizing that the subject had touched a raw nerve. He was truly passionate about this matter. "Modern nationalism is a scourge, a disease which must be eradicated," he stated, somewhat portentously.

After the 1955-59 revolt against British colonial rule, in 1960, Cyprus finally became an independent republic, essentially for the first time in its turbulent history of occupation which stretches back many thousands of years. The island's geographical position, a convenient stepping stone linking Europe, Asia and Africa was too attractive a proposition for past predator superpowers. Also, previously, its metallic and mineral riches (the word 'copper' comes from 'Kypros' {Cyprus}, or vice versa) were an attractive resource to possess. Like oil today and all the havoc it causes.

The newly minted constitution provided for sharing of power between the Greek and Turkish Cypriots, while government positions were distributed in relation to population. For example, there would be a Greek Cypriot president and a Turkish Cypriot vice-president. This independence thing should have been cause for collective celebrations but it was not so for all. Nationalists from both sides were disappointed. Their ideal goal was unification with the respective 'great' motherlands, Greece and Turkey. Independence was but a

* By 'red' he meant Turkish (red flag) and by 'blue' he meant Greek (blue flag).

temporary lukewarm compromise. So, the so called '*Struggle*' was not over for a few determined factions. Also, the majority Greek Cypriot government felt that there were serious problems in the just-signed constitution because, they claimed, it was unfairly weighted in favour of the minority Turkish Cypriots and would prove dysfunctional*. In a more mature democratic state this matter, which also contained legitimate points, would have been resolved with negotiations. Not so in Cyprus. Within just three years, the whole deal collapsed after some bloody incidents. The Greek Cypriots were left to run the country by themselves, as the Turkish Cypriots closed themselves up in 'cantons'. These were independently run armed pockets around the island. From then on violent acts between the two sides were not uncommon. People from both sides, who had previously shared the second biggest possible bond aside from blood - poverty -, were now mortal enemies, killing each other just because of dubious ancestral roots. The partnership had effectively died at its genesis.

"In any case," Mr. Aris now consented, calming down somewhat with my response, "it's not about you and me anymore. It's about the younger Cypriots. They must learn to live together, all the inhabitants of this small island, no matter whom their great-grand parents are… as if they really know. Why does it matter? Who cares, you know? Brits, Greeks, Turks… Chinese. People are people, that's all. Good people and bad people, that's the only discrimination I will accept."

"How about dumb and clever?" I was glad to change the subject.

"No way. A wise old man once told me, 'Always assume the other person is at least as clever as you are.' That will make you at all times respect your fellow man, no matter who that

* In any case, the Turkish Cypriots accepted all but one out of the thirteen proposed amendments. The one disagreement was relatively trivial, on municipal powers.

is. And also, it will keep you out of a lot of trouble. Don't you agree?"

I thought about it. I agreed. Wise words indeed. I had nothing to add.

"Believe me. I know what I'm talking about," he said with a trembling voice after a while.

Now I wasn't sure what he was talking about. Was he referring to what he had just said, or to his previous explosion regarding Greeks and Turks? At any rate, the emotional intensity of this last statement made me look directly at his lined face. I looked intently into his burning blue eyes, searching for clues. I thought I saw passion and ferocity, even pain. Did his eyes water? I decided to drop the whole subject.

So with all this commotion I had forgotten to ask Mr. Aris about his background.

And so the weeks rolled by. I still had not learnt much about old Aris' circumstances. I had decided, what the hell, let it go. But I began to warm to him. He seemed to be very intelligent, passionate, dignified and gentlemanly. Seeing him on a weekly basis was no 'job'. He was literally a fountain of interesting information. What I found to be especially appealing was the type of obscure stuff he seemed to know, especially about Cyprus. One could easily get through a whole life without such little gold nuggets running around in one's mind. But, certainly, they provided a little more texture and colour to otherwise drab every day activities and items.

For example, why do many local people, especially the older ones, add a little water to their Turkish coffee right before they drink it? Well, I had assumed, right after I had just absent-mindedly done just this, to cool it down of course, to reduce the possibility of scalding their mouths in the event the coffee was too hot. Not so, said Mr. Aris. When people drink Cypriot (Turkish, Greek, Byzantine, same thing) coffee it is a social event, a bonding ritual, like smoking a pipe of peace*. There is rarely any hurry. One could easily wait a couple of minutes for it to cool down. In any event, you don't see anyone doing the same to their Nescafe (regular instant coffee is referred to this way, regardless of brand) or their tea, do you? Apparently, he said, the habit is an old one. The Pashas, the previous Turkish rulers, would do this to ensure their coffee was not poisoned. According to his story, if the coffee had been tampered with, they could somehow tell by adding water. An old litmus test, of sorts.

* This is why you should not refuse an offer for coffee.

So I began to look forward to our driving sessions. There was usually a rudimentary plan laid out and agreed upon beforehand. This week, for example, we decided that we would put our Magnette through a different test. It would take much longer than an hour, but it was not a problem with me. We switched our rendezvous to Sunday so we would have plenty of time. We would climb up mighty Troodos Mountain, the top of the highest range on the island*. Given the size of Cyprus, this mountain range is a giant. It rises six and a half thousand feet above sea level, and apparently it is still growing by about an inch a year. Not that you would notice. It is a peaceful old mountain, relaxed in its quiet grandeur. People actually go up there to ski in the short winter season, despite the otherwise dry sunshiny climate. It is no Swiss Alps, but it seems that it is good enough. When you ascend Troodos it is like you are swiftly transported to another greener, cooler world.

"Do you feel it?" Mr. Aris asked me as we began to climb up the mountain. He had rolled the window down, letting in a huge draft, but I had not complained. He stuck his hand out of the window, catching the breeze, like kids and dogs like to do. The pine scented cool air is something to experience. Something you cannot but wish you could put in a bottle or a deodorant can. You would sell it downtown in smoggy cities. It lifts one's spirits and it makes one appreciate the true value of that oft downgraded fifth sense, smell.

Well, I felt something else too: the old MG was no alpine climber, at least not anymore. That was for certain. We had already slowed down quite a bit. The engine was breathing too hard and we were stuck in second gear. When the going is smooth anyone, or any car, can play it cool and youthful. But this was no regular Sunday drive. Any car would be stretched up here, never mind a fifty year old.

---

* The range is called Olympus. The island also has its place in Greek mythology.

"What, the car?" I asked in response to his question.

"Let the car be, look outside man!" he said, almost exasperated. "We are entering into another world now."

I looked around me. It was true. The old pine forest had enveloped us by now. You could feel that the air was thinning. It was just a bit chilly, but also fresh-smelling and invigorating. It made you feel healthier, somehow.

"We are in the middle of an ancient ocean now, Alexis!" he shouted excitedly, like a child, looking around him, absorbing things, real and imaginary, seemingly for the first time.

"But this is a mountain. Isn't the sea a little far from here?" I asked.

"Stop the car, it needs a rest," he shouted in reply, although his voice was barely louder than the noise of the revved up MG.

There was a side-road restaurant right ahead. I stopped in front of it. He quickly got out and he walked right past the establishment, as if he had not seen it. I followed him. There was a large bare rocky boulder sticking out right there and he started climbing it. I was somewhat concerned but he seemed to be doing ok. He stumbled on a loose rock. He bent over and picked it up.

"Do you know what this is?" he asked, looking at it intently with wide open eyes, as if it were solid gold.

"A rock?" I guessed.

"Well yes," he said without a hint of a smile. "But it is also a visit into ancient times, into the time of the dinosaurs. This rock is earth's underwear! It's mother earth exposing herself and all her secrets to us."

It still seemed like any other rock, possibly volcanic.

"People come right here where we are standing from all over the world to investigate these rocks," he explained. "I came across some people up here many years ago. In fact, I was only a boy. First I thought they were just your regular crazy foreigners, wandering about and rummaging in the middle of nowhere, but they turned out to be important university professors. You've heard of Oxford? And they paid very well for local workers, four shillings a day..."

He explained how he had got work many years ago on Troodos for one whole summer. He was just sixteen or thereabouts, he had lied to them about his age and they took him on. He carried equipment around for them, did odd jobs. They were very nice and civil toward him. They had some students with them, to whom these professors would give impromptu open-air lectures. He sometimes sat in the back and listened in. The scientists did not mind this, he defensively assured me.

"Did you know that any geologist worth his salt must apparently come up here in little old Cyprus and pay his respects? It's like a geologists' hajj... They say that there are certain 'natural temples' that must be visited. And this right here -Troodos Mountain- is one of them..." he pointed right in front of his feet. "The others are an erupting volcano or a geyser: all those valves, the farts, the burps of the earth!"

He did have a straightforward, yet highly illustrative way of simplifying, but still not denigrating, complicated things.

"And glaciers, those ancient frozen rivers with a million-year old waters taking their time, flowing through them... any limestone cave, where earth practises art that no man can ever imitate, with its stalactites and stalagmites. And the Grand Canyon... that's a big hole in America you know, something like the opposite of this, going downward millions of years. That's what they said... these foreigners know more about our country than we do!" he added. He mumbled something, his voice trailing off, recalling the English visitors perhaps, almost talking to himself now.

Up to that point, I had still assumed that he had never had any education at all. I do not know why, it just seemed that way, even when we had played the car bet quiz, or when he gave me little bits of information. When you see an old man sitting on a veranda you tend to see him as nothing more than that, rather than whatever he had been in another life. But this man was a real student of life. His little 'presentation' carried gravity. It could have come directly from one of the professors he had heard it from. I momentarily wondered who else had given him that other information, about the Magnette and its production year.

"We always hear about the seven wonders of the world," he interrupted my thoughts, suddenly looking up straight at me, almost surprised to see me standing right next to him, and now apologetically attempting to explain his excited outburst. "Now, don't get me wrong Alexandros. I too admire the pyramids and the Parthenon."

I did not think the Parthenon was ever considered to be one of the seven wonders*, not even in the newly anointed list. In fact I had heard somewhere that the Pyramids had been voted out of the new list of seven wonders**. Which automatically

---

* The ancient historian Herodotus' best known list of seven wonders were the Great Pyramid of Giza, the Hanging Gardens of Babylon, the Statue of Zeus at Olympia, the Temple of Artemis at Ephesus, the Mausoleum of Maussollos at Halicarnassus, the Colossus of Rhodes and the Lighthouse of Alexandria.

** In fact my source at the time was wrong, they are still in. The New Seven Wonders are: The Great Wall of China, 5th century BC – 16th century, China; Petra - 6th century BC, Jordan; Christ the Redeemer (statue) - opened 12 October 1931, Brazil; Machu Picchu c.1450, Peru; Chichen Itza c.600, Mexico; the Colosseum - completed 80 AD, Italy; the Taj Mahal - completed c.1648, India; and the Great Pyramid, Egypt. Incidentally, a Middle Ages list (unknown authorship) includes Stonehenge, the Colosseum, the Catacombs of Kom el Shoqafa, the Great Wall of China, the Porcelain Tower of Nanjing, Hagia Sophia and the Leaning Tower of Pisa.

renders that whole thing a joke. But I did not interrupt him with these thoughts.

"But we must truly stand in awe of the undisputed real wonders," he continued. "You know, not the manmade ones. Ancient whale skeletons have been found on top of the Himalayas. Now there's a real wonder for us to think about. How the heck did they get up there? Did they fly there? Did some kind of monstrous cataclysmic tsunami toss them there?"

He was on a roll. He proceeded to answer his own question: "No! One day the poor beasts were happily swimming in the ocean depths, singing or doing whatever whales do to pass the time, when suddenly they found themselves on top of the highest mountains in the world... you see, the deepest ocean became the tallest mountain, just like that," he said, snapping his fingers.

"And Troodos is the same thing?" I asked, bringing us back to earth, the one we were standing on.

"Exactly. We are apparently standing in the middle of the great Mesozoic Ocean. That's Greek you know*. It's the sea mass that separated Eurasia from Africa. And this here rock is an ophiolite, a rock that is part of the so-called oceanic 'lithosphere'. That's also Greek!"

He was beginning to remind me of the 'Big Fat Greek Wedding' film and the kimono story: All is based on Greek.

Also, he could see that I was rather lost, but quite intrigued; a state of mind which is any academician's dream situation.

"That's the ocean part of the tectonic plates," he explained, matter of factly. "This rock is 'rock solid' proof that if we travelled back in time at this very minute, we'd better have gills or we'd be quite dead. Drowned. As I am sure you know-"

"Actually my geology is on the rusty side," I interrupted,

---

* Mesozoic: In Greek, 'in the middle of life'.

too feebly excusing my obvious ignorance. He gave me a sideways look like, what kind of a professor are you.

"-the whole world was just one big landmass in the past called Pangaea. You do know that that is Greek too, don't you? It means 'One land'."

He was more understanding now, speaking slower, like talking to a child.

I nodded vigorously.

"Of course I know what Pangaea means!" Me. Too defensive.

He gave me another look: it's okay if you don't know.

"Even far-away Brazil and Africa were joined together at the hip. Look at any map. It's easy to see how they mirror each other. They fit into each other like a glove. And that was just yesterday in Mother Earth's terms: only three hundred million years ago… Anyway, Mother Earth, even though she was on the largish side, couldn't stand such a big weight on her shoulders. She was no Atlas and she was a lady too. Being single, she had no Hercules-type fellow to lend her a hand. So, being an industrious woman she cleverly split the world into more manageable pieces: tectonic plates. Brains before brawn."

He gave me the rock. I admit I looked at it with newfound admiration. My drawer's 'antiques', even the MG, gratefully resting her old bones on the side of the road, seemed like plastic trinkets at that moment.

Mr. Aris knew how to work his audience. I was mesmerised by an ugly rock.

We finally made it up the mountain. The MG had steamed up, but it was nothing a little fresh stream water in the radiator could not fix. We sat at a roadside *kafenes* and enjoyed our afternoon coffee, under big old pine trees. The sun was lazily making its way through the pine needles and comfortably warming our backs. It was really calm and peaceful… except for the rattling and banging and running commentary at the table right next to us. The two sole customers, apart from ourselves, were engaged in a *tavli** (backgammon) battle. Typical tavli boards are made of wood in Cyprus, and players noisily advance their *petres* (literally, stones, though they are made of hard plastic today).

"The older person is going to win," Mr. Aris whispered. "Let's go and see."

We went and joined our neighbours. They hardly greeted us, a slight nod from the older man and a grunt from the younger one. The mountain locals are especially friendly toward strangers, but this was no time for niceties. A few minutes later, the game was over. We gave our condolences to the younger player and sympathised with him about his bad luck. He paid for all the coffees, ours too, and they left together.

"I told you the old man would win," Mr. Aris said, matter of fact.

"Age and experience?" I asked.

"It could be that, but that's not how I guessed. Look at the way they were each reacting. The younger man kept whining about his bad luck, and because of that he was losing his

* The word has the same root as table. A table game.

concentration, still reacting to a previous misfortune. Now, the older man had some bad rolls as well. But he didn't even flinch. He calmly took his bad luck with the good. That's the way to play, that's the sign of a good player."

He leaned over and opened the tavli board.

"Fancy a game?" he asked. "I hope you know how to play the men's version."* I ignored that last remark. It was clear he meant no sexist insult to the ladies and none were around to upset in any case. He was simply defining the type of game he wanted to play. We played for a good half hour. I was soundly thrashed. Like a pro, during play I had not complained once.

"Still, it is a game of luck," I said at the end, in defence of my pitiful performance.

Mr. Aris seemed vaguely offended. "You know, this may not be as old as the Troodos rocks, but it still is a wise old game from way back. One of the oldest backgammon boards in the world was dug up right here in Cyprus you know." He held one of the pieces up in his hand. "Of course, these were real stones back then, but we still call them petres, after all these thousands of years." Then he held up one of the dice. "And this you can guess was made out of bone."

"Come to think of it, I vaguely remember playing a game called *kokkalo* (bone) as a child," I replied. "I don't recall the rules of the game or what part of what animal it was, but that bone was naturally rectangular and we'd roll it just like a die."

He nodded his head slowly, reflecting. He had probably also played this game himself as a young lad. "Imagine, people played that exact game for thousands of years," he said. "And,

---

* Only older people still refer to the international version of the game as the women's version, due to the fact that it is easier to play than the Greek plakoto.(Cypriot 'tsillito'). In this version the petres all begin at one point at the start. Hence it is harder as more strategy is needed to set up one's game.

just like that," he snapped his fingers, "you were maybe one of the last people to ever play it. You know what I find interesting but also worrying about these strange times we now live in?"

"What?"

"So many new things, like the washing machine, the car and the plane have arrived so quickly. It's like man has developed in disproportionate stages."

"What do you mean Mr. Aris?"

"Well, you know. We started by crawling, at a snail's pace… it took millions of years to learn to do something simple like use stones for tools. Millennia passed before each new invention: first the rough stone which was used to break things. Then came the carved, sharp stone to cut things and kill animals, like an axe. After that the first stone cup… these new things happened at an excruciatingly slow pace."

"No newspapers necessary back then, eh?"

He smiled.

"I'm not so sure about that. Maybe there were no innovative tools to report, but I'll bet a lot of other news would be the same: like wars between tribes on the front pages and who's the prettiest cave lady on page three. Or who could throw a stone furthest maybe, on the back ones."

He remembered his original argument. "Like I was saying, man started at a crawling pace, then he walked and walked for eons, then he started jogging, and now he is sprinting, Bolt-like. Most of us can't keep up with this insane sort of pace."

"Well, perhaps it's our destiny," I retorted. "Maybe we are literally racing against time and against our own extinction. Our internal clock is telling us to hurry it up, to develop that super spaceship or time machine which will get us off this planet before it explodes!"

"You are probably right," he reflected, to my mild surprise.

"But what a price to pay, don't you think? We are dropping age old traditions one by one, and deserting newer habits before they even have time to develop into traditions. Younger people even make fun of old Cypriot traditions nowadays."

"You are right. They call them *horkathkio*!*"

"In just a few decades I have witnessed what would have taken hundreds, if not thousands of years to develop beforehand," Mr. Aris concluded. "That's why I am glad to see some people cling on to certain old things, like bilotta**, tavli and me!" he smiled.

He looked down again and he pointed at the backgammon board. "Thankfully this game has proven resilient. It's still here, unlike your kokkalo game. I don't know for how long, but I think I know why the fascination persists. After all these millennia, it is still current. This is literally a game of life. More so than chess, which is a game of death. Can't you see it?"

Now I did not appreciate that last comment. I told him so. I love chess! It is a cerebral game, a game of strategy and tactics. It takes more brains to play that game. Surely, tavli is based on luck, heavily depending on the roll of the dice.

"Chess is a war game, with a clear hierarchy. Privileged kings and queens, knights and disposable plain old soldiers," he explained, seeing my reaction. "Your goal is to kill the enemy."

"Life itself is a war, isn't it," I rebuffed.

He paused to think about it. "You are right with that point," he conceded. "But I prefer the total equality of the petres. We all begin life with a clean slate. At least theoretically… do you

* Of the village, 'peasantish'.

** The card game 'bilotte' (resembling 'Bridge') is still often played in Cyprus coffee shops. Probably French in origin, arriving in Cyprus at the time of the Lusignans 800 years ago.

know why there are thirty pieces on the board? They symbolise time, the days of the month. Actually, the black stones are the nights, the white ones the days. Thirty stones, fifteen days and fifteen nights, a whole 'moon month'. And, count them: there are twenty-four slots to advance through: the hours of the day. Dear Alexis, backgammon truly resembles life exactly because it combines skill and cunning *and* luck. You need all these to make it. Whereas chess is less realistic: brains alone cannot get you through all the ups and downs. We all have our destinies, even if it's random. It's not fair, but that's how it is: Luck is god!"

He had a strong case.

"Think about the older man's whole outlook as he played, in the game we just watched," he continued. "I would bet that it reflected his character, his philosophy of life."

"How do you mean?" I asked.

"Well, let me give you a couple of examples. As you noticed, throughout, he was good natured and patient, he smiled frequently, a sign that he was enjoying the game. Now people who enjoy themselves in the real world, who are optimistic, tend to do better in life, don't they? Also, sometimes he slowed the game down, thinking and contemplating, and other times he would play really fast, almost in abandonment, spontaneously. That's the way to live isn't it: slow things down once in a while, at the difficult crossroads, to weigh the options and to plan ahead. But at other times, you mustn't hesitate, you must be decisive! And, although he took risks, they were always calculated. He was never reckless, like his more inexperienced opponent. Isn't that what we are supposed to do in the real world? He 'chipped' at his rival, little by little, unlike the young man who was constantly looking for that 'big' move that would win him the game. Why that's like trying to hit the jackpot in the national lottery to solve all your problems. It could happen, but it probably won't."

I saw what he meant.

We sat silently, each absorbed in our thoughts. The sun, the day-giver, symbolised by the white *petres*, was slowly making way to night, the black *petres*. We had advanced another twenty-four hours on the board of life. The never-ending game of life, in full swing, on top of an ocean-mountain.

Christmas

> *"And so this is Christmas*
> *And what have we done?*
> *Another year over*
> *A new one just begun"*
> (John Lennon)

The days became weeks and then months, easily passing by, like a smooth ride in a Magnette. And quicker than usual, or so it seemed, Christmas was upon us. They say that the older you get the faster time flies, the reason being that when you are younger each day and year amounts to a bigger chunk of your lifetime experiences. For example, a year for a six year old child constitutes a sixth of his whole life, whereas for me it would account for a mere one forty-fifth. Or something like that. Hence the 'long' summers of our youth. Seems unfair but that's the way it is.

Christmas time is anything but white in Nicosia and the plains of Mesaoria. Soggy brown if you are lucky. A couple of weeks of torrential rain interspersed with a generous dose of icy sunshine. Still, people put on their warm winter coats and pull on their thick boots, with this obligatory gesture somehow contributing to a semblance of 'the Christmas spirit'.

In fairness, city municipalities do their best to also dress up for the season. The main streets are decorated with bright lights and the central square of Nicosia, which proudly holds the somewhat inexplicable name 'Eleftheria (freedom) Square'*, is the centrepiece. It is also bathed with the sounds of the usual Christmas carols. 'Dreaming of a white Christmas' (literally

* Eleftheria Square, in the heart of Nicosia, used to be called Metaxas Square, after the Greek leader who said 'No' to the Italian and German annexation demands in World War II. This resulted in a military invasion and heroic resistance. The name of the square was changed when Cypriots 'discovered' that Metaxas was a dictator who is not revered at all in Greece. However, a neighbouring square is still called 'Ohi' (No).

dreaming) is a perennial favourite. This year it alone boasted a high-tech feature: a couple of real live sheep in a 'manger', which kids loved and animal activists hated.

It all bears a rather provincial feel, but it generally does the trick: people dip into their pockets and lighten up a little.

But the season also offers itself for people to take stock. This is when they sit back to assess their lot, to decide whether they have done anything worthwhile during the year and if they are doing all right, by and large. This almost mandatory self-evaluation exercise is fine and rewarding if things are in order, but it is a traumatic experience if you are, or think you are, messed up.

I was sitting in my living room, distractedly looking around me, in a philosophical mood. What is it all about? Am I happy or sad, neither or both? Does anyone give a damn? Such and other not as politically correct questions danced in my mind. They mainly just hung there in mid-air, unanswered, like mysterious dark and bright Christmas ornaments.

I glanced toward my miserable excuse of a Christmas tree. Plastic of course, but that is politically correct these days. Except, whoever heard of a tree which you could buy all set up, decorations, lights and all on their appropriate branches? '*Just open box, pluck in*!' boasted the Chinese manufacturer. The McDonald's of Christmas trees!

You could tell this whole house was a glorified bachelor pad. Living alone in a big house. There should be more people around here. Little and big. What a waste of space, that pool table. Used a couple of times a year, if that. The kitchen? What was that for? And the three bedrooms upstairs. One a real bedroom, the other an office, the third a walk-in dump.

This was all too depressing. I needed company. But who? I searched my mind. In desperation, I dialled Maria.

Maria

My relationship with Maria could be described as superficial, at best. You could say we were acquaintances, certainly not friends. Both of us were on the rebound when we met, social wreckages from recent ugly divorces. Her gruesome details are still a matter of conjecture, as she had not offered any information when I asked ("*You really do not want to hear it*"), and so I left it at that. Mine involved a lengthy and difficult escape from a lunatic case, leaving me full of invisible scars and scared to death of any kind of close relationships.

So, as I saw it, that was about the whole of it, as far as having something in common was concerned. We had met at a pub, some friend knew some friend of hers or something like that. Nothing exciting happened. We almost too hastily shared our 'dirty' little secret. Perhaps surprisingly, as the big 'D' is still big in these parts of the world. Many couples continue to kill each other, little by little every day, rather than face the 'humiliation' of a failed marriage. At least, thankfully, neither of us had any children.

Our common fate brought us together once or twice. We shared a drink or watched a movie when we happened to bump into one another, but neither side was willing to punch holes through our respective impenetrable walls. So, there were no real breakthroughs, just polite exchanges. And certainly no fireworks.

Come to think of it, all I had was acquaintances those days. And to be honest that mostly suited me fine: trouble-*free*, with emphasis on the second word.

She was probably taken aback when I telephoned, given her reaction. In fact, it took her a second or three to figure out who was calling. ('Who *is* this?' she had inquired. I had almost hung up). We met at a downtown café. It seemed that we both needed the outing. She gave me a broad guilty smile and then quickly mumbled a feeble excuse and an apology for her abrupt outburst over the phone, adding that she was really glad I had called. The festive spirit of shoppers passing by did us no harm. Soon we were wandering from shop to shop, along with the crowds. She decided to buy a couple of gifts and I opined over her choices ('*People really wear that?*'). We were also having a laugh with the virtuosity of the carol-singing choirs and the time passed, so now it was my turn to be surprised by the phone call on my mobile phone. I could hardly hear the voice on the other side, the sound of 'Rudolf the red-nosed deer' was too close for comfort.

It was Mr. Aris. He was wondering if I would be coming, because I was a little late. I had completely forgotten, I had almost stood him up! I assured him I was on my way, that something urgent had come up and delayed me. I hung up and hurriedly proceeded to explain to Maria my bet and subsequent commitment to the old man. I told her how he was a bit different, how he talked a lot when he got to know you and about the obscure pieces of information he always seemed to have up his sleeve. I was not trying to 'sell' him at all, but she was intrigued. On the spur of the moment, I asked her to come along with me. I told her I was sure he would not mind.

As we drove toward the old house I was not so sure anymore. Mr. Aris and I had forged some kind of a special relationship and maybe he would not be too enthusiastic about the idea of another stranger sharing our ride. Too late.

Once a ladies' man… (?) Suddenly Mr. Aris was looking more like the older version of Paul Newman. He quickly recovered when he realised there were two of us coming out of the car, one of them a lady and he turned on the charm. It did not seem odd or funny or embarrassing, more like a down-on-his-luck elder English gentleman conversing to a younger lady.

"Ah, Maria, a beautiful name…" he commented when they introduced themselves.

"Thanks, but you don't need to flatter me Mr. Aris," she smiled. "You know as well as I do that if you shout my name out loud right now, three Marias will answer back!"

"I didn't say it was rare, but it still is ethereally beautiful and powerful… one of the women gods of old. Us Cypriots, we've always revered the power of women." He meant it. Still, I momentarily remembered how he had called the backgammon game.

"You know what your name means?"

"Not quite sure, Mr. Aris," she replied.

"Well it means, 'of the sea'. In antiquity your full name sometimes appears as 'Stella Maris', Star of the Sea. What a beautiful name, don't you agree Alexis?"

"It is."

"Lots of peoples in this area revered women. Think about it. The most famous temple of all time is dedicated to a woman!" he added.

"And which would that be?" I asked.

"What do you think Professor? The Parthenon, of course! It means, Temple of the Virgin. Sorry Maria, but before your namesake's virginity in Christianity, there were many other celebrated virgin goddesses. Athina was one of them."

"No offence taken," she said, smiling.

"Maria, Astarte, Isis and our very own Cypriot goddess, Aphrodite. Probably all these are one and the same… the same super-lady reinventing herself," he added, reflecting audibly. "All of them have been referred to as 'stars of the sea' at one point or another; can you believe it Stella Maria? You know, we in Cyprus have so many churches dedicated to Holy Mary because they are built right on top of the old Aphrodite Temples, which themselves were built on top of previous female deities. A real shame that they would do that. Couldn't they put them all next to one another? So we could choose?"

He took a bit of a risk with all this. What if Maria took religious offence to this association? But she did not.

"Now, Aphrodite that *is* a nice name," she commented instead.

"'*I will sing of stately Aphrodite, gold-crowned and beautiful, whose territory is the walled cities of all sea-bound Cyprus*'," he replied, poetically. "You know who said that? That blind poet Homer. Of course you know that the goddess of love is a fellow Cypriot, but do you know how she came to be?"

"Well, didn't she like basically rise up from the waves* over at that big rock near the city of Paphos? *Romios Stone*?"

"Right you are, though it is also said in mythology that she actually surfed over to Cyprus on a giant shell," he said.

"Sort of on an ancient speedboat?" she asked.

"More like a dinghy, I would think," I said.

---

* Aphrodite: Aphro- foam (of the waves), dite- emerge.

"Whatever. Like in Botticelli's painting, if you've seen it." He abruptly got up and disappeared in his house. Two minutes later he was back with a book about Aphrodite, a.k.a. Venus. It contained all kinds of images and statues of the goddess, most of them beautiful like the deity: e.g. Andrea Mantegna, 'Mars, Venus, and Diana', 'Eros Punished by Venus', Fresco in Pompeii. And a coloured picture of the *painting* 'The Birth of Venus', by Botticelli, circa1482. Nice book.

"In any case, *her* birth was no immaculate conception, at least not in the way your namesake's was," he said to Maria when she put the book aside. "In truth, it was a pretty messy affair..."

"Oh, please give us the gruesome details Mr. Aris!" encouraged Maria with a broad smile.

He pretended to hesitate. "You asked for it," he smiled back. "There are reasons, you know, that this stuff isn't taught in schools! Well, many many years ago, in fact in the very beginning of time, Ouranos or Sky or Heaven, take your pick, lived happily with his lovely wife Gaia, otherwise known as Earth. Everything was going dandy until Gaia got kind of bored, what with spending all day with hubby and nobody else to talk to. After a few million years they'd just about covered every conceivable subject, and remember, those days, no TV."

"What?!"

"So, she started hinting at how nice it would be with a couple of toddlers running around... This prospect can be daunting even for the best of us men."

"Is it the nappies?"

"That too, but also that we get relegated to 'second-class' citizens really fast. But Ouranos had much bigger problems than that. He became convinced that should they have any kids one of them would literally murder him. So, don't ask me how, he prevented Gaia from giving birth to any of their offspring. The kids had to carry on living in the somewhat cramped environs of mum's womb. That can get pre-tty dreary for the kids after a while."

"That would be frustrating," Maria empathised.

"Indeed, it was. So much so that an exceedingly cheeky son, Kronos, castrated his dad as Ouranos was making love with Gaia."

"Ouch!"

"At least he went a happy Titan. Anyway, Kronos proceeded to toss dad's 'jewels' into the sea, and from the froth of his semen rose beautiful Aphrodite. So, as you understand, she was born from the act of separating Heaven and Earth. That makes her the oldest divinity and Cyprus the oldest place in the world!" he announced triumphantly.

"Can you prove all this stuff?" she challenged, smiling.

"Well, not exactly," he admitted. "But there is something weighty and powerful about any story that has travelled through thousands of mouths for thousands of years isn't there? It's as good and as solid as any ancient monument..."

I realised I had not said much yet. But that suited me fine, we were enjoying ourselves. All three of us then packed into the Magnette. Today, she (he??) too was putting on the charm. No backfiring and purring like a contented cat.

There is something about the Mediterranean Sea that attracts people from all over the world. Perhaps it is the convivial colours or the calm warm waters. Or maybe it is something deeper. Because, when staring out into its waters, there is certainly also a quality of mystique mixed with a sense of history and at the same time a distinctly uplifting feeling. They seem siren-like welcoming, in contrast to ocean waters which tend to appear challenging, wild and daunting.

We, the three of us, made our way toward the beach of Larnaca, on the East coast and a brief half hour ride from Nicosia. Even in winter, the short drive through the desert of barren chalky-white hills is rather intimidating: like a drive through the craters of the moon. So it is always good to see the big round-about on the city outskirts. Go straight and you head into the city. If you take the first turning on the left and drive a further hour down that highway you will reach the world famous party spot, Ayia (Saint) Napa resort: The Ibiza of Cyprus. A modern Sodom and Gomorra, one could say. Mr. Aris read the big traffic sign out loud.

"Ayia Napa… Ever heard of that saint?" he asked us, smiling.

"Not really," I admitted. "Okay, tell us how she was martyred for the Greek Orthodox Church," I suggested, suspecting he would anyway.

"Well that's just the point," he answered. "Have you ever heard of anyone called Napa? None of the locals ever-ever-call a child of theirs 'Napa' after their matron saint… strange, eh?"

"That *is* strange," agreed Maria. At least in Cyprus it is.

"Well, it's because there is no such name! The name of the place is a syllabic anagram for the honorary title of Mother Mary or even a previous goddess. Probably Aphrodite herself, maybe," he said, looking at Maria with a smile.

He paused for effect or for us to figure out what he was on about. He gave up.

"Pa-na-yi-a," he paused between the syllables, so we could get his point. Panayia literally means 'her total holiness', the absolute goddess. When people in Cyprus vocally call upon Panayia's help* these days, and they still do this often, they now refer to Mary, the mother of Jesus. But 'Panayia' conveniently does not mention any names. It just alludes to the fact that an almighty female deity is invoked. The name could apply to any all-powerful goddess.

"A-yia-Na-Pa. It's a hidden code, an anagram of *Panayia*, to mask the locals' true reverence to the ultimate goddess... and, you know, quite coincidentally, there is an ancient sanctuary dedicated to Aphrodite at exactly that spot. They recently found a likeness of a goddess in a cave there, from 500BC, her hair still retaining its red dye."

Ayia Napa has beautiful sparkling beaches with white sand, like natural enormous swimming pools. On the other hand, Larnaca, toward which we headed, is not graced with the most attractive coastlines on the island because of its brown-grey sand and arid surroundings.

Still, the old man was unfazed.

"Welcome to the home of our great ancestors, the mighty Phoenicians," he announced as we entered the city. "We Cypriots really should be proud of them as well. Not only of our great Greek grandfathers. The Phoenicians were excellent

* 'Panayia mou!' like 'Mia Madonna!' for the Italians.

tradesmen and first-rate ship builders. And our greatest Larnacean philosopher, that father of anarchism, Zenon the Kitian, was Phoenician, of course!"

"Are you sure about all that Mr. Aris? The father of anarchism? Not the founder of the Stoic school? And Phoenician, not Greek?" I asked doubtfully.

He did not reply.

We reached the beachside. As it was December, swimming was not an option, not even in the Mediterranean. Even the few scattered 'crazy' British tourists were not braving it, despite the bright sunshine. At least some of them were keeping to form by wearing their shorts complete with sandals and socks.

"The Cypriots, or the Alasians, as they used to be called, were in the thick of things three-four thousand years ago, you know. There are documents proving that at some point in time they were at least on equal footing with the mighty Egyptians. In an ancient platter the Egyptian pharaoh refers to his Cypriot counterpart as 'father'-"

"I'm sorry, how do you know all this stuff Mr. Aris? Are you some kind of a Cyprus history professor?" interrupted Maria, sounding genuinely impressed. The question I had been meaning to ask ever since I had met him and he had played quiz master with me, getting this whole affair rolling. This old fellow would have made his namesake ancestor, Aristotle the philosopher, the first guy with encyclopaedic knowledge, really proud. On the other hand, I am not sure how his most famous disciple, Alexander the Great would have felt about me. Would I at least qualify as 'Alexander the Good Enough'?

The old man gave Maria a big smile in reply, seeming almost too proud of himself for my own liking. Was he showing off or what?

"When we get back to Nicosia, I'll show you something," he finally replied.

"But first, let us enjoy the view," he suggested.

So, the three of us sat there for a while. The smooth, warm black and white flat stones were surprisingly comfortable. We looked out at sea, enjoying the soothing rays of the sun on our faces. Not a bad place to be. A state of nirvana, of sorts.

"We are sitting on the original backgammon *petres*", he realised, picking up one of each colour. "Millions and millions of days and nights…"

Maria surely had no idea what he was on about. But she made no comment. She just stared at him in a scrutinizing way.

"I'd give a lot to go back ten thousand years right now," he said breaking the silence again.

"I'd give the same just to go back twenty years Mr. Aris," answered Maria with a smile.

"I know what you mean," he said, "in that case I'll take more like fifty years, please!"

"You look pretty good right now, Mr. Aris," she assured him. He clearly enjoyed the compliment. He gave her an equally obvious look of approval, the male to female type. Who says flattery will get you nowhere? Flattery will get you everywhere. He reciprocated with an even more flattering comment.

"Actually, what I had in mind is," he went on, "if we went back a few thousand years we would maybe now be staring out at the most glorious civilisation of them all: Atlantis! Isn't that what they said on the news? Somewhere over there," he added, pointing out at sea, at an indiscriminate mark. He was squinting as if trying to make out something in the distance, probably imagining the supposed site of the ancient city. We stared in the general direction. "We'd almost certainly be able to make out from here the outline of the greatest temple ever built. The one of god Poseidon, master of the seas!"

"I've heard that Atlantis story on the radio too," I said. "Some American professor is it not?"

"Yes, well actually I think he is more like an explorer, I think they said. Like a treasure hunter or something. Off the coast of Cyprus, near Larnaca, is Atlantis, he claims."

"Don't be so sure," I interjected. "It's an old story Mr. Aris, don't go down that road... others have placed this Atlantis kingdom all over the world. They get their fifteen minutes of fame and then another wacko comes along with another place. Why would this guy be right? For all we know, this is all just a big fairytale to begin with: perhaps there never was an Atlantis".

"Perhaps it is so, but I think it is really more likely that there was one. You know who started this? Plato! Tell me, why would a clever man like Plato lie to us about a thing like that?"

"Maybe whoever told *him* the story, the Egyptian priests or Solon or whoever was pulling his leg."

"But why? Anyway," he dismissed me, "I like this man's Cyprus-Atlantis story best." He smiled. Something like, 'I may be deceiving myself a little' but who cares?

"Let's look at the facts..." he went on. "The oldest surviving civilisation, say four five thousand years ago was that of Egypt wasn't it? Just a stone throw away from where we are sitting. It was really close by, even in ancient times, don't you agree?"

We both nodded agreement.

"Could that possibly if truth be told be the beginning of

civilisation as we know it? I think that that is impossible. First there was nothing and then suddenly there is something as grandiose and architecturally perfect as the pyramids and the Sphinx?"

"I do see what you mean," said Maria. She's an architect.

"Well not exactly," I corrected on contemplation. "Before the Egyptians there were the Babylonians, at least. They were an important and developed empire weren't they?"

"That's exactly my point," he said. "History seems to suddenly begin at about, say, ten thousand years ago… Just like that. All of a sudden, this whole civilisation thing is nicely set up. Beautiful constructions which would even challenge today's architects." Maria nods in agreement. "The pyramids, the Hanging Gardens of Babylonia… it just doesn't make any sense."

"Didn't you say that we humans evolve first by crawling, then walking and then sprinting?" I reminded him of our conversation up on the Troodos mountains. "Perhaps that is when we finally decided to pick up the pace and start to run like the wind."

Maria looked puzzled since she was not with us on Troodos, but again she said nothing. I think she wanted to see where the old man was going with this.

"I don't think we simply decided to up and run, unless aliens visited us," he argued. Was that what he was leading to? 'Chariots of the Gods'? Little green men?

"First, you need a foundation," he continued. "You must first have a typewriter before you can make a computer, don't you? You need to know what you are doing. That foundation never existed or, I think, it has somehow disappeared. Perhaps it was swallowed up by a mass destruction."

"Something like the Noah's Ark story?" I suggested.

"Exactly."

"Well, that story does have a few minor glitches you know," I countered. "For one, Noah was supposed to have lived for almost one thousand years, like his granddad, Methuselah. And he was a really bright baby too. The moment he was born he recited a prayer!"

Maria and he seemed interested so I continued.

"Actually, Noah's legend varies depending on your source. According to the Koran's more plausible approach, it was not in point of fact a world deluge he dealt with, but rather more of a disastrous regional event which only affected Noah's people and the surrounding area. Also, according to this same source, God was upset at humanity because in nine hundred and fifty years of preaching Noah was able to convert only eighty three people in total! Don't laugh! That is really what it says in the Koran."

"That's a pretty poor rate by anyone's standards," laughed Maria. "Noah would have made for a lousy salesman."

"Yeah. Noah must surely shoulder a share of the blame," I replied. "Fewer than nine believers converted every century... Jehovah's witnesses take heart."

Although Mr. Aris had heard what I said, he still went on with his own line of thinking.

"Maybe that story lets in water," he punned, "but nevertheless something must have happened. An earthquake, a mass flood, something literally earth shattering...Is it not a big coincidence that the Cataclysm* is most celebrated right here in Larnaca, of all places in the world?" he wondered.

What he said is true. This so proclaimed biggest flood in history, when apparently everything was covered in water and

* A total, devastating flood.

nothing survived except Noah's family and a few animals, according to the bible, is truly a big event in Cyprus. The central point in the entire world, of these celebrations, happens to be the city of Larnaca. It is a big festival involving a motley blend of modern concert style activities intermixed with ancient water rituals, the roots of which cannot be traced, or the original significance of which has long lost its meaning.

"I feel certain there was an Atlantis, or even a number of relatively advanced cities, well before Babylonia and Cairo and Jericho, perhaps tens of thousands of years before," said Mr. Aris. "My gut tells me this centre was real close to where we are sitting, perhaps even a mile or so below us".

"If that's the case," I said, "we'll never find Atlantis. It will now just be molten rock or something. That guy is wasting his time".

"Very possibly," he consented. He held up one black and one white smooth stone. "These hold the answer," he said. "They were around when all this was happening. But they keep silent. They won't tell us."

It was dark when we arrived in Nicosia. We had sat and talked of ancient imaginary worlds, right there in our own little 'centre' of the earth, fantasizing them as far more shiny and glorious than even today's mega-cities and skyscrapers, until the sun went down. In fact, we got up to go immediately after. As soon as the direct sunshine was gone it got to be considerably chilly.

Mr. Aris invited us to his home for a cup of coffee. As he unlocked the old wood and stained glass door it occurred to me that I had never actually been inside his house. What we saw when he turned on the single bare light was shocking. Everywhere you looked, I mean everywhere, there were books. On the shelves. On the benches. On the tables. On the walls. On the floor. Both Maria and I stood at the entrance, agape.

"Sorry about the mess," he said, carefully making his way through a narrow corridor left between the books. "I don't get too many guests these days."

We waited at the door until he cleared some books and dusted off a small table and its chairs with the back of his hand.

"Please come in," he encouraged us, seeing our hesitation. He was a bit embarrassed now, given our reaction, you could see.

Maria found her voice first, though not overly articulately, especially given the zillions of words surrounding us:

"Wow!"

"I know. I must find a way to organise all this stuff, but I was never the organising type… but, really, there is some sense in this mess," he added apologetically. "You name a book, I can find it immediately... Or at least I could a few years ago," he corrected after looking doubtfully around him at the knee high stacks which were behind other piles of other stacks.

"Have you read all these books, Mr. Aris?" I eventually found my voice too.

"Most of them. No one ever gave me an education, so I had to go out there and grab it myself," he answered in defence. "Some of these books aren't really worth the time but I don't have the heart to put them down or throw them out. Someone, somewhere, no matter how poor a writer, put in hundreds and hundreds of hours to write each and every one of these books. Each word laboriously linked to another to put together a sentence, then more sentences to make paragraphs, and then chapters. Obviously, all these people who wrote these books, every single word in each of them, thought it was worth the effort. Who am I to judge them? That's why they stay."

"Did you buy all these books?" Maria asked.

"A lot of them yes. I have bought a whole load by the box, or by weight or even by the inch. Or for pennies. But I also inherited a lot of them. Most of them. And also you'll be amazed at how many people and organisations just give books away. Copies of publications they already have, new editions replacing older ones, donations of books they don't need, 'obsolete' ones and so on."

"Still, this is an awful big haul," I remarked.

There were virtually thousands of books in that house. Most of the ones I could see around me seemed to be reference volumes rather than fiction.

"I've been around for a while you know, Alexis," he replied in his defence.

He disappeared in the next room. When he opened that door I momentarily glimpsed the old-fashioned yellow kitchen cupboards, even the stove. But I also caught sight of something else. Loads of books. In the kitchen! Maria saw too. We gave each other an identical wide-eyed open-mouthed look.

"Are there special sections in different places?" shouted Maria leaning toward a row in front of her, referring to his claim of some kind of organisation.

"There used to be," he replied, coming back from the kitchen. "But then it got a bit out of control, especially when I happened to get a lot of books at once... and sometimes I had trouble deciding where books would fit. Geography, geology, archaeology, theology, anthropology, history, I couldn't quite tell them apart. So I put them where I could find them. You could say that my books are organised according to priority. What is, or what was, more important to me, is easier to access. Any book you can reach out and pick up, well that's more essential. To me anyway."

He reached out to pick up a book, perhaps at random, to demonstrate his point. Although it was not a big book, it seemed heavy in his hands, as if the words inside weighed a lot more than the ink used to put them in the book. He put on a pair of thick glasses, apologetically remarking how he was finding it harder and harder to read these days. He slowly read out its title: "'*Bibliotheca: Books One to Three*'." He took off his glasses. He did not like to wear them, you could tell. "You heard of this one, of course?"

We had not, really.

"Well, it's one of the oldest books around. Its title means 'library' in Greek, as you know. Written in the first century AD. Or thereabouts. It's actually a combination of four books. The three are right here in this volume, the fourth is lost forever."

"I wonder which is actually the oldest surviving book," I said looking interestedly at the one he was holding.

"Well this one does not quite rank up there," he replied. "I mean I have read somewhere that there is some kind of a Chinese script that is around eight and a half thousand years old. And anyway this here, of course, is a reproduction. But the actual story it tells is very old... Now, let me think... I believe I have read in a newspaper that the oldest original and surviving 'multiple-page' book - isn't that what we mean by a book, a script consisting of many pages? - is one that was found in Bulgaria or Macedonia about sixty years ago. Some man apparently found it in a tomb there. Now he is very old, about ninety, and he decided to donate it to Bulgaria's National History Museum in Sofia. On condition of anonymity, and that they don't throw him in jail, I presume. The book is estimated to be from 600 BC. And it is still kicking around! More than two-and-a-half thousand years old!"

"That is amazing Mr. Aris. So you do know which is the oldest surviving book!" said Maria, impressed once more. "What is it made of, papyrus?"

"Good guess Maria. In fact, there is actually a papyrus script of about the same age still in existence today. From Egypt of course. Its text is apparently quite boring. It's an accounts' statement or something. But I don't really count that sort of thing as a book. Papyrus was made in rolls, not pages. Even though those rolls could extend to quite a length. As much as half a football field sometimes! Anyway, the sheets of the - let's call it - Bulgarian book were made of something else. Something much more durable than papyrus. And more valuable: solid gold, twenty four carat, of course! That's why it hasn't rusted or disintegrated."

"It must be priceless. Who wrote this Bulgarian book then? What is it about?" asked Maria.

"Actually, it's not a Bulgarian book per se. It is written in the Etruscan language-"

"The what?" I asked.

"E-trus-can. Heard of them? The Etruscans? Don't worry, neither has anyone else. It's one of those ancient peoples nobody really knows anything about. They were definitely from around this area and they were seafaring people. Maybe they came from where western Turkey is today. Some people think they had to leave in a hurry after the fall of Troy. After the Trojan War that is. I don't know. I am just telling you what I've read. Later they ended up in central Italy. In any case, their written script apparently resembles the Greek alphabet... Is it even older? I don't know that either. From what I do know, this particular book basically only contains illustrations. I have seen pictures: a mermaid, soldiers, a harp, a horse rider. Things like that."

"What happened to them? The Etruscans I mean?" I asked.

"They were probably completely wiped out by the Romans about four-five hundred years before Christ's time. Just another little case of genocide. The usual. That's why they are such a mystery today. There aren't any of them left and there exist very few written records about them. But thankfully they have left us something extremely valuable haven't they, bless their souls. That golden book."

"The history of mankind, repeated," said Maria. "One step forward two steps back."

"So what's this *Bibliotheca* about?" I asked, pointing at the book Mr. Aris was holding. He handed it to me.

"This is a really interesting book," he answered. "It is a good summary of Greek mythology. It's got all those excellent legends in it. Hercules, Theseus, the Trojan War, they are all in here. It sweepingly goes through the creation of the universe, Greek style. Not quite the same take as the Bible's. In any case, mythology was their religion, and their history, before it was downgraded to just plain fairy tale 'mythology'."

"It even has the author's name on it," I remarked looking at the cover. "Apollodorus. No surname. Like Brazilian footballers."

"Yes. It's kind of a shame for him, though," said Mr. Aris. "Nowadays he is apparently referred to by scholars as 'Pseudo-Apollodorus', an unfortunate allusion, if his name really was that."

"Why do they call him that? Was he a fake or something? Did he copy what he wrote from somewhere else?" asked Maria.

"I am sure he didn't think up all these stories himself," he replied. "Nobody did. That's why they call it mythology. These stories are truly ancient, even for Apollodorus, pseudo or not. He simply put down myths that 'poet singers' were singing by memory out on the streets and in squares for centuries. Before written script. Like Homer himself... He too is probably not the original poet of 'his' epics. At least not wholly. He too was just a person who could recite entire stories off by heart... Homer never actually wrote anything down, as you may know. He had no idea how to, apart from the added handicap of apparently being blind. Which would surely make it hard even if he knew how to write."

"I've heard on TV that the last of these people, the street story tellers, still do their business in Algeria," I remembered. "Some people are videotaping their 'performances' now so that they don't get lost forever. Putting them on 'You-Tube'."

"Another great tradition disappears then," said Mr. Aris, sighing. Despite his broad knowledge, I suspect he was not quite into the internet yet. "In any case," he went on, "our Apollodorus here was called a false one for other reasons. The problem scholars have, apparently, has to do with dates. A couple of centuries BC there was another original Apollodorus from Athens who first wrote this stuff... now this 'real' person was a student of Aristarchus of Samothrace... ever heard of him?" he asked hopefully.

Neither of us bothered to answer.

"Aristarchus is truly an important figure in the world of books, so I feel I owe him a lot," he said, going off on yet another tangent. He held a key job in antiquity, a prestigious job: he was the Head Librarian of the most famous library in the history of mankind: the Great Library of Alexandria!" he announced, dramatically.

"The one that was burnt down," I said.

"That's the one. The crime of the millennium," he replied. "So many answers, gone forever. It's such a shame. I am certain that the mystery of Atlantis would not be a mystery at all if that library still existed. And so many other things from what we call prehistory."

"There is actually a new library in its place. Well, almost in its place. The actual location is now below sea level. The new building is, you could say, a modern architectural wonder," said Maria. "It's in layers, like a gigantic wave of knowledge hitting the shores. Or something to that effect. It is right on the edge of modern Alexandria."

"Anyway," said Mr. Aris, nodding interestedly, "this Aristarchus character is responsible for re-organising the Homeric Epic and dividing it into chapters and then into two complete books, the Iliad and the Odyssey. Some claim he may have overdone some of the editing – a bit of adding, some subtracting... He died right here in Cyprus. He was in exile at the time. Rumour has it that he starved himself to death..."

"Poor man," said Maria.

"Yes. Now, the student of the Librarian Aristarchus, the real Apollodorus, wrote a comprehensive manuscript on Greek mythology a couple of hundred years *before* this Apollodorus text we have here in our hands. We know that this version is a later one because it cites some person who lived in the first century BC. Much later, that is. You see?"

"Got caught by a slip up eh? My students do it all the time," I said.

"Anyhow, if you ask me, I think the pseudo- and the original are one and the same," said Mr. Aris. "Only this is like the tenth edition, updated by an unnamed scholar. We'll never know for sure, of course. The answer was lying right there in Alexandria until..."

"Why did they burn the library down?" asked Maria, reflecting on 'the crime of the millennium', as Mr. Aris had put it.

"Good question Maria," he answered. "Indeed, why would anyone commit such a terrible crime?" Anger in his voice.

"An effort to conceal damning evidence? To make history disappear?" I suggested.

"Perhaps. It's all a big riddle really. Evidently the library was established under someone called Ptolemy the Second*, an eccentric ruler of Alexandria. He was called 'Philadelphus'. Not because he was friendly toward people in a brotherly way, but rather because he got overly friendly with his sister, Arsinoe, even dumping his original wife to marry her instead."

"Kept it in the family, eh?" I asked.

"You could definitely say that. The Philadelphias of today

* Actually, it was his father who established it, after he took over Egypt, following the death of Alexander the Great and the division of the empire among the generals. But it was Ptolemy the Second who expanded the library to its acclaimed glory.

originally derive their name from this king. I wonder how many know that! In any case, maybe brotherly love wasn't too big a deal back then. At least he didn't marry his horse. Anyway, this Ptolemy character of course knew how great he was. He declared himself a god. That was always a good approach to ensure people didn't mess with you: '*I am god, leave me alone.*'" Mr. Aris said this with a 'godly' voice.

"But I do agree with him," he continued. "He was great. He was a believer in the power of knowledge. He consolidated Greek and Egyptian wisdom. He was a bridge between the east and the west. And as his crowning glory he founded the Great Library of Alexandria which was said to contain over five million manuscripts at its height."

"When did all this happen?"

"About in the middle of the second and third centuries BC. Almost two and a half thousand years ago."

"And when exactly was the library burnt down?" asked Maria.

He hesitated.

"... It's your word 'exactly' that makes me hesitate. This is where the story gets muddled, probably due to religious interference from many sides. The official take is that some Islamic Caliph ordered it burnt down because it contained information contradicting the then new religion: Islam. Apparently he uttered something like, '*if these Greek books agree with the Koran then they are not necessary to have around. If they disagree then they should be destroyed*'. So, using this crazy logic, they were burnt without even being opened. Now, if this is all true it would mean that the library lasted for about eight or nine hundred years, which isn't too bad. Given us humans' terrible record of general destruction."

"Well isn't it all true?" she persisted.

"I have no idea. But this story about the 'bad' Islamists is first mentioned round about the *thirteenth* century AD! Somebody thought to write about this big catastrophe only five hundred years later! Strange, eh, don't you think? And isn't it logical that previous fanatics from other older religions would also be tempted to destroy these books which surely contained pagan stuff like the original Sun and Moon oriented religions?"

"Who do you mean?" I asked.

"The early Christians of course. I don't think we can quite put them in jail with what we can present in court, but circumstantial evidence isn't too favourable I am afraid: they were hanging around in the neighbourhood at the time of the crime. They were the ones to first bring down Alexandria. They arc the ones who said that knowledge was evil. Look at what happened to poor Adam just for wanting to know. Apart from doing away with the even more ancient religions, if they were even still kept alive there in the library, they had to also rid themselves of those almighty wily Greek gods: the Zeus-types."

"You are blaming the Christians for eliminating the Greek gods?" I asked.

"Of course. Like every new religion does or tries to do. Eliminate the previous one, I mean. Greek mythology was Greek religion before it became mythology, like I told you. That is why every Christian church in our parts is built right on top of an Aphrodite, an Apollo or a Zeus temple or whatever."

"So it was the Christians who burnt the library then?" asked Maria still trying to unravel it all.

"Like I said I am not sure. I think that nobody is. But they must at least stay on our suspects list... you know, to be honest, whenever I try to play detective, to uncover an ancient controversy, to decipher 'the truth', I just get all tangled up: Too long ago, too much missing evidence, biased statements, questionable sources, theories which require giant leaps of faith, eliminated witnesses, fragments of things said taken out of context, and so on."

He pointed toward another bookcase and a neat row of similar books. "The *Encyclopaedia Britannica* over there says it was the Christians, if you want to believe it. But it has also been said that the library may have been destroyed by Julius *Cesar*, a few years before Christianity. Of course if these stories are *all* correct, then the poor library was burnt down several times. So the blame shouldn't go to anyone or any group in particular. Blame should go to the collective stupidity of humankind. We build and then destroy. That's who we are. There's no escaping. The more we advance, the higher we build, the more sophisticated ways we devise to bring it all right down. We build skyscrapers reaching the heavens, but we also build nuclear weapons which can bring them down in a flash. That's why one day we'll just blow this whole damn place up. We should all be on trial."

Today's drive was very very special. Not because of our destination. The two of us just drove aimlessly around the old part of town. It was special because something interesting happened in Mr. Aris that afternoon. He was very quiet for a long time, like that first drive when we had first met. Out of the blue, but like he had finally reached a decision, he started talking about his past. Just like that. I do not believe I had even asked him anything to trigger the unstoppable flow of words. He simply began his narration as if answering a question. Suddenly, quite unexpectedly then, the floodgates opened. Like the small talk was over. Of course, I did not quite realise it that day. After all, what I got was only a very brief introduction. But it was the start. I basically just kept quiet and listened, a practice I was to apply many times and perfect in our next outings.

"I am not going to tell you about the good old days. It would just be foolish to do that. When I think back, life seemed invariably rough and cruel and unforgiving back then. You can't imagine. People were poor. Dirt poor. And as tough as granite. All of them. Not just the men. Any Cypriot woman back then could beat up a seventeen year-old boy of today. Kids were tougher than many grown ups I see these days. Everyone was used to hardships. Ten year old children were more mature than people are today at twenty five.

I know it is only a bit over half a century ago. You may think I am making it like it was a thousand years ago, or that I am talking about another country. Or another planet. But things were so much different then, believe me Alexis. My family was at the very bottom of the pile but there were really no rich Cypriots anyway. Not the way we think of 'rich' today. At least I had never personally seen one. Not even from a distance… if there were any, like let's say like some of the clergy or people who were favoured by the English, their wealth really had nothing to do with present standards. I believe they still all lived in relative squalor like the rest of us. They too were trapped in this barren, dry forgotten land. They also were mercilessly attacked day after day by the same remorselessly bright sun. There was no hiding. No air condition or even fans. For the life of me much as I try I cannot recall dreamy images, like soft rays caressing people's faces and such. We were all constantly cowed by hard, white-hot bolts. It was like we were living in a big oven. But then again we didn't mind as much as you might think. We were used to it. I don't remember anybody burning from the sun. Except the snow-white English of course! The *Englezi*! Ooh, now that was a sight to see! They'd burn like lobsters! But our skin was hard and thick as leather. And dark. Cypriots were much darker then, believe me!

Just take a look at any old pictures of Cyprus. Everyone appears dark grey. And you should take notice of their eyes. They always looked directly at the camera, timidly. That's because you'd be lucky if you had your picture taken two or three times in your entire life. Of course, all pictures were black and white then. But even if they had been coloured there would not have been much difference. Everything was actually blander. There really were fewer colours around. Buildings weren't painted, clothes weren't dyed as bright.

I tell you, we were tough but pitiful people too. Why lie? You know another little detail you don't get to experience when you see old pictures from those days? The stink. Yep. Pheeeew! Of course, thankfully, our noses were desensitised. Do you think pigs stand around all day asking, in pig-talk, something smells bad in this pen? Everyone, not just us, even the softy English, smelled a lot worse in those days. To give you a rough idea of what it was like, go stand in the middle of some farm animals and take in a nice deep breath. It was not much different. We had no showers then and precious little water. It seemed a pity to waste such a valuable and rare commodity on something as frivolous as washing yourself. We lived in a dry dustbowl, so what was the use anyway? A wash every week or two was quite enough. Basic hygiene was barely sufficient and oral hygiene was nonexistent. Many people over forty or fifty had no teeth.

There even seemed to be fewer trees, they mostly were dusty greyish olive and carob trees, since for the most part the other 'decorative' kinds had been gradually chopped down in foolish desperation in order to provide heating during the bone-numbing winter months.

I remember that I was permanently hungry. So much so, that I learnt to live with it. It is always there in the background, it niggles at you, but you pretend you're not listening. It's like a game. You can tame it. You ignore it and it goes away. Or at least it leaves you alone for a while. You have heard the story about the clever 'hodja'*, of course?

No? Well, it's quite interesting. You see, he decided to try and 'train' his donkey to live without food. He almost did. Unfortunately, just when he was about to succeed, the silly beast died!

Survival, that was the word then. Other words, fancy big ones that you hear today, like opportunity, investment and development, they were not in anyone's vocabulary. Of course, come to think of it, once you get to learn these kinds of words, well, strangely, they tend to make you less human. More selfish. Like today, when it's more me-me-me.

* Moslem cleric or teacher.

Still, I hear other old people make all this silly talk about people being kinder, more 'human' back then. What rubbish! As if human biology could magically change in just twenty thirty years! Still, to be completely honest, I'm not going to say this was not at least partly true. People probably did care more for their friends, their extended family, their neighbours and their community those days. They were all together in this ancient sinking boat full of holes we called home. But, you know what else I think it was back then? When you've got nothing to give, the only thing you can offer a fellow human being is a smile and a kind word. So that's what you give.

'*Nashis tes eftches mu*' (my best wishes to you - bless you), old ladies would say if you helped them cross the road or did something nice for them.

I remember this type of words carried real weight back then, as we saw it, as if these kind ladies had some special power to grant wishes. Equally, when in anger a batty old lady laid a curse on us kids, it rang in our ears for days, as we waited for something bad to happen to us, as if she had direct contact with the devil himself!"

"You know the other day, when we talked of the oldest surviving book, Mr. Aris?" asked Maria. She had asked to come with me to see Mr. Aris. When I telephoned Mr. Aris to enquire if that was all right, he said never to ask again. She was welcome whenever she wanted.

He nodded that yes, he remembered the other day's discussion.

She was digging his stories and he was lapping it up.

"Well, I was thinking, when I went home, who is the most ancient author, Mr. Aris? Do you know *that* one?" she asked, openly challenging the poor man, but not in a cruel way.

He contemplated. It seemed that she got him there, for once.

"Good question," he replied, eventually. "I don't think anybody really knows… And in any case, what kind of 'author' do you mean? One who draws pictures? Because through pictures they'd tell stories in old times, you see. Or are you thinking of someone who writes his own stories? Or just anyone who simply writes? One who writes books?"

"I am not sure what I mean, now that you put it this way. I guess I was just looking for a name," she answered frankly.

"Because cave men were painting pictures on walls, like stories of mammoth hunts, tens of thousands of years ago. Even Neanderthals did that, no offence implied to our 'relatives'."

"Didn't they actually have bigger brains than us?" I asked, remembering I had read that somewhere.

"But did they use them?" asked Maria.

"Do we use them?" I asked.

"Perhaps an author must be someone who writes, who narrates, one way or another," said Mr. Aris. "And one, like you said Maria, whose name we actually know. Because there are thousands of ancient scripts which are anonymous. Most of them are, in fact."

"So, is there an actual name for a first known author, Mr. Aris?" I asked.

He took a deep breath. "Ok, let's think," he answered. He closed his eyes, concentrating, going through his old books in his mind. We waited. Then he said, "To get our answer, first of all, we must search for the most ancient written scripts, isn't that right? Who could actually write?"

"Well who?" I asked. "The Cypriots?"

"No, we weren't quite the first, but we were pretty close," he answered seriously. "But still, we were only a couple of thousand years late." He opened his eyes. "I think we must travel further from here, in the neighbourhood of Mesopotamia to find who we are looking for. The Babylonians, the Sumerians..."

You could almost see this great 'uneducated' man's brain ticking, as fast as a flying Magnette on the open highway about to be ticketed. You could sense him searching with his mind around his immense library, looking for a book with the information he was seeking. You could almost see him quickly flipping through pages, narrowing in on what Maria had just asked. Not quite the Google search, but close enough.

"So, it will have to be the gloriously beautiful Enheduanna," he finally announced. "That's who you are looking for Maria, I believe. That is probably the oldest author known by name," he replied to her with a winning smile not unlike the one he had given me when he had won our bet.

"Enhe-who?" Maria stammered.

"En-he-du-anna," he said slowly. "A bewitching Sumerian High Priestess."

"No wonder the name didn't survive to this day. It's too hard to pronounce," I remarked.

"Well, her friends probably just called her Anna," he conjectured, still smiling. "So it did survive."

"How do you know En...anna (she mumbled the middle part) was beautiful? Have you seen pictures?"

"Not quite. Her name means 'jewel of the sky', or something like that."

"Someone could be called Aphrodite and still be ugly though," she said.

"Yes, but she actually claimed she was alluring herself, in her own writings. I'll take her word for it," he answered, in good spirit.

"So she wasn't exactly humble was she?" I asked.

"No, I wouldn't call her that," he agreed. "In fact she openly boasts of her past glories and she even comes out and proclaims herself a goddess. That she is the earthly embodiment of the goddess Ningal, or Inanna, who was the wife of the Moon god Nanna."

We were no longer awestruck by these little nuggets of cool information. He just knew this kind of stuff. I did not even bother to question the correctness of what he was saying by then.

"So when did this lovely lady priestess live?" asked Maria.

"About four, four and a half *thousand* years ago," he replied, emphasizing the 'thousand'.

"Wow. That is a hell of a long time ago Mr. Aris. And what did she write about?" I asked.

"The usual stuff for back then, I suppose, especially given her profession. It's about religion, of course. It is about how upset she is that some 'idiot' king took over her native city and destroyed the most glorious temple of her time. But it also gets very personal. It describes how she was subsequently kicked out of her job at that ruined temple. And that she personally knew people in high places, very high places, who would get her back her job. Her supposed 'husband', an important god called Nanna- the one I just told you about-, would take care of it for her. He would deal with the bad person who did her in."

"So, same old problems back then eh? A dog eat dog world?" asked Maria.

"Yes. She probably thought, '*Ok, I got fired. It happens. Now, hmm, who do I know to get me my job back? Ah, wait a minute, I know God! I am married to him!*' That kind of usual thing… The story is quite interesting because she switches with ease from the third person to the first, at will bringing herself right in the thick of it. She exalts her supposed husband as the most important god of the Sumerian Pantheon, but then he praises her right back! '*I am yours, it will always be so*', she says. And later on Nanna replies, '*My Lady, I will proclaim your greatness in all lands!*'"

"That's so sweet," says Maria. "I wish someone would proclaim anything about me in all lands!"

I momentarily think of proclaiming something nice about her but I hold myself back.

"It is sweet, like you say. In fact, we Cypriots must thank Enheduanna. She is often credited for first injecting gentleness, femininity, eroticism and love into gods' personalities. In contrast to the macho tough, vengeful and unforgiving characteristics of most gods back then. It's a chain, and we are part of it: Ishtar was our own Aphrodite's predecessor, and she was much more warlike to start with, before she became a goddess of love. Aphrodite is Ishtar's exquisite combination with Inanna."

"Make love, not war," said Maria, not quite on the subject I thought. But Mr. Aris agreed.

"Exactly," he said.

"Are there any other really old authors you know of, Mr. Aris?" I asked.

"Well, I almost said Pta-Hotep instead of Enheduanna before, in answer to Maria's question. This person is a really close second I think. He was from that other great old Empire, or maybe I should say, the greatest ancient empire of them all: Egypt."

"Another easy name," joked Maria. She did not try to repeat the man's name.

We were on the porch. Through the open front door we saw Mr. Aris scanning a collection of books in front of him, on the floor.

"Aha!" he exclaimed. "Here it is."

He came over to me and handed me a little brown book, a typically Egyptian figure on its cover. I opened it. 'The instruction of Pta-Hotep'. Dated 1909, this translation itself was vintage. One hundred years old.

"He was a vizier, a high ranking official. He wrote down the advice he was given by his father* on how to do his job well. I think there is a copy of this at the Louvre or some other big museum."

"It says here that this is the oldest book in the world," I said, looking inside.

"Not true, but close enough," he offhandedly dismissed the

* Actually, 'The Maxims of Pta-Hotep' are now attributed to the grandson.

translator's claim. "Now, after these two," he continued, on a roll, "there's another Babylonian man from maybe over three thousand years back, I don't quite recall his name. He was a professional exorcist-"

"-Did they advertise for those kinds of jobs?" I asked.

"He wrote about a hero-type king and his friend's high-risk adventures.*"

"Like Batman and Robin?" asked Maria.

"Yes. Unfortunately this is before Hollywood so there is no happy ending. The friend dies I believe."

"More in the French film genre then... How come we've never heard these stories, Mr. Aris? Because, I assure you, they don't teach them in schools."

"I think it's the usual culprit, to be honest," he said. "Like I told you before. It's a case of one religion eliminating another, getting rid of the previous one. Sometimes I am amazed that these ancient accounts and more so those of the Greek gods even survive at all. They probably made it through only because we disguised them as fairytales... Anyway, after these old manuscripts comes the Hebrew Bible, not surprisingly, which I believe is quite like the Old Testament. Certain authors are mentioned there too I believe. Of course these types of stories were probably around for hundreds of years, if not thousands, before they were eventually written down by someone... and after them come Homer's stories, although I am not sure he even wrote them himself, like I think I also told you."

"I am surprised you didn't bring Cyprus into this story yet, Mr. Aris," I remarked, knowing his tendency to relate almost everything to this place.

"Well you are right on cue there Alexis! I just did! It has been claimed that the great man himself was originally from

---

* The Epic of Gilgamesh

Cyprus![*] That Homer's father was taken hostage by the Persians when they took over Cyprus. There is some credibility to this story. First, it comes from an ancient source, and second, why was Homer blind? Have you wondered? As you may know, hostages were blinded those days by their captors in order to hinder the possibility of escape. And of course, Homer means 'hostage' in Greek, doesn't it? That's not a real name, of course. It is what he was, a hostage, an *Omiros*."

"I always thought he was from Alikarnassos[**] or somewhere like that, or even an Athenian..." I said, thinking about it.

"Well, most areas in Greece have claimed him as their son at one time or another," he replied. "The Athenians that you mentioned, especially, forget about them! They 'Athenianised' the whole story, in order to instil a localised patriotic flavour: they made sure that Athenians were heroes within the Homeric epics. They had a chance to edit the Iliad and the Odyssey because it was an Athenian tyrant, Pisistratos, who first put together a committee to assemble all of Homer's poems, in fear that they would otherwise be forgotten. He brought in singer-poets from the streets, who would sing with a lyre in those days, to recite their stories so they could put them down in writing. Of course, any lines he didn't like or that denigrated the Athenians were promptly removed and in other places new, favourable and heroic paragraphs were added... this was all done in the middle of the sixth century BC, at least two hundred years *after* Homer's time, you see. Given the lack of

---

* It is a fact. This was claimed by Pafsanias, an acclaimed ancient traveler/geographer who lived in the time of Alexander the Great. The reader will note that I have added several footnotes regarding this whole conversation with Mr. Aris. The reason is that, afterward, I sought to confirm or disprove some of the less believable things he had mentioned. The notes reflect what I found out. The reader can judge for himself or herself whether the old man was right in his assertions, especially regarding Cypriot connections.

** Now modern Turkey.

reliable communications back then, I bet you that even they weren't sure back then if Homer had made up the whole epic thing... Of course, these epics were subsequently edited on numerous other occasions, later."

He continued:

"Even other peoples claimed Homer's birthright, like the Egyptians. So, due to lack of sufficient evidence, I'll take the Cypriot version!" he smiled. "Homer was a Cypriot!"

"I am not sure that would go down well with mainland Greeks!" Maria said, also smiling.

"Well, there is a clincher you know. Of course, there can be little doubt that Homer's Iliad and the Odyssey are an amalgamation of the many ancient poems that would be sung by many professional singer-poets* as they roamed around the old cities. It was their job, they did it for money. Like a street theatre. But did you know that the introductory chapters of the Iliad, the 'Homeric' book about the Trojan War, were actually originally written by a true native Cypriot?"

"Are you sure?" I asked, doubtfully.

"As sure as the next man," he answered, whatever that meant. "It was the great epic poet, Stasinos, a native Cypriot, who wrote the *Cyprian Epics* before Homer**. These provided

* As he mentioned previously, they sang with the accompaniment of a lyre. Hence, they were called 'lyric poets'.

** Some claim that Stasinos was Homer's son-in-law and that Homer gave him the 'Cyprian Epics', rather than the other way round. Even if this were the case, and it is likely that we will never know for sure, the fact that Homer was here, sharing stories, marrying his daughter off to a Cypriot etc. admittedly only strengthens Mr. Aris' Cypriot-influence case for the epics. Pafsanias even mentions the name of Homer's mother (Themisto), who was a citizen of Salamis in Cyprus. The Cyprian Epics, which are essentially an introduction to the Iliad saga, are usually presented in eleven books and are considered to be part of the 'Epic Cycle', the group of Epic poems which were amalgamated to create the Iliad the setting for what was to follow: the Trojan War. They contain the well known story of how Paris stole beautiful Helen from her hapless husband, Menelaos. How he and the others launched a thousand ships to get her back, and so on.*"

"Stasinos first wrote all that stuff, huh?" asked Maria.

"Well yes. You know why Zeus instigated the Trojan War? Because the world was becoming overpopulated. A bit of old fashioned population control: kill a few, problem solved."

"Or rather, have them kill each other, you mean," I said.

"Not me. Stasinos or Zeus or whoever," he replied.

"It's kind of ironic that we never learn about the Cyprian

---

and the Odyssey. The complete account of the Trojan adventure, from the gathering of the Achaean army to Odysseus' death is derived from several 'lesser' epics (this so-called epic cycle): the Cyprian Epics, (by Stasinos of Cyprus), the Aethiopis (by Arctinus of Miletus), The Little Illiad (by Lesches of Mitylene), The Sack of Troy (by Arctinus of Miletus), The Homeward Journeys (by Agias of Troezen) and, finally, The Telegony (by Eugammon of Cyrene). See "Many-Minded Homer", W.F.Jackson Knight, George Allen & Unwin Ltd., 1968 for details. Now, 'The Cyprian Epics' were originally considered by some to be written by Homer, but Herodotos wrote that "The Cypriot epics are not of Homer but of someone else" (Book 2, 117)...

* It may well be that even the great Homer was passing the baton. Pafsanias refers to an even older great poet, a Cypriot by the name of Euclus, who may have passed the poems down to Homer who then may have passed them down to Stasinos. The possibility that Homer got the poems from someone else is very likely: Did hundreds of years pass before someone, like Homer, thought to tell the story? Surely people 'sang' the war right after it finished. Why would they wait for hundreds of years to remember it and its glories? In truth, not much is known about Euclus, Homer or Stasinos. We draw conclusions from random quotes. For instance, Socrates quotes Stasinos in 'The Euthyphro': speaking of Zeus, Stasinos says the 'Machiavellian' "where fear is, there also is reverence," but only to disagree with the poet's concept of God. Incidentally, some Arcado-Cypriot words and intonations are still used in today's local Cypriot dialect. If you want to get as close as possible to a rough idea what Greek sounded like in ancient times, go listen to a peasant Cypriot talking.

epics while going through an education in Cyprus, isn't it?" said Maria.

"It *is* kind of strange," I said. "Like it's a conspiracy to hide something."

"It's a shame because Stasinos' account is quite rich, even in terms of moral dilemmas: he describes war as a primitive and naïve way to sort out problems. And he recognizes the importance of awe and shame as motivational forces."

"Well at least we have honoured the man by giving him a street name: Stasinos Avenue," commented Maria. It is true. One of the best known avenues in Nicosia goes by that name. It is the one that goes round the ancient Venetian walls of the city. The one I drove around with Mr. Aris in my first ride in the Magnette. But ask any Cypriot if he knows who the hell Stasinos was. You will get a blank look.

"Did you know, in Bodrum, that's in Turkey, in 1995, an ancient inscription was found. It's still there, of course, so go check if you don't believe me. It tells of a 'Kyprian', who is the poet of the Iliad. That would be Stasinos or possibly that Euclus character…," said Mr. Aris. "Unless of course, this Kyprian is Homer himself, like I said! And, anyway, let's not forget that much of the Iliad is written in the ancient Cypriot dialect… Homer mentions Cyprus here and there, too," he went on. "Of course, he too exalts the beauty of our very own great lady: '*Tell me the deeds of golden Aphrodite the Cyprian, who stirs up sweet passion in the gods and subdues the tribes of mortal men*'.

A beautiful quote, I thought: irresistible Aphrodite, both to men and gods. Apart from Mr. Aris, I did not know anyone else who could quote Homer.

Also, his evidence of the Iliad's Cypriot roots was not shabby. Quite circumstantial, one could say, but still.

He was on a roll and he had a receptive audience. So he continued:

"... And then, after Homer in the line of ancient authors, probably comes that other great lady poet from antiquity, Sappho," he continued.

"The lesbian?" asked Maria.

"Yes, the Lesbian, with a capital 'L'. As in from the island of Lesbos. I am not sure if the lesbian label, as in preferring women rather than men, completely fits the actual person. After all she did die for a man, didn't she?"

"Did she really?" asked Maria, intrigued once more.

"Absolutely," he replied. "Well maybe. Or perhaps not! But does anyone care? And does anyone really know anything about her? It's another one of those detective stories. It too has Cyprus connections," he added, smiling quizzically. "Perhaps another time I'll tell you about her, if you'd like."

So young

We are chasing the moon
Just running wild and free
And it really doesn't matter that we
don't eat
No it really doesn't matter, really
doesn't matter at all
'Cause we are so young now, we are so
young, so young now
(The Corrs)

Maria could not make it to the weekly drive this time. So, unsurprisingly, Mr. Aris continued his reminiscing like it had not been two weeks since he had last done so. It was as if we had not talked of other things, like ancient authors and suchlike, in the meantime. I believe it was on this day that I first thought I noticed a couple of patterns which were to prove right with time. One, he was saving his recollections only for me. When Maria was there with us he would still be talkative but he got onto other subjects. At those times, he would move onto other subjects, inviting our contribution. And two, these meetings were different. He did not need much probing at all to start off and to ramble on. He just talked and talked, a monologue, until he decided he was done for the day. Now, as soon as the Magnette engine started, off he went as well:

"You know, of course, amid all this doom and gloom I was telling you about the other day, there still was one thing in that far away world that was infinitely better than today, no matter how you see it: I was young!

And a lively little rascal I was too. A little survivor. You had to be. No food, filth all over, mysterious diseases that would strike without warning and which none of us had any idea where they came from or how to cure… The heartless reaper would take as many of us as he wanted; whoever he chose, and then leave us alone again when he chose to, for a while at least. You see, just like all other things, life was much cheaper too.

Almost every kid I knew had lost a brother or sister. Some of my friends passed away before they stood a couple of feet off the ground, Alexis. The minute you were born you had to be ready for battle… no wonder that Noah character could recite prayers as soon as he was born…

I was roaming all over our village surroundings, for miles, before I was six or seven. We'd follow sheep and goat herds, like hungry little wolves, attempting to steal a chance to suck some milk, directly from the source. Not an easy thing to do! The goats themselves had little milk to offer, given the arid conditions, and they rather preferred to give it to their little ones. And the shepherds, they would chase us away with sticks and stones, same as they would do to other irksome beasts meddling with their herd.

We miserable souls, we were the natives of Cyprus. On the other side of the fence, many times literally, were the current 'owners' of this ancient land: the English and the almighty British Empire. Maybe it was in its last throes, but how were we to know? Most of those people walked around as if they were royalty themselves and not the mere 'subjects' that they were. Noses high in the air. Doing their best to ignore the dirty, bothersome, parasitic, ignorant natives. But, as I am sure you know, the Englezi were not all like that. And I had first hand experience of this fact. I will tell you about that later.

I grew up outside a small village called Sihari. You can see it from my veranda if you look up at the Pentadaktylos range. It is right there, just to the right of that big ugly Turkish flag*. It's only twelve or thirteen miles from Nicosia. But it could be

* Since the Turkish invasion of the north of Cyprus in 1974, the occupying army has put up a gigantic flag right on the side of Pentadaktylos mountain, facing the free side of Cyprus. It is made of white-washed stones and lights, which switch on and off at night, like a monstrous and ominous Christmas tree. A reminder, lest we forget.

a million. That was very far, back then, even for us little wanderers. There were grown ups that had never ever been down to the big city, the capital. You hardly ever saw any type of vehicle pass by our parts of the world. Why should it? For a Sunday excursion? It would be reckless to waste good petrol on such silly ventures. To sell us something? With what would anyone buy goods? And anyway, what would we peasants buy even if we had the money? People made their own clothes. Now don't start thinking something like a full wardrobe or Armani suits, but those rags did what they were supposed to do. Grown ups got by with a single pair of shoes, which they fixed and re-fixed all their lives. We kids, we were like goats, we never wore any shoes at all. Our feet were so tough anyway, a nail couldn't get through. And food? We were mostly of the hunter and gatherer tradition, coupled with some farming. And fishing, if you lived near the sea, which we didn't. Soap? Perhaps once every six months. Very carefully used. Soap bars were bigger then, the green type, do you recall them? Maybe they are still available for sentimental old coots like me. They were all purpose, they washed anything and everything: clothes, hair, plates, you name it. Anyhow, most things that were taken up there were brought the regular way: via the world famous, good old, reliable, and stubborn I should add, Cyprus donkey. Now where did those fine-looking beasts disappear to, Alexis? I don't care for much from that period of time but I do miss the sight of them. Those expressive beautiful big eyes… there was more intelligence in those eyes than in some of the inbred kids I used to hang out with, I can tell you!

I remember some nights sitting by myself at my favourite spot, on the top of a big boulder next to our house. If I looked up I could see a black sky exploding with dazzling stars. Pitch darkness will do that for you: give you a brilliant starry night of a sky. I would look up for hours, sometimes till I fell asleep, trying to figure out my place in the universe. Once I dreamt I was falling. I woke up to find myself in mid-air literally falling off that rock!

Gazing down, I could see the sparkling bright lights of the big city. Don't you imagine a Las Vegas or something. The whole of Nicosia had a couple of thousand lights, maybe. But of course we still didn't have electricity at our village when I was a young boy. TV? Never heard of it. Radio? Perhaps down in the city. We rose with the sun, slept when the sun went down.

Sitting on my rock, I could also see the top of our whole house easily. We constructed it on government land, I believe, since we never bought it and nobody ever threw us out. My father built it with his own hands with the help of my mother and my three older brothers. I vaguely remember bringing sticks and stones, trying to help but being in their way and being shooed away by them all. It was made of mountain rock, plithari*, and wood. Built on a slightly crooked surface, it always was a bit downhill in there. Good for water drainage though! And I tell you, water did drip through the roof, often.

The house was no more than five by five yards, the whole thing. You could say it was designed in a modern, 'open plan', you know? It featured just one multifunctional room which was kitchen, bedroom and living room, all in one. Luckily, ours was a 'small' family by the standards of that time. There were only five of us kids, plus our parents. For some reason my mother couldn't have any more children after the birth of my younger sister. So, we really had a reasonably comfortable dwelling. I am serious. To give you an idea about what I mean, compare us with our neighbours, living in the next house down the road. The Koteros family. They had fourteen children. I think they were fourteen anyway. They probably

* Mud bricks.

weren't so sure themselves! You could find those rugged Koteros kids all over the village in nooks and crannies. And I've been running into Koteroses all my life since, in the most unlikely places. They are all over!"

It was Maria who eagerly brought up the same subject again.

"So what's the detective story on that lesbian Sappho, Mr. Aris? How did she die then?" she asked, taking a sip of her Cyprus coffee on the old porch. He did not answer immediately, as if he had ignored her. Or he had not heard. He finished off his coffee, making a loud noise as he sipped. He waited till we got into the Magnette and the motor was running. Maria sat in the back seat so he had to turn around, to face her. He had his captive audience where he wanted it.

"Now, you want to hear about Sappho?" he smiled good-naturedly. "You know, I am really not sure at all what to tell you. Her story is not an easy one to tell. It's a classic example of that telephone game, where the original tale is so distant and so down the line that no one really knows what's true anymore. You see, what we do know of her comes from her own poems of course, which are in any case often open to interpretation. Also from Greek comedies, which may or may not be accurate. That's in addition to what we have gathered from French pornographers and Roman sources ... and Greek philosophers. It's a big mix-up I tell you. Most, as I see it, are pretty dodgy sources, you may agree too. The majority of the reports were written long after her, hundreds of years after she died. How can any story stay intact and accurate for so long? What we do know is people's interpretations piled on top of other people's interpretations... so just by going on with any story about her I'm on shaky ground myself here."

"Don't worry, we are naïve Mr. Aris. We'll buy any yarn you spin!" Maria assured him.

"Unless you tell us the Lesbian is a Cypriot," I corrected.

"She could be," he smiled back. "There are ties... Anyway, let's recount the supposed facts first. She deserves the title of 'the first female voice of the West' I believe. And we do know that she was one of the greatest poets of antiquity, that she was at least in Homer's league. Being a woman she was certainly more passionate, more soulful."

"Homer the Cypriot?" I teased.

"Yeah, that one," he agreed. "Anyway, Sappho, who, not many people know, was born in Cyprus-"

"No!" we both shouted simultaneously. All three of us laughed.

"All right, all right! Sappho, from the island of Lesbos, now she was a pioneer, a wise person, a teacher," he said, warming up to the story. "She lived over two and a half thousand years ago, at around six hundred BC. She was the head of a school devoted to the Muses. Its headmistress, so to speak."

"Remind me, Mr. Aris, who exactly were these Muses?" Maria asked.

"Ah, the Muses were really important in antiquity. The first question we should ask is, how many were they? Because even their number varies. I know that originally there were supposed to be just three of them-"

"-I thought there were like nine of those ladies," I interrupted, vaguely recalling this number from my school days.

"Eventually, yes," he agreed. "In fact, Plato refers to ten muses. He says Sappho is the tenth one!*"

* It's not only Plato. Antipater of Sidon, and Plutarch (Amat. 18) also refer to her as a Muse.

"Wasn't she supposed to be really ugly? What was she doing among all those beauties?" I asked.

"Who knows? *Was* she ugly? We know that Sappho had dark hair and a beautiful blonde daughter, because she says so herself, but not much more than that as far as her looks go. No pictures back then… there are statues, of course, but those were made after she was long gone. They depicted her like an archetypal spinster type! Plato naturally had not seen her with his own eyes; he couldn't have, as he was born a couple of hundred years later. He theorised about her too, just like we are doing right now. And perhaps we are missing his point. Maybe he was only giving her the ultimate compliment. Like someone today referring to a beautiful woman as a goddess or as Miss Universe, even though she has never been close to heaven or a beauty pageant. Anyway, whatever the case, the muses purportedly represented everything beautiful."

"There were nine of them, right?" I asked, insisting on the number.

"Initially there were just three, not nine: Meleti, which means 'study', even in Modern Greek. 'Mnemi', which still means memory. And 'Oedi' which means music. Think of the importance of these ladies, what they each symbolize, to this day. Honestly, where would we be without them? Where would we be without knowledge, recollection and music in our lives? Nowhere. Or swinging in trees."

"Where did they come from? Were they goddesses?" asked Maria.

"Pretty close I would say," he replied. "Hesiod, the historian, claims in his seventh century BC Theogony that they were daughters of Zeus himself. Who knows where these divine creatures sprang up from?"

"Our rich imagination, most probably," I suggested.

"Later," Mr. Aris continued, "like you said Alexis, more of these Muses were to be born. Most sources do talk of nine, all stunningly fine-looking. And, it is also agreed, they represented the arts and anything aesthetic. Words like 'music' and 'museum' come from these Muses... That's who Sappho's school idolised: these superwomen."

"So she had a school like those of the ancient philosophers?" asked Maria.

"Yes, only this school, obviously, precedes the famed Athenian philosophical schools."

"Was it something like a 'Fine Arts' school? I asked.

"It would appear to be so," he replied. "It depends on how broadly you define 'Fine Arts'. But it was the first of its kind, as far as I know. It was basically a poetry and music school-"

"-Like that one in the film 'Fame'?" asked Maria.

He looked at her, seemingly contemplating.

"Anyway," he said, not understanding I think, "women from all over the 'world' got to know about this top school, so they went to her island to study under her."

Yeah, literally.

"So these were her girlfriends?" I asked out loud.

"Well, that's not too clear. What we do know is that there were some '*hetaerae*', maybe friends of hers or fellow teachers and there were also some '*mathitriai*' in the school. Some of their respective names are actually preserved to this day."

"Now wait a minute," said Maria. "The '*mathitriai*' part I get. That's what we still call female students or pupils in Greek schools. But what's with the 'hetaerae' ladies? That means 'prostitute' in Greek, doesn't it?"

"Well now you have opened a big Pandora's Box and you'll find us Cypriots crawling around somewhere in there too," he replied. "You sure you want to know? You sure you want us to go there?" he toyed with his audience.

"Yes!" we replied simultaneously again, making us all laugh.

"All right then. First of all, 'hetaera' does mean prostitute these days, but it also means other things, like partner or peer. So this whole 'nasty' story might simply be a misunderstanding!"

"Lost in translation," I commented.

"Also, even if it isn't, you must get out of your mind the 'sex is bad' thing that has been fed to us for thousands of years. Can you do that?"

"We can try," said Maria smiling innocently.

"So what kind of a teacher was Sappho then? A sex teacher?" I ventured.

"Perhaps you are right. Yet, perhaps she just taught her pupils how to love. Then again maybe her declared passion for her girls, her pupils, is asexual, platonic. And speaking of Plato, didn't his teacher, the great Socrates also 'love' his students, in 'interesting' ways? You see, these things were quite different back then."

"So she loved her students in interesting ways?" asked Maria.

"Perhaps," he conceded. "But really, we do have to take a closer look at the deeper significance of love back then. For one, the whole idea of love-making and child bearing is a miracle, even today, would you not agree? Imagine back then. This double power which women had, to drive men, even gods, crazy and to bear children. Effectively, to give life. To ensure the survival of humankind. That is why women goddesses have such a central role in ancient places like Cyprus and Babylon. It's all about fertility, because fertility means eternity."

I thought about it. He had a point. Don't all religions somehow spotlight eternal life? Is that not our ultimate desire?

"Now, the brightest representative of love and fertility in antiquity is, of course, our very own Cypriot goddess, Aphrodite. Admittedly, like I said before, Aphrodite, or the Roman equivalent, Venus, is a metamorphosed amalgamation of Sumerian Inanna, Ishtar or Astarte, the Persian Anahita, the Phoenician Tanit etcetera, etcetera. All these were erotic goddesses associated with love and fertility. Not in a venal way, mind you. But in the most beautiful, divine sense."

"And how does Sappho fit into all this?" asked Maria.

"She's right in the thick of it," he replied. "First of all, almost all her poetry is directed toward love and its deity, Aphrodite. One could say Sappho's school was clearly dedicated to her adulation."

"Therefore you could call it the 'Aphrodite Fine Arts School'," I conjectured.

"Surely. Her poems are laden with Aphrodite references: 'Come, goddess of Cyprus, and in golden cups serve nectar delicately mixed with delights,' says Sappho. It's this link between Sappho's work and Aphrodite which makes things fascinating and which leads to all kinds of conjecture. For Aphrodite temples, apart from the fact that they were equally as impressive as those of any other Greek god, featured another unique characteristic: they were staffed with 'hierodules' or 'hetaerae', women who would provide special services to pilgrims."

"They were employed at the temples?"

"So to speak. Like nuns, or monks in monasteries. 'Hierodules' means 'holy or sacred slaves'. I am not sure that they were actual slaves, although many experts seem to write so. I think they probably got it wrong. Even today, in our Greek Orthodox Church, when someone gets baptised, the priest says, 'Vaftizete o dulos tu Theou…' ('This slave of God is getting baptised…'). The insinuation is that we are all God's slaves. Now, holy slaves, in my mind, are more important than plain old slaves. Back then this must have only meant some kind of holy person, a priest. A priestess."

"Sappho trained women to be sex priestesses?" Maria asked.

"It's likely. Or just good wives, for all I know."

"If I understand this correctly then, Aphrodite's temples, which Cyprus was full of, were populated by prostitute priestesses?" I asked.

"Well, bluntly put, yes. Of course, the World Centre of the Aphrodite faith was right here, in the city of Paphos. Hence she is referred to as the Paphian by Sappho and others."

"So my Cypriot ancestors were all sluts?" asked Maria, feigning shock.

"Not in today's sense. Let us say they facilitated immortality, rather… It wasn't just Cyprus anyway. The same was practiced in places like Babylonia and Kappadokia before us. And the most infamous such Temple of Aphrodite was the one in Corinth, in Greece. '*Wealthy Corinth*' that place was called by the famed Strabo, on account of its bustling trade. He visited the place a couple of times, thirty and forty years before Christ."

"If he went there twice, maybe he didn't just go for purely scientific reasons," I guessed.

"I readily indulge him some fun, considering what he has done for humanity. Because we owe him a lot, for his momentous work, Geographica. It's made up of seventeen books which not only summarise the work of geographers before him, which is magnificent in itself; they also provide his own insight, from personal experience. He travelled all over, he claimed. He was an empirical researcher as well as a meticulous chronicler. Incidentally, in book fourteen he wrote of Cyprus."

"It's good that his work survives," I commented.

"Part of his work survives, you mean. Strabo was first a historian and then a geographer, although he himself admitted the lines between these two sciences are blurred. Before Geographica, which he compiled when he was quite an old man, in his eighties, he wrote a historical account of all the countries in the 'known world' in forty three volumes. Sadly, none of that work survives."

"Someone did not like his view of history."

"Probably. Destroy the old books and then manufacture a new history, as you like it to be told. An age old trick. Fools people every time."

"What did Strabo say about Corinth?" asked Maria.

"The Temple of Aphrodite there was so rich that it housed over a thousand hierodules, or hetaerae. Imagine the range of choice! He wrote that because of these hierodules the city was always crowded and it became wealthier and wealthier, as sailors would easily fritter away their money with them."

"On them, you mean."

"Whatever. Maybe with them. Maybe they were entertainers like Geishas, accomplished companions, or even more than that, since they were sacred too. A union with the divine is something we all seek, isn't it? Who knows?"

"Their social status doesn't seem too clear," commented Maria.

"It's true. I've only found bits and pieces, little clues. Pindar, the poet, stated that they were '*free from reproach*'. These ladies were Aphrodite's representatives, so they must have shared some of her power, don't you think?"

“Do we know any of these women by name?”

“As a matter of fact, we do. Books mention a couple of them. One, rose-cheeked Rhodopis, even became queen of Egypt! It’s a lovely story.”

“But is it a true story?” asked Maria.

“Does it matter? Well, some of it probably is: the great Herodotus wrote of Rhodopis, a ‘courtesan’ from Thrace and a slave of a certain Iadmon, who was taken to Egypt by pirates who had stolen her, to be sold. There she got her freedom and then proceeded to make lots of money on account of her beauty and possibly a whorehouse she may have opened in Naucratis, a Greek city on the Nile Delta. It was even claimed that she became so rich that she later financed the building of a pyramid, though Herodotus doubts that.”

“How did she get her freedom?” asked Maria.

“It was bought for an incredibly large sum of money by a man called Kharaxus. He was a very wealthy old merchant living in this city… You’re interested? Well, one day he went to the Naucratis market, to kill some time-”

“-Window shopping?” asked Maria.

“Exactly. Without the windows. He saw her, on display, literally. He was so mesmerised that he bought her on the spot. He proceeded to give her her freedom and then to lavish her with beautiful gifts. He even bought her a house of her own.”

“Which she turned into a bordello?” I asked.

“Again, maybe. The nice story goes otherwise. One of the favourite gifts Kharaxus bestowed on her was a dainty pair of beautiful ruby-red slippers. One day while she was bathing in her private ‘swimming pool’, an eagle swooped down and stole one of these slippers. Later, the bird dropped this single slipper into Pharaoh Amasis’ courtyard. He picked it up, wondering whom this delicate, beautifully adorned rose-red slipper belonged to. He cleverly realised that God Horus had obviously 'delivered' it to him through his envoy, the eagle. But why? He considered it and made his decision. In his infinite wisdom, he issued a decree: '*My messengers will travel to all the cities of the Delta, even beyond, to find the owner of this slipper. They will declare that when this woman is found, she will be my bride.*' A bit of a risk, wouldn't you agree? What if she proved to be an ugly bat? Fortunately, she turned out to be beautiful beyond the Pharaoh's wildest imagination. So they married, and lived happily ever after. Until the Persians took over, that is. Amasis was the last Pharaoh of ancient Egypt."

"Are you sure this is not the Cinderella story you're telling us, Mr. Aris?" asked Maria suspiciously.

"Of course it is," he conceded. "But it's an older version. By the way, guess who the man who bought Rhodopis' freedom was? That Kharaxus chap? I'll give you a hint: he was from Lesbos... Yes, he was Sappho's brother!"

"Small world," said Maria.

"The way you say it, it seems that everyone who was anyone was related..." I said.

"The way Herodotus says it," he corrected me.

"Do you know any other hetaerae Mr. Aris?" asked Maria.

"Not personally," he replied. "But I've read of a couple more. They didn't quite make it to queenhood though. Still we know what one of them looked like, exactly."

"How's that?" I asked.

"Phryne, the hetaerae, she modeled for Aphrodite statues. In fact, one of the most famous statues, the Aphrodite of Knidus, was sculpted by her boyfriend Praxiteles. When you think of Aphrodite's divine looks, you're basically envisioning Phryne."

"So she was a model?" asked Maria.

"Probably one of the oldest confirmed models, yes. Her story is just as thrilling as that of Rhodopis. Exactly because of her modeling career, posing as a Goddess that is, she got into a heap of trouble. She was formally accused of impiety, not a charge to be taken lightly. Remember, Socrates was put to death for the same offence. Anyway, her able lawyer, Hyperides, who of course was also her dear boyfriend, among a hundred others, was having a hard time defending her in court at the Arios Pagos. For a mortal a claim of having divine attributes was a terrible crime. In desperation or in a moment of brilliance, he ordered Phryne to drop her garment. The judges, naturally, were dazzled. They had to concede that, indeed, she had godly attributes. So, Phryne became the only woman in history to be declared divinely beautiful by order of court."

"Was she rich too, like Rhodopis?"

"Yes, immensely so. It was well known that she adjusted her prices according to the customer. For example, when the King of Lydia asked for her favours she demanded an outrageously high fee. You see, he was an ugly chap and she wanted nothing to do with him. Anyway, desperate idiot, he paid it! Eventually Phryne became so rich that she offered to rebuild the walls of Thebes on one simple condition. That they would have the inscription, '*Destroyed by Alexander the Great, rebuilt by Phryne*'. The city turned down the offer. The fools! A shame isn't it?"

It was this subtle running commentary that I enjoyed most in Mr. Aris stories. We had been driving for quite a while now, but we were hardly paying attention to our surroundings. The 'steamy' action was all inside the car.

We drove silently for a while. I was envisioning Aphrodite statues.

"Any other 'great' ladies worth mentioning, Mr. Aris?" I asked.

"One more. Last but not least, as they say. This lady, the

equally stunning Lais, was one of the thousand courtesans I told you about at the temple of Aphrodite in Corinth. Demosthenes, the famous orator, was said to have offered ten thousand drachmas for her companionship!"

"That sounds like much higher than the going rate, even today," I remarked. Maria looked at me strangely.

"The figure is exaggerated, surely," answered Mr. Aris, taking my point seriously. "To give you a rough idea, Athenian hoplites (soldiers) were paid just one drachma a day. It would take any one of them a lifetime to amass that kind of money. Eight drachmas could buy you a pair of 'shoes' to last a lifetime and one hundred and sixty would get you a whole slave. To give you an even better idea, it's been estimated that one drachma in the 5th century BC was worth about forty US dollars in 2006."

"Maybe Demosthenes was on a different pay scale," I said.

"Definitely," he agreed.

"Or maybe he liked her so much that he was willing to break the bank," I ventured further.

We were stuck in traffic now, in the middle of Nicosia. We hardly bothered. Still, I hoped the Magnette would not voice a complaint.

"Lais is mentioned in Karl Marx's PhD thesis, you know," he added, offhandedly.

"You've actually read Marx's PhD thesis?" asked Maria, amazed.

"No, I have a copy somewhere, but it's really too boring to go through. But he mentions Lais at the start. His PhD is about Greek philosophy. It deals with the differences between Epicurean and Democritean philosophy. To illustrate these differences he writes that it is as though one wanted to throw the habit of a Christian nun over the bright and flourishing body of Lais."

"I think it's clear whose side he is on," I said.

"But they're both from the same philosophical school," he commented.

"Plato mentions Lais as well," he went on after a while. "It's a sorrowful address to Aphrodite. It goes something along these lines:

'I Lais, who laughed exultant over Greece, I who held that swarm of young lovers in my arms, give my mirror to the Paphian. Since such as I am I will not see myself and such as I was I cannot.'

"That is touching," said Maria.

"Yes. It's about old age of course. Lais sees herself as an old woman in the mirror, but she longs to see her young beautiful face. Since this is impossible- no photographs back then- she has no use for her mirror so she gives it to Aphrodite... Oh well. In any case, she can't have looked that bad when she died. She was stoned to death by jealous 'regular' women, outside the Temple of Aphrodite."

How about the love story?

"I tell you, someone will remember us,
even in another time."
Sappho, (c. 630 BCE)

I parked the Magnette in the garage. Mr. Aris stepped out and headed toward his home. He did not invite us to join him. He seemed tired - and old.

"Mr. Aris, you didn't tell us about Sappho's love story," Maria called after him, apparently oblivious to his mood. Or maybe because of it. He invited us to sit on his porch and he went inside to prepare coffees. Maria followed him in, to help him out. It was a lovely evening. I could smell the faint but distinct aroma of jasmine in the air.

They emerged from the house laughing about something. Mr. Aris was back in form.

"There's really not much to talk about. Rumours have it that Sappho was in love with a handsome local boatman by the name of Phaedon. Her feelings were not reciprocated or there were complications since she was supposed to be already married, in any case. As a result, she leapt to her death from a forlorn lover's 'favourite' spot, a steep hundred foot rock on the island Lefcada*. She was, the story goes, dressed in white from head to toe like a bride."

"She committed suicide then?" I asked.

"If this particular tale is to be believed. Even if she did jump it is possible that she survived the fall anyway. Many did. You see, the rock was also used as a test of guilt or innocence. They'd throw alleged criminals down, dressed up in white bird's feathers-"

"-What's that for? To help them fly or to soften the fall?" I interrupted.

* The island is near Ithaca and Kefallonia (in the 'Eptanisa').

"Sort of, believe it or not."

"Sounds like the trusty 'witch test' of the Middle Ages: toss her in the water. If she floats she's guilty. If she stays under, she is innocent!" said Maria.

"Very much so. But some people did make it through the fall and if they did there were men in boats ready to pick them up. Then they would set them free... it is highly likely, if this episode ever happened, that Sappho lived to be an old lady. Evidence has recently emerged from an unlikely source. Archaeologists were unwrapping Egyptian mummies when they realised that the 'package' was more important than the 'product'. One mummy was draped with an entire poem by Sappho, a twelve line lyric meditation on aging:

'This state I often bemoan;
but what's to do?
Not to grow old, being human,
there's no way.'

"Reminds me of Lais," commented Maria. "This age thing..."

"Reminds me of me," he retorted.

"But that was lucky, the wrapping 'paper' I mean."

"It was. But the most fascinating story relating to Sappho was uncovered right here in Cyprus in 1894. Archaeologists found poems of a contemporary of hers, of a courtesan by the name of Bilitis."

"You didn't mention *her* before," said Maria referring to his recount of famous 'ladies' while we were in the Magnette.

"I'm old, she slipped my mind... Well, three entire 'cycles' of her work were discovered on a tomb here in Cyprus, in Amathus*. They dealt with three stages of her life: when she lived in Pamphylia **, then in Lesbos where she met and worked with Sappho and finally in Cyprus, where any Aphrodite priestess worth her salt had to come sometime. This whole work gave enormous insight into the life and philosophy of Sappho. Appropriately, when they were published, the '*Songs of Bilitis*' caused an enormous stir around the world... just like the discovery of Hitler's diaries did a few decades later."

"Yeah, but those proved to be fakes, didn't they?" I asked.

"You are right. But so were the amazing poems of Bilitis! The 'translator' fabricated the whole thing! There was quite a stir when the songs were 'discovered'. The author was so well versed in Sappho's work and in the ancient Greek language that he expertly made up every single line. Even esteemed experts were fooled because he referenced the work with real sources and because the style was so 'genuinely' old."

"Wow. That is amazing," I said. "I mean what this guy did. Shows how easy it is to bamboozle us naïve academicians."

"Anybody can be fooled, as long as one is meticulous. I sometimes wonder how much of history is just the figment of some 'wise' persons' imaginations. You know, a mere exercise in nationalistic propaganda."

We finished our coffees. He picked up the tray, bade us good night and walked into his house.

---

* Limassol today.

** Pamphylia was in the south coast of today's Turkey. Right across the sea is Paphos, where Aphrodite emerged from the waters. The two names, Paphos and Pamphylia, may well be related.

"So tell me what is it that you do, exactly Alexis? What do you teach at that college?" asked Mr. Aris. I could see him looking directly at me from the corner of my eye, from the passenger seat next to me.

I was mildly surprised. He had never really asked me 'personal' questions before, so I had concluded that we had an unspoken understanding: 'I don't pry into your business, you stay out of mine. Unless I choose to tell you it'. But, in fairness, maybe now that he had started talking about his past he wanted to know more about me too. I suggested offhandedly that he could come to a lecture at the college.

"Is that allowed?" he asked in genuine disbelief.

"Of course it is," I replied, somewhat puzzled. "Why wouldn't it be?"

"Well don't you have to pay or something? And also, I don't exactly look like your average student do I? I couldn't exactly slip in unnoticed... What with me being so old-" he waved his hand, dismissing the whole idea.

"What are you talking about, Mr. Aris? Of all people, I didn't think you would consider age to be a barrier to knowledge. Don't you worry about it. It really is no problem at all. We can go together tomorrow."

I walked in the lecture room with Mr. Aris by my side. Sixty or seventy students were already seated in the amphitheatre-style room. I am proud to say that my lectures are often filled. There was the usual commotion, students chatting with each other. I started setting up my notes and the overhead projector. Mr. Aris stood right next to me, dressed in his suit. I had expected him to find a seat for himself but he just remained there immobile, frozen and bemused. Like a child on his first day at school. I was taken aback a little.

So as the class quieted down and they looked down toward us I introduced him as a distinguished scholar of life. Perhaps the students didn't quite get it, for they clapped as if I had introduced Noam Chomsky. He bowed in response, awkwardly, even more nervous now. I pointed to an empty seat and he gingerly made his way there.

"Ok, now, let's put ourselves in a pleasant situation," I began. "After a few stress-filled, tense days, or weeks perhaps, you have finally plucked up enough courage to ask that pretty classmate you have been eyeing in my lectures to go out with you. Of course, you half expected her, or him, whatever you prefer (*smiles*), to put you in your place with something like 'me go out with a worm like you?'" (*Grins all round*)

"But she doesn't. She says yes, she will go out with you. So that's the first and perhaps easiest hurdle, successfully overcome. Now begins the real hard part. The actual going out together."

"That doesn't sound too hard," calls out a student from the front.

"Perhaps not at first," I concede. "Anyway, a friendly tip for the first date: don't order a big meal, eat at home. Either way you see it you lose: if you eat like a pig in front of her, commenting 'I'm hungry', with your most charming smile, with your mouth full, you probably won't impress her all that much. On the other hand, chances are you won't even touch any of your food. And, in any case, you need to be able to make a hasty retreat in case the date goes horribly bad or you find out you are dating a freak. You can't do that with a plate full of food in front of you!"

I notice that a few students are actually writing this point in their notes. Oh well. Maybe I should include it as a question in the final exam.

"But let us go through this whole thing a little further," I continue, hoping they are generally still with me. "During those early days, during those first dates, how do you behave? What are you thinking?"

"How to get her in bed?" A suggestion from the back, not loud but everyone hears.

"And good luck to you my friend," I reply with a smile. "But how do you behave, are you nice, are you bossy?"

I answer my own question.

"Of course you are nice. And she's nice too. You open every door for her; she laughs at all your jokes. Actually, you agree on just about everything don't you?"

Some nods.

"Now, let's take this little adventure one more step further," I continue. "You've been going out for a few months. By now you are officially 'a couple'. Or, lo and behold, after a year or two, you are actually married to each other!"

"From here on it's all uphill," I assure them and they smile understandingly. They probably know my marital status. They know I'm qualified to tell this story.

"Now you both begin jockeying for position. Perhaps you want to show him or her who's the boss around here. Maybe you just argue about where to go or what to do. Or, if you live together, you can't agree about who will do the dishwashing and who will take the garbage out. And about other important things: should the toilet seat be up or down? Welcome to harsh reality!"

"What you have experienced in this story is actually very normal. It's typical of the development process of a team. Any team, be it a football team, a 'family-husband-wife-kids-team', or a business team, like a department in a company," I say, in order to establish the desired perspective. The course is on leadership and team building.

"All teams, and you already belong to several, be it your family or your friends, typically go through several stages before they can be 'good' teams, harmonious and productive teams, happy teams. That first stage in our story, during those first dates when everything was fine and dandy, well that's the 'forming' or 'genesis' phase. And the second period, when arguments and politicking began, that was the 'storming' stage. Only if you are lucky, or you know what you are doing, you can reach the latter more productive stages, 'norming' and 'maturity'."

And so the lecture went on. At the end I put up on the overhead projector a few team-related old Cypriot sayings*. I asked the students to copy them down and to contemplate what they mean, whether they are universal or unique to the locality, and if they still hold today:

"Δώσμου στην ρίζαν να σου δώσω στην κούζαν"
(Give me for the root and I will give you of the pot)

"Το σταφύλιν το έναν θωρεί το άλλον τζιαι μαυρίζει"
(One grape sees the other and darkens {ripens} too)

"Ο συγγενής εν γαίμαν σου, τζιαι ο φίλος εν αρφός σου, τζιαι ο γείτος σου νυκτημερόν εις το προσκέφαλον σου"
(Your relative is your blood, and your friend is your brother, and your neighbour is night and day at your bedside)

"Ψήλα με να σε τραβήσω"
(Hold me up so I can pull you up)

* The Cypriot dialect is a form of Greek. In actual fact, mainland Greeks have trouble understanding it!

After the class was dismissed a few students came down to ask me some questions while the rest slowly drifted out. Mr. Aris waited until the very last student was gone before he got up from his seat to come toward me.

"Now you know what I do for a living Mr. Aris," I said.

He said nothing. He only held out his hand to firmly shake mine, fervently. And very seriously.

He was also quiet on the way back as we drove the Magnette to his home. After I parked the old car in the garage I made my way to my own vehicle. I opened the car window to bid him goodbye. He leaned in and shook my hand once more.

"Thank you," he said.

"Hello Mr. Aris, how are you doing? No, no I am coming over today. I'll be over, same as usual. I just wanted to tell you, this man who claims lost Atlantis is in Cyprus – the one we were talking about the other day - is here in Cyprus these days," I said. Mr. Aris was on the other end of the telephone line. I was referring to our previous conversation at the Larnaca beach, when we had sat on the black and white pebbles. I was also affected by his positive response to my lecture at the college. "He is probably looking for sponsors, but there is a presentation today and it is open to the general public, as I understand it. Just now, I received an invitation at the college. I mean, he is speaking somewhere else, but I just got the invite. If you are interested, I can arrange for us to go listen to him. Perhaps Maria wants to come as well. Maybe we can meet him too, if we get a chance."

He agreed to go. So the three of us went to see what this Sarmast (his name) explorer was about. Was he, like others before him, chasing rainbows? Probably, I thought. But we all three enjoyed what he said and especially how he said it:

'The whole world is going to shift to Cyprus. It will be the greatest archaeological discovery in history. It will change religion, it will change politics, science. The implications are almost endless…'

And so on. That kind of thing made Mr. Aris swell with pride. Powerful stuff. We loved it! He had some decent evidence too: for example, how Plato had basically described Cyprus when referring to the geographical characteristics of

Atlantis, but enthusiasm is what he really had brought along with him. And that is like an epidemic. It's palpable. You can touch it, you can catch it. We really hoped he would succeed. I wished that, somehow, I could some day know with certainty if what he claimed was true. I doubted it would ever happen.

Both Maria and I had agreed to visit our respective relatives earlier in the morning. So the three of us met for Christmas day lunch at Mr. Aris house. I had invited them to my place but he insisted. I brought with me a cooked turkey (it looked good!), bought from a local catering service. Maria 'chipped' in with homemade potatoes (she said) and a Mediterranean salad.

It was a wonderfully clear but chilly day so we settled inside, around the old fireplace in the living room. No central heating in this house. Mr. Aris had already set it up when we arrived, so the fire was blazing invitingly. We sank in on the slightly decrepit and weathered couches, a little too deep, holding our plates in our laps. It made me momentarily wonder what, when and how Mr. Aris ate on a daily basis. The small dining table was predictably overflowing with books. Still, the combined smell of the food, the burning pine and olive logs and the old books all around us was particularly pleasant.

There were no Christmas decorations or lights around. Most of the lighting came from the fire itself, easily eclipsing the bare electric bulb on the ceiling. Staring at the crackling and dancing fire was soothing. Way better than any TV show. I looked at the faces of the two people. Both seemed content. It occurred to me that it is the little things in life that matter: Companionship, sharing the little moments. It really is all about the little picture. The big picture is for the gods to contemplate.

The flickering flames warmed their faces and softened their features. Mr. Aris glowed, almost saintly. Maria looked – just beautiful.

After we ate, Maria went to the car to bring the Christmas gifts. Maria told Mr. Aris that she and I would exchange our gifts later but he asked her to do it there. So we first unwrapped our gifts. She had given me a nice watch. I was surprised. It was very nice. I held it in my hands.

"It's used to tell the time," she helped. My reputation preceded me.

Mine was less glamorous. A Parker pen.

"People used to write with that thing you know, before the advent of the computer," I informed her. She seemed impressed.

Now it was Mr. Aris' turn.

"You know what is most valuable to me," he told Maria. "The two of you and my books. Oh yes, and that Magnette outside! Let's not forget her. She may be listening in on us! Anyway, I want you Maria to walk around the house and take any book you want for yourself."

She was suddenly moved to tears. "I can't do that, Mr. Aris. These books are right where they belong. Here, with you."

But, of course, he insisted. "Yes, and I will take them all with me to the grave," he said, irony in his voice. "I will read them when I am dead, to kill time," he joked.

Some books in that house must be quite valuable. Especially the very old ones. I had flipped through books in good condition, from the seventeen hundreds. I think Maria was careful not to go for any of those. Or any of the easy-to-reach ones which were, as Mr. Aris had said, more important to him. She eventually picked out a 'newish' one (1971) called 'Mediterranean: Portrait of a Sea' by Ernle Bradford.

He flipped through it. "I remember this. Good choice," he said. "Not too much on Cyprus though," he critiqued.

She gave him a small key ring, gold or perhaps gold-plated.

It was octagonal, with the letters MG inscribed in the middle. On the back it said 'Magnette'. He put on the old key, the original.

I then handed over my gift to him. He could tell what it was, though he deliberately guessed wrong when Maria asked him. He said it was probably a radio, but it turned out to be a magazine when he took off the wrapping. It was a National Geographic, dated July 1928.

"The college was getting rid of some old books and magazines and I literally found this in a heap," I confessed. "It's got an article on Cyprus." I pointed to the first article entitled '*Unspoiled Cyprus*', within the signature yellow frame of the periodical. Written by a certain Maynard Owen Williams, apparently the magazine's first foreign correspondent. He became famous for his reporting of the unearthing of the Tutankhamen haul in Egypt.

"They threw this away?" asked Mr. Aris in amazement.

"They need the space for more computers Mr. Aris. Forget about books and magazines in the near future. They take up too much space (his house was testament to this but I hadn't connected the fact and meant no offence), they use up too much good wood and get worn too quickly."

I thought of telling him about e-books and suchlike, but I changed my mind.

He looked at me as if I was crazy. Then he dismissed it all, as if I was kidding. Perhaps stubbornly, I persisted.

"Libraries are closing down everywhere Mr. Aris. Remember the days when people used to actually check out books from libraries? The most popular ones had to be returned within a few days. Just like DVD's. Where's the 'American Centre' library in Nicosia? Closed. Does anyone even know if there are Cypriot libraries anywhere? And how about the 'British Council'?

"Did it close down too?" he asked in shock. He seemed genuinely hurt, like it was a personal matter.

"Its library, yes."

A moment of silence. As if news of the death of a distant sick relative had just come in. Maria broke the stillness.

"Wasn't fifty U.S. cents quite expensive back in 1928?" wondered Maria looking at the price on the magazine.

"Most definitely in Cyprus it was," answered Mr. Aris. "You couldn't make that much in a day, in a week for most people probably."

"You can tell that by looking inside," I suggested. "It looks like for many Cypriots there was no such thing as money."

He flipped through the sixty six relevant pictures stopping at some, pointing at things he recognised. I had read the article before I handed it over. Cyprus was not described in the most flattering of terms, and the pictures corroborated the reporter's statements. He portrayed the island as the most backward of the Mediterranean lands. The mostly black and white pictures accentuated the misery in the locals' faces and the desolate biblical surroundings. The road we had taken from Nicosia to Larnaca a few days ago, barely a half hour drive in the Magnette, was seen as a '*barren ride through a chalky wilderness, enough to repel a very Romeo amongst travelers*'. Hardly anything was complimentary. Mr. Aris read out loud, slowly and with a heavy accent:

"*Cyprus roads are run on the theory of a farmer with a hole in his roof. When it rains they can't be fixed, and when it's dry why fix them?*" He laughed.

"Good point," I said. "Seems reasonable."

"Some habits are so hard to break," commented Maria.

Further on he read, "*one cannot walk through a thicket or along a beach without tangling his feet in legend or history.*" He wasn't exactly sure what that meant in English so I translated for him. This statement satisfied him far more than the previous one. He nodded in agreement.

He flipped to the end: "*Aphrodite's isle, given by the lovesick Antony to Cleopatra, preached to by Paul and Barnabas, seized by the Lionhearted to avenge an insult and sold within a year... fled to by Crusader refugees... conquered by the Turks... now occupied by the British... awaits the visitor in a sheltered nook of the sparkling sea.*"

He closed the National Geographic, reflecting on what he'd read. Then he got up, suddenly.

"Now it's your turn," he announced excitedly, almost like a child. He appeared more happy giving things than receiving them. He disappeared in another room, returning almost as soon as he left. He was holding a large rectangular wooden item in both his hands. I immediately recognised it for what it was.

"A backgammon board!" I exclaimed, smiling.

He handed it over, almost ceremoniously. This was obviously an important moment to him. As I took it in my hands I started to realise why. This tavli board was not the usual type. For one, it was heavier than normal. I run a finger along the smooth wood.

"Solid oak," he said proudly.

It was not as precisely dimensioned as the usual factory-made boards. And it was beautifully, if unevenly, engraved. There were burnt-in designs on the borders of the matt-lacquered wood.

"Took a week to put together," he announced.

"Did you make it?"

He nodded.

"Actually, not recently. I made it years ago, but it got broken. A sour loser threw it at a wall. Could have killed him right there and then… So, all I did was fix it up again. And I added your name on it."

I looked all around the board to spot my name. I couldn't locate it.

He smiled. "It's right there," he said pointing at a corner. That did not look at all like my name. This is what I saw.

"I know. It doesn't look at all like your name," he read my mind, smiling. "But it is. It is our very own writing, and most of us Cypriots don't even recognise it. Even you, a big shot professor! It is called Cypriot Syllabic, Linear A. It is, as its name suggests, a syllabic language, so your name actually reads 'A-le-xe-se'. Near enough. But people used to speak that way too. Even today: old villagers still say 'a-tho-ro-pos' (anthropos – human), don't they? It is of course, an ancient form of writing. It existed even before the Greek alphabet. We here in Cyprus were in a unique position to develop a writing form and we did. We already had the Phoenicians here, who had their own writing, and we also had another great civilisation living here: the mighty Minoans, of Minotaur fame, the people from the island of Crete. They too had their own writing. We sort of drew from both these sources, and others, to create our own. Of course…"

He went on but I did not hear. It had hit me. I recognized these symbols. They were similar to what I had seen stashed in the secret compartment of the Magnette. I almost blurted it out but then I thought better of it. I caught the tail end of Mr. Aris' presentation.

"Our very own writing and it dates back to 1100 BC! Actually, even further back. The mighty mainland Greeks hadn't come up with any letters at all yet back then!" he boasted.

He opened a book. There was a crumpled piece of paper inside. Obviously, it had been frequently used. Here is what it said:

a	e	i	o	u
ja			jo	
ka	ke	ki	ko	ku
la	le	li	lo	lu
ma	me	mi	mo	mu
na	ne	ni	no	nu
pa	pe	pi	po	pu
ra	re	ri	ro	ru
sa	se	si	so	su
ta	te	ti	to	tu
wa	we	wi	wo	
xa	xe		zo	
ga				

Ancient Cypriot syllabic script. Decoded.

"You can keep this too if you want," he said handing me the piece of paper. "I have had some practice, I know most of the symbols off by heart."

"You must be the only one in Cyprus," said Maria in approbation. "You and a couple of archaeologists, maybe."

Mr. Aris went on and on animatedly about Cypriot language and culture, late into the night. His favourite subject, Cyprus was. He informed us that although Cypriot is ancient, the Sumerians in the Mesopotamia area are credited with developing the first ever written language. Five thousand years ago! Chinese symbols are also very old, appearing about a thousand years later, around 2000 BC. A few hundred years later than that, Cyprus was to catch the written language 'craze' too. Since the island was a cross-cultural crossroad, it was open to many influences. Hence, its first writing was not Greek or alphabetic at all. In fact, the original Cypriot inscriptions are among the oldest worldwide, they are about three and a half thousand years old. Those, apparently, have still not been deciphered to this day. The first readable script appeared four hundred years later. It was the name of the owner of a certain funerary object. Mr. Aris did not know the actual name of the person or the exact nature of the object. He said his sourcebooks on languages did not provide that little piece of information. But he did know that Cypriot writing was originally mainly used for short dedications and funerary texts. Later, it was also used for more elaborate writings, like historical accounts. All in all, Cypriot writing existed and survived for quite a long time, for over a thousand years. Toward the end of its life, for a while, it coexisted with the Greek alphabet, which had been developed in the mean time. In fact, thank god for multi-script engravers of the past. Some plaques from that Classical period displayed both scripts. That is how the writing was deciphered. Much like in the case of the Rosetta Stone*. My namesake, as Mr. Aris put it accusingly, wagging his finger at me, the grander one between the two of us, brought the death knell to Cypriot script. Extensive colonisation of the island during the next period, the Hellenistic period, at the time of Alexander the Great's expeditions in our neighbourhood and beyond, led to an eventual complete abandonment.

It is interesting to note, added Mr. Aris, that around this time another famous Greek was around. One of the greatest thinkers of all time, Plato, born about sixty years before Alexander, who got the written language idea all wrong, as he was fervently opposed to it. He labelled writing a detriment to human intellect, arguing that it made the brain lazy and decreased the capacity of memory. Surely, Mr. Aris argued, Plato would change his mind if he was around today. How can any brain, no matter how sharp, hold a whole world of knowledge in its tiny confines? How can something a mere sixteen centimetres 'long' hold all this information we have been patiently gathering for thousands of years?

We had a great time, the three of us, that night. We chatted, we laughed. Mr. Aris provided us with interesting information and told stories. We drank a lot of cheap local wine, which tastes great and can make you happy, but can still give you a thumping headache the next morning. Still, in the back of my blurring mind, I kept thinking about Cypriot syllabic and the crumpled piece of paper in my pocket. I was eager to decode the old notes I had found in the car. In my dizziness, I was thinking how to get hold of the Magnette by myself so that I could open the secret compartment and get my hands on the hidden notes.

When I got home I remembered that I had made copies.

---

* The Rosetta Stone, featuring the same text in three languages, helped archaeologists finally crack the code of Egyptian hieroglyphics. (At London Museum).

I brewed some strong coffee and then I spread the two copies out in front of me on the kitchen table. I placed the decoder in front of me and carefully proceeded to write the message in Latin characters, below the ancient Cypriot ones.

The first one came out to this:

Pa-po-se te-ka te-ka.

"What the hell is this?" I said out loud. Was this English or Greek or something else? Or was it just gibberish? I momentarily wondered if this script wasn't Cypriot syllabic after all.

"Papose teka teka, papose teka teka," I repeated a few times, in an attempt to force my mind to make some sense of it. I tried various accents. It sounded like an Indian dish... Chinese seemed to fit best... Could Mr. Aris possibly know Chinese? I realised that my mind was not quite at its sharpest at that moment.

So the two same words at the end, if indeed they were words, were 'teka teka.'

I noticed that I had not 'translated' the 'SS' symbol that both papers bore at the end. Well, 'SS' was indeed a syllabic symbol in old Cypriot which translated to 'ZO'. Was this the author's signature? It occurred to me that I did not know Mr. Aris' surname. Were both these notes written by someone whose initials were 'Z' and 'O'? I tried thinking of some names: Zack… Zenon… Zeus… that was a bit of a dead end! Not too many names begin with a 'Z' I realised. Perhaps those latter ancient Greek names were aliases, a pseudonym, I considered, because they really are not common at all these days. Who on earth would call anyone 'Zeus' after all? It then occurred to me that maybe the two letters were meant to go together. After all, 'ZO' means 'I live', like for example in 'zoology' which is of course a Greek word that means 'the study of life'.

I turned my attention to the next document. Let us see what nation's food this one will bring up, I thought.

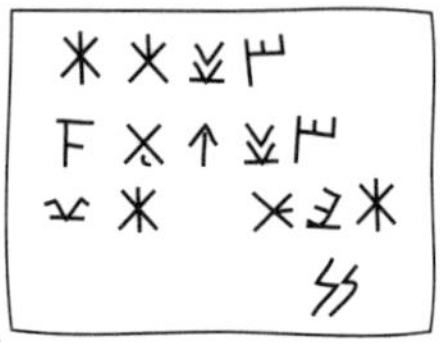

Apart from the Nazi-style signature, there were four 'words.' First word:

A-i-o-se.

Here we go again. What's this? A Japanese delicacy? Second word:

To-me-ti-o-se.

And what's that? Tomatoes?! Was this about food after all? I noticed that both words rhymed, they ended with 'iose', though of course that did not help any. Next word:

Mi-a. Mia? 'Mamma mia!' That's 'my' in Italian is it not?

But wait a minute, that's also number 'one' in Greek! A breakthrough? Last word:

E-ni-a. Enia… Ennia. That is number 'nine'! I went back to the other copy. Teka Teka. Could that be 'theka', as in 'ten' in Greek? I searched the 'decoder' for a 'th' sound, like in 'the'. There was none. Cypriot syllabic, I realised at that moment, did have its limitations, not all sounds are included. So, yes: a breakthrough. Both documents end with numbers. The first one with 'ten', repeated twice. The second with a 'one' and a 'nine'.

I tried the first two words together, out loud.

"Aiose tometiose."

Aiose? Does that not mean 'rusty' in the Cypriot dialect? It does! Was I on a roll?

Rusty tomatoes one nine," I read. Hmm.

I tried reading them together: "Papose ten ten and Rusty tomatoes one nine." That papose thing didn't even sound like a vegetable.

Perhaps this is a coded message in multiple layers and I have just peeled one off, the first one. I mean, really, do we ever refer to anything or anyone as a rusty tomato? Maybe 'rusty tomatoes' really means something entirely different… Deflated, I realised that even the numbers could be a coincidence. After all, I had kind of forced them to be numbers, had I not?

I was not making much progress so I went to bed to sleep on it. I dreamt of fresh bright red tomatoes. They were fine to begin with but they turned rusty toward the end. I bit into one. That left an ugly metallic flavour in my mouth. I woke up and then went back to sleep. Silly dream.

We were driving, at a legal pace, toward Paphos city, the old home of Aphrodite.

A week ago, during a meeting on Mr. Aris' porch, with a map spread out in front of us, the three of us had agreed to take the scenic route to that city, that is, by going via the road that goes over the Troodos mountain range. After all, we already knew that the Magnette could handle that particular challenge.

It is considered a longish drive, given Cyprus distances, especially since we were taking the round about route.

When you reside on a small island, you tend to live and think in a different way. You could compare it to a goldfish living in a small bowl. It only grows a couple of inches. Put him in a lake, that adorable little fish can reach gigantic proportions. In the same way, staying on this island changes your perspective. When I lived in the USA and the UK I didn't think twice about making a two or three hour trip. Now that would seem an eternity.

The voyage to 'distant' Paphos would be our longest excursion yet. A whopping two and a half hour drive! So I suggested we take my Volvo, what with the air conditioning and smoother ride. Mr. Aris said nothing but his expression spoke volumes. If we went without the Magnette it would be like leaving a good friend behind. It was out of the question. I never suggested an alternative ride again.

Mr. Aris was in a good mood. He was rambling on about his favourite subject: books.

"We all pretty much know which is the best selling book of all time-"

"-I know that! It's the Bible right?" interrupted Maria.

"Yes, I do think so," he confirmed. "Maybe it depends on who's counting and what they are counting. The Koran must also be up there, I'd say, as well as Mao's Little Red Book."

"I believe that in terms of fiction, it must be this Harry Potter series. And that Lord of the Rings series as well," I chipped in. Mr. Aris, I suspect, was not so up on such fictional stories. He did not give his opinion.

"Some also claim that the Bible is actually the first book too, at least as we understand the concept of a book, with many many pages and a cover: the Old Testament that is."

"But isn't the Old Testament a clever combination of other more ancient scriptures?" I said. "A way to substantiate the existence of a single God?"

If you, dear reader, are ever in Cyprus, do not go starting such conversations on the strength of what you read here. Talking about these things is generally considered taboo in Cyprus. Most people, especially older ones, would rather play it safe with religious matters. 'What's there to lose?' retorted my grandmother once when I challenged her. 'If He exists, then fine, I'm in His good books. If He doesn't, then it doesn't matter, does it?' Irrefutable logic.

But Mr. Aris was a thinker. He had obviously read widely on the subject and he could not help but ask the difficult questions.

"Yes, you are right. In fact, in the Old Testament itself several deities come in and out of stories and play their cameo parts. There are fire gods, war gods, and so on. The ancients later combined all these superheroes into one almighty Lord... Or, more accurately, I should say, one of them beat out the rest of them. But I still do like the oldness, the crudeness and brutal honesty of that Book - the Old Testament- best."

I believe he was comparing it to the New Testament.

"When was the Bible actually written?" I asked.

"Well, it would really be impossible to place a single date on its writing, didn't I tell you before? Like you said, it was written by many people, probably more than we can imagine, it includes ancient fables and scriptures and its authorship literally spans several hundred years. I guess you could say that it was put together, assembled, at the so called Council of Nicaea. Some claim that this was the most important conference ever. Constantine the Great, a heathen himself, wanted to find a way to cement all the disputing factions in his empire. He thought a common religion could do that, hence he got all these priests together in order to reach agreement. After heated argument on which scriptures to include and which to reject, they hammered out a common reference: the Bible.*"

"What do you mean by what you said before, that 'one of them beat out the rest of them'?" asked Maria.

"Exactly that," he answered. "People originally had different gods, as was logical, like the Olympian gods. Depending on their locale, their surroundings, their superstitions, their experiences, their priorities and their needs. Then suddenly all these had to be consolidated into just one. Not an easy task to make gods disappear. Even little ones don't go quietly, they can be especially feisty. But that's what happened, eventually."

"But who is the god that wiped out the rest of the others? Our God?" Maria meant the Christian God.

---

* The list of books to be included in the Holy Scripture was actually physically drawn up at the Synods of Hippo (393 AD) and Carthage (397 AD). But it is true that the Council of Nicaea (325 AD) was the first attempt to create a common canon on what was to be referred to as Christianity. Important agreements were reached, for example regarding the dates for Easter and Christmas, resurrection and crucially, that Jesus was indeed of the same status as God.

"Yeah, that one. The One and Only. It says so in the Bible itself. He actually has a name, as you know."

"What's His name then?" I asked.

He looked at me like I was pretending not to know. He answered anyway.

"Well, it's hard to pronounce. It's four letters actually, YHVH. Hebrew has no vowels, which isn't very helpful. Anyway, no one was supposed to actually say His name out loud, so the vowel omission probably helped things rather than the other way around. Today we guess that the name was 'Yehova' or Yahweh, or something like that."

"Like Jehova's Witnesses?"

"Yes, it's the same," he confirmed. "Since the name could not be said, He was referred to as 'Kyrie'* most of the times, over seven thousand times actually, in the Bible."

"So who did He fight against? Who did He wipe out?" asked Maria.

"Some of the adversarial entities are known to this day: that evil up-to-no-good Prince of Darkness, for instance. However, some of those deities were well and truly defeated. For example, female goddesses were generally wiped out for the sake of phallocracy. Like Asherah, who is mentioned in the Bible. She may actually be Astarte or a derivative."

"Astarte? Isn't she an Aphrodite 'relative'? Or something like her?" I asked, remembering what Mr. Aris had said at another occasion.

He nodded. "Then there's another chap called Baal, supposedly he was the son of god to many people back then. He was the son of El, the Canaanites' highest god. You may be interested to know that every year his death and resurrection were celebrated by the Canaanites."

* 'Lord' in English.

"You mean he was crucified as well?"

"Not at all. It was more a fertility ritual, perhaps a gruesome one too. It may have involved human sacrifice and even temple prostitution. Remember that? The Greeks apparently identified Baal as Cronos. Remember what he did to his dad, Ouranos?"

"The one who cut off his dad's things?" asked Maria.

"His things, right. Baal, like Aphrodite was a fertility god. The Phoenicians 'spread the word' about him all over the Mediterranean. So he was popular with the Jews too. Given his popularity, Baal was considered particularly dangerous by Yahweh or Jehova. So he had to be especially vilified."

"This Baal is in the Bible?" I asked.

"Absolutely. He is often referred to as Baalzebub or Beelzevul, as one of the fallen angels in Satan's camp. There are other gods in the Bible. Dagon, the Philistine fish god, and so on. Temples of these gods could be found next to Yahweh temples. But unlike Zeus, He did not tolerate them. He had to be alone."

"You make Him sound tough and unforgiving."

"And so He was, at first. He had to be too, given the undisciplined motley crew that his 'chosen' Jews were. Although, by the time of the New Testament we are really talking of a complete transformation. A kinder persona. We go full circle, from 'an eye for an eye' to turning the other cheek."

"Sounds like a different God," I commented.

"It is, if you ask me," he said. "That's what you get when you try to amalgamate too many gods from too many cultures from too many different eras. But it worked, so who am I to judge? Anyway, like I was saying, the original Yahweh was a war god, much like Aris in Greek mythology."

"Seriously?" asked Maria.

"Seriously. In the Old Testament he is often referred to as Yahweh Sabaoth: God of armies."

"By 'armies' they might have just meant 'people'. The Jewish people," I ventured.

"It's possible," he conceded, "but I must tell you, the war insinuations are all over the text."*

"What is it that you have against God?" I asked.

"Nothing. It's just that in the name of any given number of gods, so many people have needlessly suffered or died. Entire cultures have been wiped out. So much ancient wisdom, painstakingly gained, has been destroyed. Entire libraries full of invaluable books, like that famous one in Alexandria, have been burnt to the ground. All in the name of some god. Apart from these things, I have nothing against this whole deal."

He was a bit peeved. He went on:

"It's when God takes on nasty human attributes, like destructiveness and vindictiveness that I get upset."

"You can't blame God," I countered. "You must blame us, the people, who actually do these things. It's like blaming a car for driving fast. Or a gun for killing people. After all, bottom line, these things are us. That's our nature... The scriptures say that God fashioned man in his own likeness. But really, we fashioned God in our likeness."

"'*They are not hid from my face, neither is their injustice hid from my eyes*'", he replied mysteriously. "I know that. I figured it out too, Professor. What I just quoted is from the Bible, Jeremiah 16:17. I've read the Bible, more than a couple of times, unlike most Christians who vaguely follow the Word. It says it clearly: Yahweh has a face, lips, a tongue and breath, a beard even**. I also know that God has human attributes. Yahweh

* It is truc. E.g. Exodus 15:3 'The Lord is a man of war, his Name is Yehova'.

** E.g. Isaiah, 30:27, 33

regrets his actions in Jonah, he feels sad in Genesis and he discriminates by choosing the Jews over the rest of us. And He doesn't always seem to know everything that goes on. That's not too omniscient is it? It sometimes takes Him a while to find things out!"

Paphos

Cyprus, Paphos, or Panormus
May detain you with her splendour
Of oblations on her altars,
O imperial Aphrodite.

Yet you regard, with pity
For a nameless child of passion,
This small unfrequented valley
By the sea, O sea-born mother.
(Sappho)

We dropped that deep theological discussion to enjoy the changing scenery. We were in among the pine trees of Troodos once more. The minute we went over the top of the mountain we caught sight of the sparkling sea way down on the other side. Mr. Aris pointed toward it.

"The city of Limassol is right down there. That used to be the ancient city of Amathus, of course," he informed us. We knew that. Who didn't?

"Under the sea right there is buried one of the greatest harbours of all antiquity. It was really a technological masterpiece. Made of five thousand square stone blocks, each weighing three tons! They used an ingenious pulley system to construct it. One of the first winches ever, basically." We didn't know that. Who did?

We were getting closer to our destination. It was always inevitable that we would have done this Paphos trip in the Magnette some day. This entire ancient city has been declared a 'world heritage site' by whoever makes such declarations.

"Where does the name 'Paphos' come from Mr. Aris?" asked Maria when she noticed a road sign bearing the name of the city which had been the capital of Cyprus in Jesus' time. She was fully expecting him to tell her.

For once he seemed stumped.

"I don't know," he admitted after a while. I was almost glad. "Possibly comes from 'pan' (all) and 'fos' (light): 'All-light' emanating from her bright holiness, Aphrodite. Or something."

"How about 'pathos'" I proposed. "You know, all that steamy love over there with the goddess of passion living among the mortals: Pathos-Paphos... not much of a difference for a couple of thousand years is it?"

"You are right," he agreed. "But there's a problem: Paphos was always called exactly Paphos as far as I know. At least the two greatest poets of antiquity referred to the city by this name... You know, Homer and Sappho."

We drove on.

"Is it not interesting that Paphos is an anagram of Sappho, the lady who sang of Paphos and its glorious goddess?" he commented.

Did he just figure that out, I thought, impressed.

We drove on.

"There was a man called Paphos, of course," he stated. He had been thinking about it. He wasn't letting go.

"A person or a god?" asked Maria.

"Well a little of both, I guess. He was the son of a mortal, Pygmalion. This Pygmalion character was a sculptor of exquisite skill. So much so that he literally fell in love with a particular statue that he had made."

"The perv," I said.

"No, the 'Pyg'," said Maria.

"At least the statue was a woman, carved out of ivory," continued Mr. Aris. "Apparently Pygmalion had got sickened by real women because some Amathusian women of loose morals completely turned him off."

"Why what did they do that was so upsetting?" I asked.

"Well, they prostituted themselves in public and they weren't even ashamed of themselves."

"I see what you mean Mr. Aris, but could he not think of a more normal way to vent his frustration? Like stone them to death or something?" I said. "Anyway, being an artist, he was probably too sensitive for that," I retracted. "No harm falling for an attractive statue really, especially if his feelings were reciprocated."

"It seems that you can relate," Maria teased me. "On the other hand, I'll bet 'she' was as cold as a rock."

"Well, she was, for starters," agreed Mr. Aris. "But dear Aphrodite, bless her sensitive soul, took pity on him and turned the statue into a real, beautiful woman. They had a child whom they called Paphos."

"And they lived happily ever after," Maria finished the story.

"Well we won't," I said. "You won't believe this but I think we are lost."

We were lost. This is not very easy to do in Cyprus, given the fact that distances are of map-size scale when compared to other countries. The island only measures one hundred by two hundred and forty kilometres and even that takes into account a couple of wrong turns if you get lost just a little. So, its total area is a little less than ten thousand square kilometres. To give a bit of perspective here, the United States of America has a total area of almost 10,000,000 (that's ten million!) square kilometres. In other words, if you were a god and had the inclination, you would need exactly one thousand 'Cypruses' to cover the whole of America.*

We had meandered around one too many country roads and now there were no signs to guide us. We were deep in a mountain forest, making it harder to assess these kinds of things by looking left or right.

Suddenly, we were out of the thick woods and into an open area. Up ahead there was an enormous slab of solid grey rock which was at least the height of a tall building. Under the rock I noticed a man. He was slowly heading toward us on his donkey.

Although men hate to ask for directions, and that includes me, I felt we had no choice. What if the Magnette heated up on us in the middle of nowhere? On that thought I decided to stop the car at the rock and, by the way, we could ask for directions.

When the man, who was dressed in traditional Cypriot clothing, saw us, he promptly dismounted to come and greet us. We got out of the car and waved hello. Mr. Aris took over:

"Hello old man," Mr. Aris greeted him.

"Speak for yourself! Don't you have a mirror?" replied the man with the donkey. But at least he was smiling.

* Of course, the same applies if you look at it in square miles. Cyprus is a little over 3,500 square miles and the USA is just over 3.5 million square miles. Coincidentally, the two countries even look alike. The USA looks like an unkempt overweight uncle of Cyprus!

“Sir, could you tell us where we are?” I asked him, changing the subject.

“You are standing right under the ‘Hassanpoulia’ hiding place,” he informed us.

“What’s Hassanpoulia?” asked Maria. He looked at her with too obvious approval.

“It’s ‘who’ not ‘what’. They were a notorious family of bandits,” he informed her, looking her up and down. “They lived in this area at the turn of the century.”

He was referring to the 1900’s I believe.

“This rock doesn’t look like much of a hiding place,” I commented, looking up at it.

“Yes, but there is a secret entrance. You can go in the rock. Would you like to see?”

Of course we said yes. He took us around the massive boulder and indeed, at one point, six or seven feet up, there seemed to be a crack in the smooth surface. He climbed up like an agile goat and we clambered behind him. A couple of steps further and the gap opened to a big enough aperture to squeeze through. What we saw inside was magnificent. There was a beautiful sun-drenched opening, as wide as a large room. On the soft ground there was thick short grass only broken by beautiful little purple and yellow flowers. We sat on the grass and he related the Hassanpoulia story:

It begins with this man, who went by the name of Hassan Pouli, falling in love with a beautiful local lass called Emmett. Some other person approached her in an indecent manner. That was enough to offend the chivalrous Hassan. So, on three different occasions he ambushed Hairedden -the offender- and shot at him. Because he was terrible with his aim he missed all three times. Still, of course, by then Hairedden was running scared. It is said that in desperation he proceeded to frame Hassan, accusing him of stealing sheep and goats from his herd. Hassan got a seven year jail sentence for that but he promptly escaped with only one thing on his mind: revenge! Anyone who sided with Hairedden was summarily dealt with as Hassan's aim had steadily improved with all the practice. Still, it became known that no 'honest people' need worry if they bumped into him in the mountains. He was always very friendly and courteous with them. All he asked about was the movements of the police and of other news. Hassan and the band he had assembled lived right there in the wilderness for a couple of years, constantly moving from place to place and in safe houses. There were a couple of close scrapes when the police thought they had him cornered but he always seemed to find a way to slide away. One of the biggest shootouts was right here at the 'Hassanpoulia' rock. The police were sure they had him trapped. But they did not know that there is a second exit at the back. It's difficult to master but still an exit. By daylight the police bravely stormed this place we are sitting at. They found no one. Once in a while he would visit Emmett in the middle of the night and disappear again before dawn.

Hassan became a cult hero in the whole of Cyprus. A lot of people justified and even praised his actions. Songs were composed about him. The old man proceeded to sing one. It was all about love and honour and daring and heroism. Nothing about killings.

One day, out of the blue, he surrendered. He walked into a police station, just like that. Perhaps he got tired of running. Perhaps he was ill – malaria. It was probably a combination of both. He was sentenced for murder. While in jail he was a model prisoner. He was always mild-mannered and well liked by the other inmates and the guards. He learned to read and write. He was placed in a low security section. That should have been the end of the story. But, one fine morning he got news that two of his gang members, of the old 'Hassanpoulia' band, had been arrested in Paphos. They had been betrayed by people Hassan knew. So, once more, he decided to escape in order to exact revenge. However, this time the escape did not go down smoothly. Hassan was seen by a prison guard. When he refused to stop he was cut across the neck by the warden's sword. Then, as he lay there mortally wounded, he was mercifully shot dead.

The old man got up to go. He gave us each three apples, he insisted, he winked at Maria and he went on his way on his donkey.

We got into the Magnette and followed the man's directions. Twenty minutes or so later we were cruising downhill toward Paphos.

We did the tourist thing: we went to the Tombs of the Kings and to see the beautiful mosaics, one of which depicts Dionysus handing over the secret of viticulture to Ikarios, the King of Athens. According to the guide, this is apparently the earliest portrayal of 'drunks' ever found. Fascinating.

Still, the guide had left out the most interesting story. It was, guess who, Mr. Aris, who filled the gaps. He told us that Paphos was the very first offshore stop made by St. Paul, the person who is credited for spreading Christianity. Paphos was, in effect, the first hurdle. And St. Paul almost stumbled there. Had he, the whole Christianity revolution would be a short page in history.

When St. Paul came to the town, he requested to see the king and to address the people in order to let them know the good news he bore: he was bringing them the real God. The

Paphians were not too thrilled to hear this, thank you. They had their own gods, one of which, Aphrodite, was their very own. Also, perhaps some local entrepreneurs were concerned. What would they do with all the little Aphrodite statues if this Paul character convinced the world? And where would their thriving religious tourism industry go?

So they promptly had St. Paul whipped. Thirty nine lashes, to be precise, as was tradition. However, on that same day there occurred another particular incident which was to turn the tide of history. St. Paul's biggest local adversary, a 'wizard' named Elymas*, openly challenged St. Paul as a charlatan. Suddenly, this infidel pagan priest was blinded. This was enough evidence to sway the allegiances of the king and the townspeople. The rest is history as they say.

Then we did the other touristy thing. We walked along the promenade with the calm Mediterranean Sea to our left. We headed toward Paphos castle. Maria held my hand as we walked. Mr. Aris stayed a step behind us. Maria noticed that Mr. Aris was looking at our hands, not dissatisfied, but with a hint of a poignant look.

"Mr. Aris," she asked him, letting go of my hand and grabbing him by the arm, "can I ask you something personal?"

"Sure, whatever you like," he replied, with ease. He always enjoyed her attention.

"Ok. A dashing gentleman like you, with those blue eyes of yours, how many hearts did you break?"

"Oh, the list is endless," he joked. "How could I possibly remember?"

"No really, did you not marry?" she persisted.

"I didn't have the luck to marry, no," he answered. "I did

* Famous painter Raphael has painted this scene.

know a few women in my life time, I cannot complain, but it never went as far as marriage, unfortunately."

"Wasn't there ever someone who was really very special Mr. Aris?"

He hesitated and his face turned cloudy. But he did reply.

"Well, there was this one lady, but it just was never meant to be. Timing was completely wrong if you know what I mean."

"What do you mean Mr. Aris?"

"She was married for one thing... It's best we let it go Maria," he pleaded. She did.

So there was another piece of the Mr. Aris puzzle revealed. He had never married. Presumably then, he had no children either. Which explained his aloneness.

Mr. Aris and I were sitting on the veranda drinking coffee, that routine prelude to our driving expeditions. I was telling him about a recent trip I took to Ljubljana, Slovenia, where I had given an academic presentation.

"Ljubljana… sounds exotic," said Mr. Aris.

"Well, sort of," I said noncommittally. "Nobody really knows where it is, somehow. It is a European city," I added clumsily trying to think of a way to illustrate the place. "Slovenia used to be part of Yugoslavia," I added, an afterthought.

"I know that," he said. Of course he did. "Is there anything to see there?"

"I was only there for a couple of days, I wouldn't quite know. But there are some beautiful large caves in the area. With interesting stalactites and stalagmites. You need a little train to go through the caves."

He nodded approvingly.

"You know, our city here, Nicosia, was full of natural underground caves and passages," he said.

"I didn't know that, how come nobody's mentioned it before?"

"Well, it's the truth. Most of the caves have been covered or cemented over now of course. Under this very house there was once a passageway of almost a kilometre in length. Apparently, you could actually walk most of the distance, crouched, real low, but at certain points you had to get down on your belly and crawl through."

"Does this passageway still exist?"

"Not really. I don't think so anyway. Like I said, too many new houses and apartment flats have been constructed since then. The caves have been filled with cement, probably, to strengthen the foundations. This area we are at now, as you know, is now the most densely populated in Nicosia*. So… but you can still find the odd evidence. Come and I'll show you."

He got up and I followed him. We went down to the basement of the house. We snaked our way through the masses of books, down a narrow staircase, it too laden with books. He switched on a single bare lamp. It was musty down there, a bit creepy. I suddenly heard some shuffling noises in a dark corner.

"Damn rats!" he growled. "Must remember to put some more of those pellets down again. Those bastards and me, we have similar habits. We both like to devour books. A few books down here, you'll find they've only got covers. Cheeky buggers! They eat the inside pages, leave the outside intact. Probably more tasty."

The light hardly illuminated the surroundings though again I could see that most of the shabby shelves were filled to the brim with old and dusty books. He led me to a dark corner. He picked up a hammer and suddenly turned to face me. We stood really close to one another. I nearly bumped into him.

"Look around you. Do you see anything strange"?

"Well, no," I lied. In fact he seemed strange right then, his eyes oddly bright in the dim lighting. I half expected him to shout, 'Heeeere's Johnny!'

Then he knelt down, and using the hammer, he tapped lightly at a few spots on the wooden floorboard. "Aha, here

---

* Incidentally, the area in Nicosia he is talking about is called 'Acropolis', just like the famed hill in Athens with the Parthenon. Acropolis literally means the edge of the city, as this area was before it was swallowed up by the city.

it is," he said shortly. He put down the hammer and put his fingers between two floorboards in the corner. He pulled, but nothing budged. "It's stuck," he said. "Can you help?"

I kneeled next to him and emulated his efforts. "On the count of three pull upwards, towards you." There followed a creaking sound and suddenly the narrow floorboard came undone, throwing us both to the floor behind us. He proceeded to lift another three or four boards next to the one we had just yanked out, this time they came up easily. He went to another corner and came back with a lit flashlight. He shone it at the gap we had opened on the floor. What I saw was somewhat disappointing. Below the floorboards there was solid concrete.

"Do you see here?" He ran his fingers along a crack, a perfect line, removing the dust. It shaped into a square, barely a foot by a foot. "This is it. Alice in Wonderland."

"Is that the entranceway?"

"Yes, I filled it up with cement myself. Probably left a couple of gaps... I bet you that if we opened it up again we would find a bunch of rats living happily ever after down there. I think that's where the bastards come from. From the caves."

"You really have to get rid of them or you'll have no books left... just covers."

"Poor sods," he now defended them. "We are the only ones standing in their way of taking over the world! They are the only living things, apart from us humans, which you can find on all continents."

"Well, we facilitated their evil plans. We took them along for the ride on our ships, didn't we. As we conquered the world they were always close at heel. Your Phoenicians or your sea-people started it all, didn't they?"

"So, even rats started off from Cyprus?" he said with doubt. He had taken my point seriously.

"You know," he said conversationally, "the famous pigeons in Venice, the ones at St. Peter's Square, they were brought in from Cyprus, did you hear of that? Tell that to the tourists that flock there to have them shit on their heads!"

"I am not sure the Venetian authorities are thankful to us for that import!"

"Let's get out of here," he said presently. "What with the memories and the rats for company, this place is getting depressing."

I was glad to see the bright sunshine and the welcoming old wooden chairs on his veranda. That other world, the Alice in Wonderland world, was too dark and prohibitive for my liking.

"So what did you do in the caves?" I asked.

"As kids, we knew of them, but we never went down too far. Too scary, you know? We'd hear of shepherds losing their goats once in a while. They'd fall through holes in the ground, never to be seen again. We did go down a bit of a way a couple of times on a dare, or to play hide and seek there. But later, I know that the organisation opened up these entrances a little wider and hid them with bushes."

"What organisation?"

"EOKA*. Didn't I tell you?"

Tell me what?

"No, you didn't."

I was not completely clear in my mind about this EOKA. Though everyone in Cyprus has learnt about its heroics in school, there is controversy. The organisation fought for independence from the British rulers in the fifties but it has also

* Ethniki Organosis Kyprion Agoniston (Greek for 'National Organisation of Cypriot Fighters'). Militarily active from 1955-59.

been claimed by some that it really had a mixed agenda. Its members were fiercely nationalistic (for Greece, not Cyprus) and they had reportedly simultaneously fought against communists and other local minorities.

"I was informed by one of its members of these caves. He told me that they would sometimes hold meetings down there or they would use them occasionally to hide from the British soldiers."

"Didn't they ever discover them? The caves, I mean."

"The Englezi? Not as far as I know. By the way, you know who this man I knew saw down in those caves one day? Uri Geller!"

"Who?"

"You know that famous spoon bender… the psychic chap or whatever."

"Isn't he Jewish or something? What was he doing in Cyprus?"

"I don't know, although it was him. I later found out that he had been a pupil at a local school. He was only a child, perhaps ten or eleven years old. He was apparently looking for adventure and found one. He also found one of the cave entrances near Terra Santa, his school, and he wandered down. He literally dropped in on them, through a hole in the roof."

Mr. Aris rubbed his eyes hard. He grimaced, his mouth a straight line, I could not tell if it was a smile or the opposite.

"There were four or five EOKA fighters in the cave, at a 'roomy' point where one could stand upright, barely. They were dressed in civilian clothes. Still they must have looked intimidating as they were dusty from head to toe because they had had to crawl through some parts. It must have been really claustrophobic down there. One of the fighters down there was actually the leader of the Organisation himself. He sat on a solid wooden box which was the only piece of furniture there was there. The little boy -Uri Geller- was clearly as startled as they were. Digenis, the leader of EOKA, composed himself first. He wagged a finger at Uri and told him in a stern voice that if he ever as much as hinted to anyone, even his parents, about what he had seen then he would end up into a lot of trouble. The kid was scared to death. He profusely agreed to never tell."

"What happened to him?"

"I don't know, I never heard of him again. Maybe he left the country. I was a little concerned about his wellbeing. But anyway, as you know, he is famous now, isn't he, so he obviously came out unscathed."

Mr. Aris was in a talkative mood.

"My mother was a petite lady. Quite the opposite to my father. She was always dressed in traditional dark blue and black layered clothing. Hair, long, jet black, always covered with a *mantila*[*]. She was usually not too far away from home, so we kids knew where to find her if we really needed her. But still she was out for most of the day. Sometimes she'd go help pick olives or carobs. Or do odd jobs here and there. Whatever she could find. Her reward was always in kind, never cash. At the end of the day she'd come back with some olives or carobs or a *halloumi*[**]. She took care of us as best as she could. But, with her being away for hours on end, it meant we had to fend for ourselves during the day. Of course, it was the same for everyone else. That is why you'd always see stray kids roaming all over the place.

In your contemporary eyes it would be pathetic to see her trying to make ends meet, bearing in mind her endeavours to feed six and a half mouths. To explain that half: while father, the absolute master of the house, ate first if he was home, mother ate last. She would eat anything that was left, which wasn't much, although we also gallantly held ourselves back to leave her something. And this with barely enough food to feed a single person, never mind a family of hungry children. A decent meal would include a few olives each, some crusty old bread and maybe half a tomato or some slices of a cucumber. Not much, but I hasten to add, a feast when we could get it. Nowadays, this would be called a Mediterranean diet! We

* Scarf

** Delicious white local cheese.

always lived in hunger. So much so that we learned to ignore it, like I said before. One can do that, I assure you. Just takes training. Remember the hodja's donkey. In any case, look at the bright side, Alexis. I hear that hunger is the only proven way to longevity, did you know that? Seriously. People who never stuff themselves apparently live longer.

A brave woman, mother was. Her face never revealed the sheer desperation she surely felt… but come to think of it, maybe she didn't quite feel that way. She was very religious, and that provided real comfort to seemingly forgotten souls like hers and ours. She was certain that God glanced our way once in a while. Toward our dry little island. Perhaps not every day but often enough. I once heard her say that He must be extremely busy, what with so much misery wherever He looked. A very understanding woman, she was. So we had to wait for our turn. He would give us a helping hand, one way or another, when we really needed it. And if He seemed not to, say when a kid or someone we knew passed away, her faith was still unwavering. God did what He could, given the circumstances. Sometimes the work load was too much, even for Him. That was fate. To be accepted without complaints.

I suppose she was beautiful as a very young woman. But I can't be sure. Hardship took its toll on everyone, her included. She always looked middle aged to my young eyes, as far back as I can remember and right before she died. Also, somehow fragile, despite her outward toughness. Maybe in another world she was meant to be pampered, she would be royalty or something. She had that predisposition like she was in the wrong place. I must have been about twelve years old, or thereabouts, when she passed away. What did she die of? I really don't know. One night she peacefully went to sleep, the next she just didn't bother to wake up. I swear she looked content that morning. Nothing scary. At peace.

It's a shame I don't have a single picture of hers to show you. While she was alive I mean. Or of my father for that matter. But me, I remember her as if I just saw her this morning.

My father. Now he was a tough man, no matter how you looked at it. Big and strong, like that Clint Eastwood in a western. Nothing or no person could ruffle his feathers. No one would mess around with him. Not that I ever saw him take on anyone but you just knew. And just like the westerns, he would often disappear into the horizon, destination unknown. For days, sometimes weeks.

He would reappear out of the blue, just like when he left. Often carrying all kinds of goodies. Food, mostly. But sometimes he would bring other interesting things as well. A flute that he'd made, a crude backgammon board, things like that.

That is probably my single best memory as a child. Catching sight of my father riding into 'town', on his donkey of course! Ahh, our donkey… she wasn't exactly what you would call a thoroughbred, but she came pretty close at least to us poor folk, let me tell you. We called her Maria Callas because of her powerful and beautiful loud voice. Early in the morning, she would honk and kick the side of our house with her powerful back legs, when she wanted dad to wake up and set her loose. He would get furious with her. I am ashamed to say, sometimes he would beat her. Maria was good-natured, she just took it, and she didn't react. But I remember other locals who had died from donkey kicks… did you know that even today more people die from donkeys than crocodiles or sharks or any other animal? Blame us humans though, for being asses!

But he loved her. She was a prized possession, say like a Porsche or something, which my father earned after years of hard work in the searing summer heat at the Salt Lake, in Larnaca. You know, that's where you can also see the famed

Moslem shrine, Hala Sultan Tekke*, right on that lake's shores. Are you familiar with the legend? Prophet Muhammad's 'wet-nurse', or aunt or something, Umm Haram, fell from her horse at the temple's very spot and died after breaking her neck in the course of a siege of Larnaca which was organized by the much maligned and ambitious Muawiyah**. She was buried at the site of the impressive mosque which was built in her honour. Her big stone grave is a sacred shrine. It is said to float in mid air which is something I cannot confirm or deny as it is covered with a thick blanket at all times. To this day.

My father told us this account and of other 'far away' places and their exotic stories and we listened with wide open mouths. My old man was never formally educated, just like me, but he always kept his eyes and ears open. So he picked up a lot of these titbits on his 'travels'. And he told a good story.

Now, as I was saying, the salt workers would gather the salt from the bed of the dried lake - all its water would evaporate in the summer months, so this work was limited to a couple of months in the summer - with the help of donkeys, and pile it into neat, massive rectangular heaps. He told us this and we imagined enormous symmetrical sparkling white salty mountains.

But I only saw all these things for myself years later. His stories were bigger and better than life. Better than the real thing because imagination is such a powerful, magical tool that we humans are blessed with. It can travel you to the stars. It can build twenty-four carat gold palaces, silver streams, diamond

* You can see the Salt Lake and Sultan Tekke as soon as you arrive in Cyprus. They are right next to Larnaca International Airport.

** Muawiyah fought against the Caliph Ali who was considered to be a direct descendant of Prophet Mohammad (his son-in-law). For this reason he is hated by Shia Moslems. He later became Caliph himself (AD 661-680).

towers. And all this for free! '*Imagination is everything*,' as Einstein once said. Think about it. You may agree.

I remember another time when he came back he was much whiter than ever. He looked spooky, even sickly. Usually he was as dark as coal, what with working all day under the blazing Cyprus sun. He explained how he had been working deep under the ground, in big tunnels called mines, where there were rivers of glistening copper, just waiting to be carried away. All you needed was a pick and a bucket and an appetite for hard work. He flirted with the idea of finding a vein himself. The metal was all over, he claimed. 'Cyprus' and 'copper' were the same word, he informed us. The metal had actually got its name from our island, he said. We were in Copper-land! He also told us, lowering his voice in a conspiratory manner, that he had figured out the kind of geology which hides such vast riches. One day he and Callas would come back loaded with it. But he never followed up on this dream, as far as I know. Or perhaps he did, unsuccessfully.

Anyway, he put his hand in his pocket and he pulled out two little treasures. Two ancient coins which he had found in the mines. He told us how these coins had a couple of things in common. One of the coins was from Roman times. He said it was called a '*Constantinato*' and it was quite common in that area. Many miners had found one or two for themselves. The coin's name was derived from Emperor Constantine the Great, who had declared Constantinople (literally Constantine's city, later renamed Istanbul under the Ottomans) the capital of the Roman Empire. However, Constantine only took over the 'Eastern' Roman Empire after Rome and the powers there didn't quite take to the idea. So, half the Christian Church was split into the 'Western' Roman Catholic - meaning 'aggregate'- Church, led by the Pope, and the other half was the Byzantine Empire, called the Orthodox - meaning 'correct'- Church.

Of course, this division stands to this day, as father informed us. Although admittedly the Catholic Church seems to be the bigger remaining 'Empire' these days. Only Greeks, Russians, Romanians and some others are part of the Orthodox Church. Naturally, both still claim to be the 'real' representative of God. It was, and is, a power struggle. The oldest surviving power struggle. Older than the Moslems versus Christians clash. And certainly older than the Greeks - Turks thing. So, my father continued, that coin was from around 330 AD, the time of this Constantine chap.

The other one was also from 330, but BC! And it had on its face the original great man himself. Alexander the Great! This other coin rightfully belongs to you Alexis. You can have it - both of them - when I ... bow out, if you are willing to wait a year or twenty! And if I can find them. At least I think I still have both these coins somewhere.

But I remember another of my father's returns even more vividly. His arrival that day was different. This time he came back home on foot. That big tough man sat in the middle of our one-room house on our one chair, head in his hands, broken. He wept like a baby when he told my mother how Maria Callas had collapsed and died under a big and high load of firewood that she was carrying at the time. He was blaming himself for overloading her. But we all knew that she was quite old in the first place, even when my dad first brought her home. We all cried. That is when I realised that Maria Callas wasn't a prized possession after all. She was family.

But, loss or no loss, there was no choice. Off he went, once more, after a few days. When he came back the next time he was in for an even bigger shock. He came early in the evening, as he usually did. Mother had been dead since the morning, or maybe the night before. He found us there, tearless, numb. He didn't cry at all either. He was mad though. Like I had never seen him before. And he swore at all the gods he could name, daring them to come down and explain to him, in his face, what the hell they were up to, letting a woman like that die, and leaving five children orphaned.

We helped him bury her in a shallow grave that he dug next to our house. Not at the village cemetery. He brought no priest. No neighbours. For that matter, I don't think he ever notified any authority of her passing away either. Or any of her relatives. But did anyone else care, really? They had their own share to deal with. My father looked down at the grave. I still remember that moment and how I looked up at this big man in trepidation. How I inwardly shuddered at what he said. He was dripping with sweat but he was composed and determined. His eyes rock steady. His face gleaming in the moonlight, his dirty shirt soaked to the bone. He stood tall and proud and defiant to his fate, in the cool evening breeze. He said a few words to mother, after he got his breath back. That she was a queen. That she was meant for better things, that she had found peace at last. Then he addressed us kids. He said that we were all grown up now and we were ready to take on the world by ourselves. Mother had done her job, she had already raised us. I tell you, maybe we were tough little nuts, but those words didn't console me. On the contrary, they scared the hell out of me. There I stood, a skinny little lad, not even a teenager yet, and father, this pillar of strength in my eyes, was saying I was now a grown up and ready to fend for myself. Perhaps that's not what he intended but it felt like he was washing his hands of us."

Greek Cypriots can be separated into two distinct categories these days. These divisions have nothing to do with left or right, black or white, rich or poor, skinny or fat. People are distinguished by the manner in which they voted in the ill-fated 2004 referendum, a reunification plan referred to as the 'Annan Plan', the name of the then Secretary General of the United Nations. This plan, drafted by and refereed* by the United Nations following intense negotiations between the leaders of the two main communities, the Greek and the Turkish Cypriots, called for a federation-type reunification. As a result, Greek Cypriots would either get back their homes or be granted compensation for the property they had lost in the Turkish invasion of 1974. This depending on where their land stood in relation to the new two states' demarcation lines which were to be placed on the new 'Cyprus Federation' map.

Greek Cypriots who voted 'yes' in the referendum, point to the fact that with this 'Annan' settlement most displaced persons, one hundred thousand of them, would have gone back home. That the tens of thousands of Turkish troops which have been stationed on the island since the invasion, bar a few hundred, would be obliged to leave Cyprus. That Cyprus would generally become a demilitarised country. That the steady flow of illegal Turkish settlers would be halted. That, at last, all Cypriots would live in peace in one sovereign country. The Greek Cypriots who voted 'no' claimed that the plan represented a de jure - formal to you and me - acceptance of

* Literally, arbitrated.

the de facto -existing- effects of the invasion, when Turkey occupied about a third of the island. That the new federation would be inherently racist as it consisted of two states based on ethnicity. That it really was a confederation, with loose central government powers.

Both sides consider the other as naïve and or misinformed or worse, unpatriotic. Nowadays, despite the fact that the division persists, it is of little importance what they voted. While the plan was overwhelmingly accepted by the Turkish Cypriot community it was soundly rejected by the Greek Cypriots. So the de facto borders between the internationally accepted legal Cypriot state, run by the Greek Cypriots, and the illegal Turkish Cypriot state, run by Turkey and the Turkish Cypriots, remain.

As an indirect consequence of the above, Greek Cypriots can be distinguished by yet another characteristic: those who are willing to cross over to the occupied area, and those who are not. Generally, but not absolutely, the 'no' voters tend to be less inclined because in order to cross you need to show a passport or ID, which is like recognising the existence of another country. To the 'yes' voters, crossing over is a symbol of the continuing efforts to get to know our Turkish Cypriot brethren in order to try to reunify our country.

If you have read the above couple of paragraphs a few times and you still do not understand what exactly is going on, who is right and who is wrong, do not fret. You are with company. Most people, local and foreign, feel the same way. The so-called '*Cyprus Problem*' has humbled and ruined the reputation of many a big shot international diplomat who naively got involved and attempted to solve it. It may not be as 'glamorous' (rather, read 'high profile') as the Palestinian problem but it is just as hard to untangle.

After a brief discussion, Mr. Aris and I found that we were both 'crossers'. Maria was a crosser too, but she had some other obligation to tend to that day.

So, we agreed that it was time we took the MG to the other side, the Turkish occupied area of the island which has been illegitimately baptised the Turkish Republic of Northern Cyprus (TRNC) by a local ex-satrap, Rauf Denktash. This break-away pariah territory is not recognised by the world community.

I first crossed over in early 2003, right after the borders opened up, thirty years after the war. I was among the first to do so. Those were moments to behold. They were reminiscent to the fall of the Berlin Wall. People from both sides, Turkish and Greek Cypriots, formed two massive queues, one on each side, and patiently waited for hours on end under the hot sun to cross over. Two sets of authorities viewed personal documentation. In the middle, looking foreign and blond and out of place, were lots of people wearing blue berets, the poor United Nations forces, tense as hell but acting calm. The Turkish troops stood further back, yet ominously.

When they finally faced each other, the 'victor' and the 'victim'*, there were no skirmishes, not even any dirty looks. On the contrary. In fact, total strangers hugged and kissed one another. Like long lost friends. Villagers from both communities who did know each other hugged and openly wept. They talked of the 'good old days' when they used to live side by side. Not one bullet was fired.

Stranger things happened later. Many displaced persons gingerly made their way to their old homes, the ones they had

* Quotes inserted because both the Greek Cypriots and the Turkish Cypriots are really the victims of this whole affair.

hurriedly abandoned as they fled the war. They found others living in them. Instead of hostility, they were invited in to have a coffee and take a look. Both sets of people were embarrassed, almost apologetic. 'Sorry I'm living in your home. I was also kicked out of mine, on the other side', their faces implied. 'What a mess', they said to one another.

Cypriots were upbeat during those first days. They smiled a lot. Many Greek Cypriots learned their first Turkish words: '*Barish*' (peace). '*Kardash*' (brothers).The end, the elusive solution, seemed to be round the corner, finally.

Then, suddenly, everyone woke up. It was, after all, just a dream. The sleeping beast, nationalism, stirred out of its slumber and raised its ugly head. It was 'us' and 'them' once more.

As one crosses, one can instantly feel the brute power, the formidable military presence of Turkey. Make no mistake, this is a local superpower. No one messes with this country and goes unpunished*.

So, one is not as quite at ease in this 'TRNC' as one would be in a regular democratic state. You can see that all is superficially in order. But you sense that if you dare offend the 'force' you will abruptly find yourself in deep trouble. It is there, palpable. Big brother is watching.

Make no mistake. This is a pariah state. There are implications, all summarised in one menacing sentence: no one can challenge whatever the 'state' does. Although this is not expressly stated anywhere as you cross over, you are aware of it, an invisible sign hanging in the air. The 'policemen' are firm but not rude; they will even smile on occasion. But it is there, everywhere, and that is how they probably want it to be: quietly

---

* At the time of writing, Turkey is undergoing serious reforms. In its efforts to join the European Union, the country is genuinely trying to clean up its act.

intimidating. All Cypriots know it, Turkish and Greek, even if they sometimes won't admit it.

The Magnette hesitated when our turn to go through arrived. It would not start. People in a convoy of cars behind us were beginning to get restless. A couple of mild hoots were heard. I tried the ignition for the fifth time, sweat dripping down my face. Not having air-conditioning did not seem so 'cool' right then. The car fired up, bellowing a big cloud of black smoke right into the face of the car behind us. Mr. Aris and I sighed in relief.

Going to the other side of Cyprus is a bit like being in an episode of the 'Twilight Zone' series. You suddenly step into another world. It is not just that road and other signs are suddenly unintelligible to the Greek speaker's eye. That is to be expected. It is more that, within just a few hundred yards, you go to a Cyprus of thirty years ago. It is like time stood still. It is not dissimilar to the eerie experience one gets when visiting Cuba with its magnificent old dilapidated buildings and fifties' American cars driving all over.

Soon after we crossed over we stopped to quench our thirst at an outside coffee shop. The proprietor, a Turkish Cypriot, greeted us in halting Greek. Most Turkish Cypriots are still quite friendly with their counterpart Greek Cypriots but not as much as they were in 2004. We did the obligatory discussion of the Cyprus Problem. Would it be solved? We doubted it. The dream is over. We have woken up.

I thought of opening up the subject with Mr. Aris after the owner went away. I saw Mr. Aris' face and changed my mind. I looked around at the surroundings.

The coffee shop was situated at an interesting petite olden square in occupied Nicosia. Swivel your head from left to right and you could see the ultimate flagships of separation facing one another, only a few yards apart. West versus East: in the middle, Cyprus, the battlefield. Like two burly gunfighters waiting to draw their forty-fives. Two battered, timeworn and battle weary temples: one a Greek Orthodox Christian church, the other a Moslem Mosque. Both had domelike roofs but they each also featured a customised prominent feature, their distinguishing formidable 'weapons' of choice. The church had its tall square bell tower, while the mosque had a slim and pointy rocket-like minaret.

"If you take away their respective towers, the two temples look alike," commented Mr. Aris, pointing at both of them at the same time.

"Well that and their little symbols on top," I said.

"Ah yes, let's not forget the symbols on top: the cross and the crescent. Of course you know, those are truly primitive symbols derived from extremely old religions."

"What do you mean?"

"I mean from the very beginning of time when people still worshipped nature's inexplicable wonders. When the sun was the god in the sky and the moon was also a god, its partner."

"I'm not sure I follow."

"Well, the cross, in its oldest format, comes with a circle superimposed on it. Many churches still have it. The cross divides the circle actually, depicting the movement of the sun. It divides into the four seasons, Alexis. If you look at an old illustration of a horoscope and its twelve Zodiac signs you will clearly see that it is round with the twelve signs arranged in a circle. They are divided by a cross. The actual lines of the cross symbolise the equinoxes and solstices: Season changes."

"Yes, but the cross in this case," I said pointing to the cross on top of the church, "is for the crucifixion so-"

"- I am not sure I agree Alexis. Do you have a one or two-Euro coin on you?"

I fished around in my pocket. I brought out a Cyprus one-Euro coin*. I placed it on the wooden table between us.

"Take a look at it man. It's a perfect cross, from three thousand years before the time of Christ!"

I looked more attentively at this coin we carelessly handle a hundred times a day.

"I see what you mean. Still, it's not quite a perfect cross. It looks like a squatting dwarf with outstretched arms."

"To tell the truth, it's not actually a dwarf. This same shape of statue has been found all over Cyprus. In different sizes, as large as a metre and a half sometimes, but more often as tiny little charms to be worn around one's neck for religious purposes. Just like we wear crosses these days!" he concluded triumphantly.

I took a closer look at the idol staring right at me from the 'silver' surface of the coin.

"So what is it if it's not a dwarf?" I asked him.

"Really it's not even a person. I'll tell you what: we are the only country in the world which got away with flaunting pornographic symbols on its national coin! Let me show you."

I leaned closer.

"Cover the bottom half of the little dwarf chap with your finger, including his arms. Now, what does that remind you of? Don't be bashful now... Of course you see it. It's a penis isn't it?"

* The ancient statue and next to it a Cyprus one Euro coin

Hmm.

"Now cover the top part, again including the arms. Yep, you do see it I believe. How do I say this to a professor: it's the female reproductive organ!"

"Kids handle these coins Mr. Aris!" I said, feigning outrage.

"Nothing wrong with the human body," he replied. "Now, Alexis, look even closer."

"What now?" I said, leaning in on the coin.

"What's the statue wearing around *its* neck, can you see?"

"It looks like a cross!"

"A perfect cross. The cross-statue is wearing a cross. Funny isn't it? This whole deal is, of course, not a pornographic depiction. At least it's not meant to be. The cross is an ancient depiction of life, given by the life giver, the god of all living things, the sun. And also of fertility. The continuator of life."

"So it's all about life, is it?"

"You bet. What's our biggest concern in life? Life itself, of course. Who can prolong life? Bigger powers than little old us. That's where religion steps in."

"So it's about eternal life?"

"Religion has always been about eternal life. The sun gives eternal life. Fertility keeps the human race going."

"Ok, how about the crescent then?" I turned my attention to the other symbol on the mosque. What's that about? Eternal life? Infinity?"

"Absolutely. The moon always symbolized fertility. In its crescent form it looks like the womb, the vessel of birth, of life, that is. So, both the crescent, over there," he pointed, "and the cross on the other side is one and the same. Actually, one complements the other. Check out the weird hat that sits on top of Isis and other fertility goddesses' heads: it's a sun nestling in the crescent of the moon. Male and female. Fertility. Same thing. Our primeval roots are still right here, in primitive symbols which have lost their original meaning."

"Only they are not together any more," I said.

"Stupidly so. Human beings are so similar and yet they find reasons to squabble."

"Maybe it's in our nature."

"I can't deny that. Have you finished your drink? Come on. I want to show you something."

We headed toward one of the temples, the mosque.

"Take a look at the shapes, the angles, the architecture," he urged me. Maria would have liked this, I thought.

"What am I looking for Mr. Aris?"

"Keep looking."

"All right... I can see that there is an older and a newer part, perhaps an expansion or a reconstruction."

"Good. The older parts are usually the more intriguing. Concentrate there. Describe it to me."

"It's the base of the minaret, it's more worn than the new part, it's got many sides-"

"-How many sides?

"A few."

"Count them."

We walked around the building, counting.

"Seven, eight I believe," I finally announced.

"Eight, huh? Now, let's go over to our church."

We took the short walk to the Greek Orthodox church on the other side of the small square.

"All right Alexis, now count the sides of the foundation which holds the main dome."

"Let me guess, it's eight right?"

"Sure it is. Eight, that magical number again. You are aware of the symbolism of 8?"

"What is it?"

"Infinity, of course. In mathematics, a sideways 8 ('∞') still stands for infinity, doesn't it?"

"Infinity-eternal life-fertility. Is that where you are leading this Mr. Aris?"

"You are right of course, Professor," he said. "The sun, the moon, Aphrodite, number 8, the octagon, the Magnette with its octagonal badge, it's all about our obsession for eternal life."

"The Magnette too eh?" I smiled at how he had elevated its value by including it in that privileged list.

"Yes. The MG's creator, some chap called Kipper or something, he was behind the octagonal logo. Coincidentally, he was born in eighteen eighty eight and his home was adorned by an enormous octagonal dining table."

"Lots of eights eh?"

We had picked up company. A man behind us had been casually listening in.

"Hello," he said. "Are you 'Roum'?"

"Room?" I began to ask but Mr. Aris answered yes for us both.

He started talking to us in village Cypriot. He told us where he was from, and asked us where we are from. He told us names of Greek Cypriots he knew from the past. Of course, we did not know those people. In years gone by people in Cyprus used to think that they could find someone in common, with anyone they met. So they would go through a routine set of questions in order to find who they both knew. Often they would happily conclude that they are related, even quite remotely: 'So we are related! Your third cousin's brother-in-law is my sister-in-law's uncle!' That is why local people often casually call total strangers '*koumbare*' ('best man' at a wedding). To be on the safe side.

Finally, Mr. Aris and he found a common acquaintance, a Turkish Cypriot shop owner. Of course, that made them both happy.

"Goodbye koumbare," he said as he left us, inviting us to his home for dinner. We promised we would take him up on the offer some other time. When people invite you for anything here, say to their homes for food and drinks, it is not just a polite gesture. They mean it.

"So we are 'rooms'?" I asked Mr. Aris.

"Roums yes, romioi: Greeks," he explained.

"That should be how they call Italians, Romans, would you not agree?"

"You are right. But Greeks considered themselves Romans from 200 AD onwards. Especially with the emergence of the Byzantine Empire and Constantine the Great establishing his capital in Constantinople, things got quite muddled. So Greeks were Romioi for hundreds of years, till the fall of the Byzantine Empire and even beyond. In fact, in the Byzantine period, an Ellinas ('Hellene'- how Greeks call themselves) implied a pagan: someone who believed in the idolatry of the Greeks, like Zeus and that gang."

We went back to the Magnette. We had been meaning to

drive further to a coastal old city, Kyrenia but we had left it too late and it was getting dark and Mr. Aris suggested we could do that another time, so we could see the place in daylight.

Soon we were again at the border waiting to get through to the other side, back to our side. We patiently waited in the queue of cars for our turn to come up to show our papers to the two sets of police.

"Seven-eight hundred thousand people and we can't find a way to live together," he commented.

I did not reply. We Cypriots, we have had this conversation a million times.

"You know the English word 'idiot'? Yeah? Well can you think of another word that rhymes?" he asked.

I could not right then. He paused for effect. He gave me his answer.

"Cypriot."

But I tell you a cat needs a name that's particular
A name that's peculiar, and more dignified
Else how can he keep up his tail perpendicular
Or spread out his whiskers, or cherish his pride?
('The naming of cats', Cats musical)

We were once again at our usual pre-drive spot: Mr. Aris' small porch. Maria was there too, inside, taking care of our ritual coffee. Something rubbed against my leg. Suddenly and reflexively I drew my leg away. For a second it crossed my mind that it could be one of those nasty rats from the cellar. But it was a cat.

"You got yourself a pet Mr. Aris?" asked Maria, coming out of the house and greeting the little guy as well.

"I don't think cats are really anyone's pets Maria. They're too independent to be owned."

"You know what I mean," she answered. "Does he live with you here now?"

"I think so. In a way. I'm not sure to be completely honest. He spends a lot of time here on the veranda with me in that corner over there. He comes over, says hi, and then he goes and sleeps for hours on end. He is not big on conversation… Let's just say he's my new friend."

"He looks quite old. Strange that he would be looking for a home at this age," I commented.

"It is," he agreed, initially offering no attempt at an explanation. "He was quite shabby only a couple of days ago… He's probably a stray or the people he'd been staying with have gone. But I don't know if he's that old though. A grown up, ok."

"So he just showed up?" asked Maria.

"Yes. One day, four or five days ago, maybe it was on Saturday, he appeared at my door. I heard the meowing outside and

I opened the door. I looked down and there he stood, like a guest coming for a visit. He didn't run away when he saw me. He meowed again, once, like he was saying, 'so aren't you going to ask me in'? I kindly shooed him away."

"But he didn't leave?" I asked.

"I don't know. I closed the door in his face. Later, when I came out to sit on the veranda he came in through the front gate. He rubbed against the front door, like he wanted to go inside the house."

"Did you let him in?" asked Maria.

"No. But at some stage I went in and he dashed in behind me. He disappeared down in the basement among the books. I left the front door open so he would leave in his own time."

"Did he?"

"Well I forgot about him. I was reading this book. Suddenly, as I sat here, he appeared right in front of me and he dropped something right at my feet. I looked at it and almost jumped out of my skin. There was a live rat right at my feet!"

"What?"

"Yes. This crazy creature had been hunting down there in the basement. I think that's why he wanted to get in the house in the first place. He heard or smelled the rats."

"What happened with the rat?" asked Maria.

"It was quite dazed, poor thing; you know how cats torture their victims before they kill them. But it suddenly recuperated enough to make a mad dash for the bushes over there. There was a mad chase. Perhaps it eventually got away."

"Well if it did I'm sure it's moved out of your house after that experience-permanently," I said.

"So, as you understand, Kypros is not at all my cat. He came here asking for a job. And I gave it to him. Or rather, he took it. We are partners."

"Did you say Kypros?" I asked. "You called the cat a country?!"

"Why not?"

"I don't know. Can you do that?" I asked.

"Well I have. And he doesn't seem to mind. Do you Kypros?"

He meowed 'no problem'.

"Apart from the fact that he likes it, the name fits him. Like the country, he is copper-coloured. He is little, independent, headstrong, friendly and a bit reckless."

Come to think of it he did look a bit like a Cyprus.

"Also, as you probably know," he went on, "Cyprus has the distinct honour of being the very first country in the world where people had cats as pets."

"Would that not be Egypt?" I wondered.

"Maybe. But it is here in Cyprus that actual evidence has been found of this close relationship between man and feline. At the Neolithic village of Shillourokambos archaeologists have found a ten thousand year-old grave site with two graves right next to each other: a man and his cat."

"How sweet," said Maria.

"Another world-first for us!" I said for Mr. Aris sake.

"Of course!" he smiled.

How did these two people meet? I mean, your mother and father?" I asked.

"How did they get to marry you mean? Well there were only two ways to go about it back then. The most common one was by arranged marriage. That was the traditional and proper way. Of course, such weddings often had little to do with the will of the actual prospective brides and grooms. It was frequently up to their respective parents. If each side's conditions were accepted, then they would proceed. In that case, the bride's family was obliged to provide the dowry. That was aggressively negotiated upon, based on the property of the girl's parents and her perceived 'value'. Pretty girls from 'good' families were obviously a better catch than poor ugly ones. The best case dowry scenario could include a house thrown in, the worst some hand-made linen and a couple of goats. Of course, the wedding proposal had to be made by the groom's parents. It was considered demeaning or bad form for this to be done the other way around. But it wasn't all one-way for the groom and his family. He had to 'prove' that he would be able to care for his wife and subsequent children for the rest of his life.

Such arranged marriages could be consummated quite early in people's lives, if it all worked out smoothly. Some persons I knew got married at thirteen or fourteen years old. That was a sight to see! Two young children standing all suited up on their wedding day, confounded with what was going on around them.

These weddings were the most significant events those days. We would wait in anticipation for weeks, like some people nowadays cannot wait for an important football match or a big concert. Despite the poverty, the bride and groom's parents would give it their all. They would often go into serious debt to stage a 'rich' wedding. Some weddings would last three days and nights. Rituals would begin on Thursday or Friday, with the actual church ceremony taking place on the Sunday. According to the rite, before the actual wedding the bride and groom would stay apart. The girl's mother, sisters and girl friends would prepare the bride, and the same would happen somewhere else with the groom's counterparts. Cut his hair, shave him, and dress him, all in the public eye. Professional fiddlers would sing old customary bittersweet wedding songs all the while. During the festivities, many traditions were re-enacted, all at the 'right' time. For instance, relatives and friends would pin money on the bride and groom as they performed their first dance together. That was a sight for sore eyes, for us poor folk. A man and a woman, 'dressed' up in all the bank denominations from head to toe. Five pound notes, one pound notes, *thekaselina* (ten shillings – a half a pound) notes, even *pentaselina* (five shillings – a quarter of a pound) notes! The people who pinned the *pentaselina*, say like us, would do it in a hurry, hoping no one would notice their 'stinginess' or poverty. Of course, everyone noticed. Especially the newlyweds' parents. They would watch like hawks! Anyway, that money was very important to the couple. They would never see so much cash again in their entire lives. It would be used to get them going. Despite the match-making, the whole atmosphere was all quite happy and romantic. Except for the fact that both newlyweds would be sad at 'losing' their mums! Oohh, and how the mothers wept for 'losing' their sons or daughters! They would be consoled by 'understanding' relatives! Do you know how the song went? Do you want me to sing it for you?

'Σήμερα μαύρος ουρανός, σήμερα μαύρη μέρα,
Σήμερα 'ποχωρίζεται κόρη που την μητέρα!'

(Today there's a black sky, today it's a black day,
Today daughter and mother are separated!)

How tragic!

That was the arranged marriage. That was the done way. Of course, my parents opted for, or I should more correctly say, were forced to get married the other way. The more drastic kind. Although elopement wasn't common it did occur when the normal fixed marriage procedures broke down or didn't quite work out for all concerned. You know, silly little things. Like falling in love with the 'wrong' person, not the one everyone else intended for you.

That was my father and mother's case. He told us kids their whole story one afternoon. Probably as a lesson of something to avoid doing ourselves. My mother listened in, with a mysterious happy-sad half smile. Like in a Mona Lisa pose. Here is how it went:

Just like he did after he got married, my father would wander all over the country, combing all locales, looking for work. Any kind of honest work would do. So, one fine day, he arrived at my mother's village, Lapithos, asking around for employment. He didn't ride into town on a donkey, which would have been a more stylish entrance, he said, because of course he didn't have one at the time. He was barely out of his teens, but still he was already quite big and strong. A 'dashing' young man, mother commented.

At least as dashing as one could be while dressed in rags. Anyway, he asked around and he found out that indeed, a local was in the process of fixing his house which had been seriously damaged by a landslide and that he was looking for a helper. So he got directions and made his way to said house. His offered remuneration? Food and drink for as long as he worked. And a shilling after all was done. Fair enough. As always, he worked like an ox, from dawn to dusk. He slept outside the house, of course, under the stars. His *mastros* (boss) often praised him for his hard work, his willingness and politeness.

And my father could not get his mind off his employer's youngest daughter, a beautiful shy girl with long jet-black hair, called Eleni. Yes, my mother! When he got his chance, and the nerve, he told her how he felt and that, being an honourable man, he wanted to marry her. He would ask for her hand from her father, right after the work was finished. Teenager Eleni happily consented. You can guess things didn't quite work out as planned. Eleni's father, my grandfather that is, was dumbfounded when my father made his proposal. He didn't reply for what seemed like ten minutes. When he finally found his voice, he was calm but firm. He thanked my father for his services, gave him *two* shillings and bade him goodbye. He firmly told him that he never wanted to see him again. And if he saw him around his daughter he would kill him with his bare hands. Well, not exactly the best start with one's future father-in-law, wouldn't you agree?

But my father was a determined young man. He stuck around in the Lapithos area, even though he didn't make any secret approaches to Eleni. That could ruin her reputation those days, even if absolutely nothing happened. However, every couple of weeks or so he would appear at the house, asking to speak to her father. He would summarily be shooed away. In the meantime, my grandfather had another problem brewing, this one from within. His daughter was rebelling, at least as much as she could without going too far to deserve a beating. She would cry. She would be sullen, avoiding her father as much as she could and as obviously as she could without being outright insolent.

Consequently, grandfather cracked, a little that is. He agreed to talk to my father.

"So, who are your parents?" he asked the next time he came over. "And where are they from?"

Simple and fair enough questions, don't you agree? Which my father could not answer. Neither of them. He didn't know who his parents were. He was raised in Nicosia, at a 'rich' lady's house, close to the Archbishopric. Her husband was affiliated with the church, collecting church taxes. These were not actual taxes for the church. During Ottoman and initially even during British Empire times, Cypriots were obliged to pay their taxes through the church. The two occupying empires thought it would be less trouble than collecting them from the locals themselves. They would of course allow the church to keep a big 'cut' for its troubles. By the way, this is how the Church here became so rich. Also, some locals would bequeath their estates to the church in order to avoid paying any tax at all. Church operations, you see, weren't taxed. Of course, these people continued to work their land. But after they died, or a couple of generations later, the land remained with church ownership. A dirty little 'secret', I tell you. That's how come the Cyprus Orthodox Church is so fabulously wealthy.

Anyway, my father was not this rich lady's son. He was more like her little slave. From as young an age as he could remember, he was told that he had been left at this woman's door in a basket. She could have left him out there in the cold, she told him, but she mercifully brought him in and had him fed and clothed. Also from as young an age as he could remember, he was a 'hand' at that house. By the time he was ten he was doing regular servant work. He was never abused or mistreated. He just never had a father or mother or anything resembling parental love.

He told my grandfather the truth. A terrible start to the interview.

"So who will represent your parents?"

"Represent them? No one. It will just be me at the wedding, sir."

"Who will pay for the wedding?"

"We can keep it simple," my father replied. "I will pay for the priest's services and perhaps you can contribute for a simple meal and the wine," he suggested.

"What kind of dowry are you after?"

"Nothing at all, sir. I will make our own life."

"You will eh? And how exactly will you support my daughter?"

"You yourself said I am a hard worker. These hands will support her and our children. I give you my word of honour."

And there was an additional little problem. The 'correct' way to marry off one's daughters was one at a time, beginning with the oldest one. There were two other daughters ahead of Eleni!

I don't need to tell you what happened. Once more, he was shown the door. He left, but then he became bolder. Now he would secretly see Eleni, at every opportunity. To cut a long story short, they agreed to elope. When they did it, it was reckless, even as elopements go. They had very little money between them and nowhere to stay. They just ran away with only their love to sustain them. They crossed the mountain (Pentadaktylos) and came over on the other side to my village, Sihari.

There was no wedding dress for mum, no suit for dad. No

flowers, no real ceremony. No dance ritual with money pinned on them. No dowry to help them get a head start. No family support, which was, and still is I daresay, the cornerstone of Cypriot society's welfare. They were wedded up there at the tiny Sihari church by a renegade old priest who didn't ask any questions about the father's blessings and the fact that there were no guests present. Of course, he charged a little extra to conduct the ceremony under these highly suspicious circumstances!"

Kypros was content. He was sleeping in Mr. Aris lap. The sun was warming his back. Mr. Aris was stroking him.

"And what happened to your brothers and sister, Mr. Aris? Have you kept in touch?" I asked Mr. Aris.

"We poor folk, we are not exactly pillars of society," he answered. "We disappear easily. We are the people who fall through the cracks of our wonderful capitalist system. We are the ones who fall under the radar, through the safety net, never to be seen again."

Yes, but surely he had seen them or at least heard of them later in his life? I chose to leave it alone. He looked very tired today.

We got into the car and drove off in silence.

With mother gone, my father did his best to remain in the vicinity more than ever before. He tried not to disappear for days on end like he used to, instead looking for work in the immediate surroundings, the way mother had done. But it was soon evident that he couldn't take care of us that way. My brothers took off, one by one, until there was only me and my sister left. No long goodbyes or anything mind you. In fact, I don't remember any farewells at all. Just like dad before them, I kind of thought my brothers would disappear and then reappear. They didn't. They simply vanished from our lives. The time period between losing the first member of our family, Maria Callas, and the family falling completely apart was no more than a year or two. One day, I too took the long road to Nicosia. Not that I had to make preparations or pack or anything. Everything I owned I was wearing. I just walked away like my brothers did before me. When I told my sister, Stella, she quietly wept. She didn't complain or try to make me stay though. The problem was poverty and there was no need to explain. Its presence was always there.

But I shouldn't have left my sister all alone. She was about ten or eleven years old at the time. When I left the village, that day, my father wasn't even around. I was not sure my father would have let me take off, that is why I left when he wasn't there. Anyway, like I said, she understood.

I must have been only twelve or thirteen years old, give and take… Incidentally, I should tell you, this age thing, it wasn't as big a deal in my days, you know. How old you were, well it was such a useless detail one didn't need to really bother oneself about. You started by being a '*bebi*s' or '*beba*', then a '*sporos*' ('seed'), then a '*rokolos*[*]' (regular kid), then a man and finally a '*geros*' (old man) or a '*kotziakari*' (old woman). Or maybe something in between like, you are almost a man, or, you are not a baby anymore. That's it. Birthday parties, candles, cakes and balloons, we had no idea about such things. Name days were a bigger event than birthdays, if there was any kind of such selfish celebrations at all. Some people weren't even sure when they were born, myself included. Like everyone else, I was born at home with the help of a village midwife. Since we weren't born in a hospital, there was no registry. Basically, one day you would appear in the neighbourhood, barely two feet from the ground, but still, sooner or later someone or other would notice you. Where did you come from, shrimp? And, what's your name? they'd ask. You told them, and bam, just like that, that was your identity. That was your passport.

Years later, the authorities tried to pinpoint my day and year of birth so that they could provide me with documentation. Proof that I was alive and a human being, so to speak. It was a driver's license for the Magnette that I needed, to be precise. Eventually, I had the '*mouktaris*'[**], the village mayor, sign a piece of paper which placed my birth somewhere in the summer of 1938. August 23 was quite randomly selected I believe.

Anyway, when I headed down to Nicosia, on that very day, I suddenly stopped being a child and became a man. Nothing in between. From then on, my survival was entirely dependent on one person. Me."

---

* Derived from ancient Greek, 'rokon' meaning mule. So, the term loosely translates to 'young mule'.

** Derived from the Turkish word 'Muhtar' (village headman).

Archaeology

I was reading an article in the newspaper:

In two excavation cases (Salamis Tomb 2, Lapithos Tomb 422) the figures buried in the ground were bound and so apparently qualify as 'ritual killings'. These murders were in all probability revenge killings. The article said that it is on record that only in the time of Hadrian (117 AD) was the annual human sacrifice to Zeus abolished at Salamis in Cyprus.

It occurred to me that sometimes digging in the past brings up serious dirt.

Where do the children play?

o you never had a chance to be a regular child? I mean, to just play mindless kids' games, like kids do? To have no responsibilities, no worries in the world?" I asked Mr. Aris in a distressed tone.

"You see what I've gone and done now? I gave you the wrong impression: that poverty and hunger equal misery twenty four hours a day. Not true. Not true at all. We were just like young wild animals that do not know where their next meal is coming from. Don't they play all day? Cubs will be cubs, kids will be kids.

Of course, we had to be creative with our games. Imagination played a big part. A stick could be a … stick, which is fun in itself, or a gun or a bat. A stone was a ball or a missile. A big rock was a monster or a castle. We had a lot of fun and a lot of freedom. Also, as maybe I have told you, I never really had a formal education. Those days, if you finished primary school you were considered educated. If you finished high school you were really educated."

"These days a first university degree makes you just plain educated," I said.

"Well, anyway, not going to school much gave me a lot of free time. My parents had a vague idea that we were supposed to be in school, but they never really enforced it. We were needed around the house. And besides, my parents were usually gone, so they wouldn't really know… I really regret this. That I never really went to school I mean. It's such a pity."

"Perhaps you didn't have a formal education but you still are a wise man, Mr. Aris. Sometimes people do just enough to get a degree which they proudly hang on the wall and then that's that. They feel they have done enough. But you, you have never slowed down. You have read more books than anyone I ever met. If you had gone through the formal education system you would probably now have five or ten degrees! So don't you go feeling bad."

"I thank you for your kind words, Professor. But I have slowed down now. I can't really read without wearing thick glasses. And it tires me so… At any rate, if you wish, I will dispel the miserable picture a bit. I will tell you how we passed our time when we were kids. Perhaps you will find that you did the same.

For one, we played with the other animals around us. All kinds of animals of all shapes and sizes. Goats and sheep. *Zeezeeri*, *kourkoutaes* and *helicopters** of every colour of the rainbow. Big vicious hornets, even poisonous snakes. We would catch them all. Anything and everything that could move was game. I regret to say, cruel game sometimes, at least for some kids. Maybe they took it out on the poor beasts. Maybe it was their way to show that they were not at the very bottom of the chain. That cats and crickets and slugs were below them… Animals were right around us. We literally lived with them. Many people would share their humble dwellings with their animals - oxen, goats, sheep, and donkeys - in winter in order to get some of their warmth. They were their heaters, literally.

My older brother would love to repeat the story of when he got stung by a scorpion… Two days later *it* died! But the event wasn't quite as humorous the way I remember it. It hap-

---

* 'Zeezeeros' is a type of cricket. Its name is onomatopoeia. Its midday constant zee-zee-zee sound is very common in these parts of the world. So common you don't even notice. 'Kourkoutas' is an endemic stone-age looking lizard. It can sometimes grow to over a foot long. Its name is derived from the old 'korkoutis', meaning… penis! There is a certain resemblance. 'Helicopters' are Dragonflies.

pened one night, while we were all sleeping in our small house. Scorpions you understand wander around at night. They are nocturnal. That's why you hardly ever see one. Anyhow, getting stung by one is no laughing matter I assure you. Even today, for every person killed by a poisonous snake, there are ten killed by a scorpion. Have you ever seen anyone who was stung by these little creatures? Not pleasant... My brother suddenly jumped up, howling. Woke us all up in a hurry. You wouldn't wish this kind of unspeakable pain on your worst enemy. It was a scary sight to see, like he was possessed by the devil himself. Through the night his skin turned paler and paler. He was sweating, frothing at the mouth, his eyes rolled... in any case, he eventually came out of it. But we found a dead scorpion outside our door a couple of days later. Hence the story.

Once I caught a great big vulture! The poor things are extinct now. At least in Cyprus. And we didn't even bat an eyelid while committing the crime, while wiping them all out. Just like the Golden Eagle and the Black Vulture before them*. I remember when I came down to Nicosia and even up to the eighties you could still make them out circling over the Pentadaktylos mountain top, fifteen miles or so away. I tell you, a beautiful sight. I don't know why some people think vultures are ugly. Cypriot vultures were majestic animals. In flight and even on the ground. Due to their size, they preferred to hop and open their wings for speed, but they would also walk with a stiff swagger, like English gentlemen, like they owned the place. Grown birds were over a metre long with a wingspan of two and a half metres. That's big. That's a bigger 'wingspan'

* The 'Cyprus vulture' is the Griffon Vulture. Apparently there is still a remaining colony in the area of Acrotiri, Limassol, but Mr. Aris wasn't aware of this. The 'black vulture' is the Aegyptius Monachus. The Griffon Vultures have been documented to be present on the island since as early as 1553. Locke stated that "there are many in this island." Mariti, who was in Cyprus during 1760-67, stated that "one sees many vultures standing in the fields like flocks of sheep."

than the poor Magnette here, which is just less than one and a half metres wide! But hunters and nature itself wiped them all out. Not enough dead donkeys around anymore, for them to feast on… At any rate, that's a huge bird to actually catch I tell you. Not easy at all. 'Do not try this at home', you know? We 'surrounded' four or five of them as they were feasting on a stinky donkey carcass. They noticed us but they had more important business to tend to. Suddenly, on the count of three, we sprinted toward them. I was half hoping they would all fly away. They seem much bigger and scarier close up, you see. But they are awkward and not too fast on the ground. I leapt and suddenly I was right on top of one of them, my arms holding firmly onto it. Before I knew it, my nose was buried in its 'hairy' white smelly neck. Like I'd just caught a giant chicken, or rather perhaps a big turkey or something! I think the bird was more surprised than I was. It froze, it hardly reacted. The whole thing only lasted a few seconds, then of course I let go. But it was enough to give me hero status for a couple of months, even among the grown ups.

I was not among those boys I told you about who were really cruel with animals. I even defended the little creatures when I could. Not that they ever thanked me for it. Once I found a wounded sparrow hawk under some bushes. It had been shot on the wing by hunters. It would have surely died out there. So, I took it home. That was no straightforward feat, mind you. It bit and scratched me when I tried to pick it up. I almost let it be. A real predator it is. Its beak and claws are deadly weapons, let me tell you! But I was a tough little nut myself. I eventually managed to wrap it up in the old shirt I was still wearing. I found a wooden fruit crate outside the village co-op. By turning it upside down I had the ideal cage. For the next couple of months I nursed it to health. I did its hunting for it, lizards mainly. Eventually, I opened up its cage and it would sit on top of the crate. Slowly but surely it recuperated. At first it flew just a couple of feet onto my arm, tempted by the dead lizard I was holding. Clawed me deep when it landed. Strong grip, like a full grown man's. So, after that I wrapped my arm with an old cloth. For a few months, I walked around with a hawk on my shoulder! I really loved that bird. If any other kids tried to fondle it it bit them with its wrench-like beak!

In its final days under my wing, so to speak, it could fly high in the sky above my head in circles. One day it flew half a mile away. I desperately ran after it. It sat on a tree and watched me from up there, twisting its head downward toward me the way those birds do, like it needed to take a better look. I begged and I coaxed it to come down. After a few minutes, it reluctantly flew on my shoulder, I could tell. The very next day it took a bee line in the same direction but it stayed high up in the air. I ran and ran after it until I was so tired I could go on no more. I was mortified. It had left me, just like that, with not even a last circle above me to say 'goodbye, thanks for saving my life, thanks for the memories'. I cried as I walked all the way home, but my mother explained. Hawks and eagles are wild birds and really proud. Nobody can 'own' them, they have no masters. They are the kings of the skies. Such birds are not meant to be in cages, or confined in small areas. They need to fly wherever they want. They are the symbol of freedom, and such talk... I was still inconsolable! To this day whenever I see a sparrow hawk I stupidly hope it's 'my bird' coming to say hi.

We also played lots of fun games. Like *skatoullika* (literally, the 'shitty game'!) You know that game? Do kids still play it? I didn't think so. It is a great pastime. Don't be fooled by its name! It's a game of skill, speed and timing. You simply pile four or five flat stones on top of each other. One player, the skatoullis, has to protect this pile from all the others who try to knock it over with their own stones from behind a line about twenty feet away. Anyone who fails must stay put where his stone has landed. If one of the throwers knocks over the pile then the skatoullis has to reassemble his stones before he can chase and try to catch anyone who picks up his stone and is rushing back to his home base behind the line. It's not as complicated as it sounds. Think bowling, only more dangerous. I don't know how many people have been struck with stray bowling balls, but I assure you many heads have heroically cracked from being hit with stones in the name of the shitty game. Still, iron out some of these minor problems and this game should be in the Olympics.

The most fun game we played, however, was another, called *lingri*. For this game think cricket or baseball. A small thick stick is balanced on two big flat stones set about a foot apart. Those stones are the batter's base. The bat, or lingra, is another bigger thicker stick, naturally. We would wander around the village, searching for nice and straight olive branches to cut down, covertly of course, to turn into prized custom made lingras. Now, the batter's task was to place his bat under the small stick in order to raise it in the air. Then, while the stick was still in mid air, to swing his lingra, hitting it as hard as he could. He had three chances to achieve this. His points were the equivalent of the distance, approximately in yards, that the stick travelled. If one of the outfield players caught the flying stick he got all the batter's previously earned points. That took a lot of skill and courage to achieve. For one, you had to guess the direction where the little stick would be hit, so you would be standing in the right place. But the hardest thing was actually catching it. It would travel at speed in a swirling motion. It could effortlessly whiz by you like a missile full of splinters.

You may think the resemblance to cricket and its younger cousin, baseball, is just coincidental. It probably is. But I've also read that the origins of cricket date back as early as the eighth century. And, like other old leisure imports such as chess and backgammon, these sports may have travelled into the European continent via Persia and through Constantinople, the capital of the Ottoman Empire. Remember, both these empires were present in Cyprus. Indeed, there are eighth and ninth century accounts of such games being played in the Mediterranean region, sometimes as church-sponsored events to maintain community. The theory that games such as lingri are a direct ancestor of cricket is based on the notion that the Normans brought it into England after the 1066 defeat of the Saxons. So 'owzat!

Of course, the very best game was also the most productive one: scavenging. Searching here and there, looking out for and discovering all sorts of things to eat. Most people today would look down a valley and see nothing, but we could clearly see potentially tasty food sources right, left and centre. Like in those cartoons where they see a chicken and they imagine it as a delicious cooked meal on a plate. With time, you get pretty good at it. Like an eagle spotting its prey from a mile away. You know what's good and what isn't. For example, you soon find out that most wild mushrooms are not edible. Usually not deadly either, but certainly not edible. '*Porti tou Garou*' (donkey farts!) the most common ones were called! So you can imagine their taste. You wait for the land to successively offer you its delicious fruit, like the *mosfila*, growing in the wild. Those ripen in October. The Mosfilia tree is a thorny ugly tree, but its yellow fruit taste better then any apple, I swear. And have you tasted a sweeter fruit than *papoutsosika* (literally 'shoe figs') growing on gigantic prickly cacti. Those we ate in the summer. We would even devour some of the thorny bushes themselves. Peel off the outside and there you have it. The most mouth-watering low-fat meal you can imagine.

Now you see why I told you we were not really starving at all. Just constantly hungry. In fact, as I found out, it was much worse in the city."

So I finally made it to the big bright lights of Nicosia. From up at the village they shone even brighter than Venus and the North Star in the night sky. They were like beacons of hope. Hope of a better and even, dare I say, a 'glamorous' life! We had heard of the cinemas, the skating rinks. But down in the city, up close, you saw them for what they were: Unsightly bare street lights. Ugly buildings with tall walls. All the lights did was shed a naked glow on all the misery. A bit like shining a torch to reveal a bunch of rats in a dark pit.

We street kids, we were the rats, by the way. That's why I have a soft spot for the ugly rodents, even though I do have a right now to declare them official enemies of the state, the way they go through my books. But I was one of them, you see. I have been there. So I understand them. Nobody wants you, everyone fears you. You want to be liked but it is impossible. You want to look endearing but no matter how hard you try your whole countenance scares the hell out of decent folks. A tramp is a tramp, even when he smiles. Is that not the fate of the rat? Was that not exactly our fate? Stray kids were and always have been considered pests. There is no room to feel sorry for them. You feed one, a hundred will appear out of nowhere to ominously surround you.

I spent the next two or three years of my life as a resident of our 'lovely' capital city. I slept in the open air, in animal sheds, in alleys, in passageways, just about anywhere I laid my head down. I don't know if my father ever looked for me but I never got word of anything. Not that he was to blame. I wasn't exactly the easiest person to find, what with no home address and no phone number (*and no e-mail*).

Well, around 1956 or thereabouts, 'business' in Nicosia, was not exactly going swimmingly. Too many street rats like me were hustling for too few 'employment opportunities'. I also had a nasty situation brewing. An older homeless thug began picking on me for no apparent reason. Well, not exactly, I should say. Perhaps it had a little to do with the fact that I was younger and a little more convivial than him. Of course that didn't take much doing. That boy would scare the living daylights out of Count Dracula. Anyway, when ladies or even gents came in our direction looking for a helping hand for some odd job, they would invariably pick me over him even though he was obviously stronger than me. So, in light of these generally adverse 'work conditions', I was keeping all my options open. And in any case, knowing that the other side of the hill is always greener, even in the Cyprus 'desert', even for a homeless boy, one always keeps his eyes and ears open lest word of greener pastures comes up. One such occasion was a little adventure I had up on Troodos Mountain with some foreign scientists. I think I told you about that one.

The other 'greener pastures' news, came from the seaside city of Limassol. Once in a while, and I mean quite rarely, like maybe once or twice every week, that city's port would welcome ships containing goods to unload, and more importantly, 'rich' eccentric foreigners coming to Cyprus for all kind of weird reasons: to study the natives, to take pictures, to dig up rocks. These 'strange' people, it was rumoured, were always in need of a service. They would perhaps ask for someone to carry their luggage or equipment, or someone to simply lead them to suitable accommodation. For such trivial help, they were willing to compensate you with absurd amounts of money, say a shilling or two. As much as we would make in a whole month!

In Nicosia payments were in *bakkires* (pennies). So I decided to take the long road to Limassol. This was almost an epic voyage, even compared to the one I had made from my village to Nicosia. The distance was, and still is of course, over sixty five miles. Such a move would take at least a week, I knew. But I didn't care. It wasn't as if I had something urgent to do or as if I was leaving friends behind or as if I would have to shut down the office and pack. I hadn't exactly accumulated much in my three or four years in the capital. Although I should point out that now I was the proud owner of an old pair of shoes. An old man gave them to me as compensation for a day's work. It was like I'd hit the jackpot that day, I tell you. The other boys were green with envy. To be honest, wearing that first pair of shoes in my life did not give me the pleasure I thought it would. The fact that they were about three sizes bigger than my foot didn't help, I grant you. But the confinement in that thick coarse leather was almost unbearable, given my previous complete freedom. But I stuck to it. I think because of the suddenly achieved dizzying social status those shoes promoted me to. In any case, perhaps they did assist somewhat in the many miles I walked in order to get to Limassol, though then again I often took them off to walk barefoot, tying the laces together and hanging the shoes around my neck. After all, I reasoned, this preserved them for more necessary or 'formal occasions'. I truly intended to hold on to those shoes for the rest of my life. But shortly after that hike, subsequent events put that notion to rest.

It took me just three days to make the trek. I was proud of that record, considering the fact that I was not picked up by a single car. It was not really a matter of drivers not willing to pick me up. It was more the case that the passing cars were packed full of passengers. Rarely would a vehicle travel to another city without a big number of relatives, friends etcetera wanting to join the owner. Such trips were put to full use by everyone, you see. Very few cars passed by anyway. In any case, to be honest, if I was in their place I wouldn't have picked me up either! Mostly I walked but I also rode donkey-back for a while. But I 'crawled' along the biggest distance riding on the fender of the back wheel of a slow old tractor. The driver mostly didn't take the main road. He went on shortcut dirt roads, through valleys, even over hills. This proud owner had just purchased the tractor for a hundred pounds, he said. That was a princely sum those days and he was making his way back home. In order to buy it he said he had to sell some land his shepherd father had left him. Ten donums!* That's a lot of land for a tractor. In today's land prices he bought that tractor for about a million pounds!

The 'formal occasion' I was telling you about for the shoes came just a day after I arrived in Limassol. In fact, my relocation away from the capital city only lasted for that one day. I guess it was all because I got lucky and also because I instinctively followed that wise saying, 'first impressions count'. As I made my way to my new abode of employment, I spruced myself up as best as I could. I actually paid for a haircut and to have my shoes shined with the last of my money. You might think that was a big and reckless risk, but I was used to that. I never really had money on me most of the time so it wasn't as if it was the end of the world or something. I also washed my face and shirt at one of those taps you find outside of Moslem mosques. They use them to wash their feet before entering the mosque. I kind of took a full body shower there. So, you could say, I arrived at my new place of employment looking and smelling like a rose. At least compared to the other tough and scruffy dockhands.

When I got to the port, I was a bit disappointed to realise that the police were guarding the port entrance and that they

* An old unit of measurement (A third of an acre or 1.338sqm)

would not allow us to actually go in where the ships arrived. Only the professional dockers were in there. But there were other kids my age and even grownups standing or sitting outside the port entrance, so I figured that that place was as good as any. They were friendly enough and I didn't spot any Dracula look-alikes among them. There were both Turkish Cypriots and Greek Cypriots in that bunch. Although they sort of made two separate groups they all generally had a friendly disposition toward one another and joked with each other. I recall thinking, 'I like it here. I could be friends with some of these people'. So I was really glad about my decision to go there. Of course, it turned out that these thoughts and feelings did not matter.

The news about the imminent arrival of a ship came hours before anyone saw it. There wasn't exactly an arrivals board or anything somewhere but I heard the news spread among the others on the outside. A ship would be arriving from England sometime later that day. My more experienced 'co-workers' weren't moved at all by the leaked news. They simply stayed sitting or lying in their chosen spots, in the shade under a couple of trees. But I was excited. For one, I had never even seen a boat in my life before, never mind a whole big ship that could apparently travel thousands of miles to get here! So I stood and waited, craning my neck, squinting and trying to spot a speck, anything, out in the sea. It turned out that somebody else spotted the vessel before I did. In fact, it took me a couple of minutes before I could make it out even when another boy pointed it out to me.

When it finally docked I was very impressed by its size. It wasn't exactly the Titanic, I am sure, but to my young peasant eyes the impression was equal. First the passengers came down the wooden stairway. They all looked very white and well dressed and fresh, like they had just come from around the corner. Or from another world. There were quite a few of them, maybe about thirty or forty. From there, as I was informed, they went inside the small building to take care of their papers and to buy themselves some refreshments. Don't think 'restaurant' mind you. An old-fashioned fridge and an old man to fish the drinks out of the ice-cold water was all there was, apparently. Do you remember those stylish red Coca-Cola fridges?

However, it would be a while longer before the passengers actually came out the gates because first their things would have to be unloaded. 'That is a lot of stuff for so few people', I recall thinking as the dock-hands came in and out of the ship's depths loaded with cases and big square boxes.

Then, I saw it. It seemed to come right out of the vessel's gaping hull. I just stared. A whole car had just been driven onto the tarmac, straight out of the ship's guts. Yes, it was this Magnette. This dark green gleaming beauty sat there confidently staring out on this alien land, blinding us mere mortals in the sunshine. I couldn't take my eyes off it. Of course I had seen cars before, little Morrisses and Volkswagens, but never anything like it. Its grand entrance onto my life's little stage did it I think. Or its big, shining grill, I don't know. Like one might gape today at a convertible Rolls Royce or a yellow Lamborghini. Presently, a tall skinny man in a suit and wearing steel rimmed round spectacles walked to the car, seemingly to survey it. He walked all around it, leaning toward it and away, carefully scrutinizing, searching for scratches or whatever. When he was satisfied, he opened the door and got in at the driver's side. He opened his window and asked someone a question. In response the man pointed toward the gate where we were all standing. So the owner of the car drove toward us. He showed his papers to the policeman and a couple of minutes later he was out. He parked right in front of me and he got out, half way, one foot in the car the other out. It goes without saying that it was immediately evident that he was an Englezos. About ten kids and grownups gathered round him, though they did not smother him. They stood at a respectful distance.

He asked, "Does anyone know the city of Nicosia well?"

Most Cypriots, as you know, do understand English. Being occupied since 1878* can do that for you. Despite the man's accent, which I later learnt was from the North of England, I understood what he said. Still, as it was my first day at the port, I did not immediately pipe up. But then, when the foreigner asked the same question again, slower this time, and still no one responded I raised my hand.

"I Nicosia milord," I said to him with my fluent English, but he understood what I meant. "I from Nicosia."

"Do you know where the Governor's Palace is? Or the English School?"

I told him I knew both those places. In fact, I showed him with the palms of my hands, they were close by. He nodded, then looked me up and down, sizing me up. He had this penetrating look, like he could see exactly what you were thinking. But I held my nerve. He made his decision.

"Could you please show me the way to these places? I will pay you ten shillings for your trouble." Ten shillings? That was

---

* Cyprus became part of the British Empire through a simple two article agreement with Turkey. If Great Britain would accept to guarantee the protection of Eastern Turkey from Russian aggression then Turkey would hand over Cyprus to the Brits. On the fourth of June 1878 the Convention of Defensive Alliance between Great Britain and Turkey was signed. Incidentally, it may be interesting to note Article 6 in the Convention's Annex. It stated that if Russia restored to Turkey various territories taken during the last war, then England would end the agreement, in effect handing the island back to Turkey. When Russia did return the contested territories England did not return Cyprus to the Turks.

a bloody fortune! Should I take such an outrageous advantage of this man who was so obviously naïve? I figured I could use the money. Of course I would have to make my way back to Limassol and this goldmine port once more but so what. So I sat in a car, this car we are sitting in right now, for the very first time in my life. I could not believe the Magnette's interior. The wood, the leather, the MG badge! I wanted to touch everything, to absorb the sheer class. But I didn't. I figured it would be bad form to do that, so I sat as still as I could here in the passenger's seat, where I am sitting now. I know this car is in pretty good shape even now, but it is still over fifty years old. You have to imagine it brand new, Alexis. The smell, the shine. And it was dizzyingly fast, a rocket! I looked out of the window and everything just whizzed by, a mere blur. I soon figured out that it was best to keep my eyes straight ahead, or I else I would throw up, I was sure. Of course I was comparing the Magnette's performance to donkeys and the tractor that brought me part of the way to Limassol. In truth, any old mule could easily beat that piece of junk. I could have sprinted faster than that tractor. But this! A royal carriage drawn by twenty thoroughbred horses or more couldn't keep up with it. Thinking back now, I guess we can't have been going much faster than forty or fifty miles an hour. The roads were really bad, full of potholes, and people would routinely and casually cross streets. They weren't used to cars you see. Also it would be all but impossible to drive all the way from Limassol to Nicosia without running into at least one flock of sheep crossing the main road.

We completed in a mere two hours a 'trek' that took me an epic three days and that included a stop half way at the tree-lined village of Skarinou for a coffee. The English man introduced himself to me as Stanley Edwards. He said he was from a big coal mining city from the North of England with a population almost as big as the whole of Cyprus. This city was called Newcastle. He was what they call a Geordie. He said he would be living and working in Nicosia for at least the next five years and that he had been told that his house was somewhere near the English School and the Governor's Palace.* He asked a lot of questions, half of which I didn't understand. The other half I couldn't answer! He wanted to know everything about Cyprus. Its population, its geography, about the armed struggle against the English. It was embarrassing. I really could hardly answer most of his questions. That day I realised how little I knew about the country I was living in.

When we got into Nicosia I led him toward the address he had given me. It wasn't hard to find the house he was looking for. It was literally the only house in the area. The only other building in the vicinity was the English School. There were just empty fields around us, except for the high eucalyptus trees of the school grounds.

Given the location I just described you have probably figured it out, Alexis, that the house we went to was the one I am currently living in. Of course it is now surrounded by those ugly monstrosities that city people live in. Anyway, it still stands out like a sore thumb, you will admit. I opened the gate and he parked the car in the dusty driveway. By now the Magnette looked like it had been in the Cyprus Rally. It had accumulated a healthy layer of dust along the way. He had a key to the front door of the house. We both unpacked the car and put all his things right in the centre of the hallway. From what I could see, apart from those things the house was completely empty. So, this house seemed even more enormous to my eyes. It even had an in-house toilet, a European one, and a bathtub! Again, please remember what I was comparing with those days. In this case, with my humble residence back at the village.

* The Governor's Palace is today's Presidential Palace.

He went from room to room while I stood there at the entrance patiently waiting for my ten shillings. I started contemplating whether he had since been having second thoughts, given the fact that, I admitted to myself, I hadn't done much to deserve that kind of money.

He opened all the windows in all the rooms to let in the fading light and some fresh air. He looked around him, thinking, ignoring me I thought. But it wasn't so.

"Do you know where I can buy some furniture?" he asked without looking at me, a tone of exasperation in his voice. Perhaps it just dawned on him at that moment that he was in a strange country and that he had a lot of irksome details to take care of. "A bookcase, a bed, some chairs?" he went on.

I indicated to him that indeed I knew where he could find such things. I figured why not help the poor man out and at least earn the ten shillings. If he still intended to give it to me. It was as if he had read my mind or perhaps he just suddenly remembered. He handed me the money we had agreed upon and told me that I had an extra ten shillings coming for showing him where he could buy the items he needed to set up house. I was thrilled. This deal was getting better and better!

Some of the items he bought we piled into the Magnette, the bigger ones were brought to the house by the sellers. It took about a week for everything to arrive. As expected, he bought a couple of beds, two sofas, a kitchen table and a few chairs, things like that. But he also purchased some incredible stuff that I'd never seen before: A 'Crown' radio which he immediately tuned to an English station. And a washing machine! Of course, it was only an electric washing machine, not automatic. I don't know if you know of this sort. It was made of a single tub and it was of the wringer-type. Over in America they already had even more modern ones: the automatic washing machines which were still prohibitively expensive in England. Mr. Edwards told me of this fact when he saw how I stared at the washer like it was a spaceship. He also informed me that no one really knew who had originally invented the washing machine, but the rotating drum prototype was first patented in 1782 by an English man called Henry Sidgier. He proudly emphasised this man's nationality. What? Mr. Edwards knew of such things! I felt like an imbecile.

I was really impressed that he was aware of facts like that. But I still voiced my doubt about the date he had mentioned. 1782? Why that sounded like way too ancient, Mr. Edwards, like the Stone Age! If this washing contraption was discovered so long ago how come we didn't have them yet in Cyprus? Did it take two hundred years for inventions to travel here? In Cyprus, you see Alexis, we were then still with the classic hand operated wringing machines, so this one that Mr. Edwards bought was space age. He laughed in reply. He said the idea was even older. One earlier design of a washer had appeared in a 1752 issue of "The Gentlemen's Magazine", an English publication. Wasn't it interesting that a product so associated with women would appear in a periodical that sounded like an early version of 'Playboy', he asked me. I had no idea what he was talking about. I asked him, what's 'Playboy' magazine? He laughed in reply and he just said it was a brand new magazine. Of course, a few years later I did realise what 'Playboy' was about! Shocking! (*Mr. Aris laughs*)

Still, I was most awed by an acquisition which was much simpler in design. Mr. Edwards ordered four shoulder-high bookcases! He laughed even harder this time, when I asked him what they were for. Of course I knew what books were but I had never seen a piece of furniture especially designed to hold a lot of them together. No one in our village had one anyway. The church had a few Bibles. That and a couple of other books you would see in some houses. That was just about what I had seen up until then. You don't believe it?

"Where are all the books you are going to put in these bookcases?" I asked Mr. Edwards in disbelief, in my broken English.

"They should arrive here in a few weeks, when my wife comes over," he replied. So I also found out at that moment that he had a wife and she would be arriving shortly. He explained that he came here first in order to assess the situation and to try and set up the basics for the house. The small details, the 'woman's touch' he called it, well he would leave that stuff up to his wife.

During those first few days when he was setting up I too slept in the house. I had a whole empty bedroom to myself. I slept on the floor and he did so too, in the master bedroom. Even though he was an Englezos, he was the best employer I ever had. He gave me one of his shirts and a pair of trousers. He took me to restaurants to eat! We drank ice cold beers! He chatted to me like we were friends! I couldn't believe my luck.

I found out from him that he had accepted an administrative position at an organisation called the British Council. He explained to me that this was like a big library which the English had been setting up in many countries. One such library had been established in Cyprus since 1940. Anyone could borrow any book he wanted from its vast collection of thousands of books. Take it home, read it and then take it back. You might guess that I was to learn that simple process well in the forthcoming years. The library's purpose was to help educate people, he said.

It sounded too good to be true. It was, other Cypriots told me later. This British Council thing was funded by the British Empire. This Council thing was the Englezi's chief propaganda machine and even an undercover centre for spying and other sinister operations. Could it be so, with a nice man like Mr. Edwards working there? Why, he was probably a spy himself, they told me.

Whatever the case was, I thoroughly enjoyed those first days with Mr. Edwards. Between the restaurants and the enlightening chats I had a lot of work to do. To clean up the house, carry things here and there, to do some painting, some gardening. I even washed the Magnette for the first of many times.

I could see that he took a liking to me. Perhaps he needed me, but I think it was bigger than that. He also wanted to help me, to get me out of my misery, even out of my ignorance. So, after we finished the house he offered me a job at the library/spy headquarters, whatever, the British Council. Nothing fancy. I was just a messenger. But it was my first real job. With a salary! Ten pounds a month! Yes, you heard right Alexis. A fortune I tell you.

I also did the odd jobs at his house. That was an extra four pounds a month. He arranged for me to live at the back of the main house. Like many other houses of that day, there was a single independent room in the back. It's still there now, though it's a mess. They used to call them *blistarko* (literally, washing room), a room with a big sink for washing things. It barely fit the small bed Mr. Edwards put in for me but it was a roof and I had my own front door with my very own key and an outside toilet. A home! I sure had come a long way in a short while.

Like Mr. Edwards had said would happen, a few weeks later we took the Nicosia to Limassol road once more. This time to pick up his wife and his books. I waved at the boys and men standing outside the port. They waved back but none of them seemed to recognise me. I didn't blame them. I'd only been with them a day, after all.

We went inside the port. Not through those big gates with the policeman where the Magnette had been driven out, but through another entrance. We made our way to the 'cafeteria' I told you about. We each got ourselves a cold Coca-Cola in those delightful small glass bottles and waited. I could see that Mr. Edwards was very anxious. He wasn't doing the usual chitchat with me. He just kept his eyes outside, smoking and looking out at the calm blue sea.

When the ship eventually arrived he went outside to greet his wife. He told me to wait where I was. Now, Alexis, you know how I love the Magnette. But I know it forgives me when I say that when I first laid eyes on Mrs. Edwards I was much more dumbfounded than when the Magnette made its grand entrance to my life.

Now how to explain without exaggerating. It was like a goddess had decided to wear normal human clothes to come and mingle among us mere mortals! But then again, she didn't look a fake like a Marilyn Monroe or something. She appeared homely, very natural and pure somehow, she had no make-up on you see. Yet, she was so incredibly pretty, like from another planet, never mind another country. Our own Aphrodite would have been fittingly envious.

He rushed toward her and he held her in his arms for a long time and they kissed each other on the mouth. Like they do in films. A big no-no generally in those days, let alone in backward Cyprus. But they didn't seem to care at all. Finally, he picked up a couple of her things and they started making their way toward me. I swear I almost bolted! Of course I know it's silly, but I was barely a man, I mustn't have been eighteen yet. I did not really know any women at the time, and definitely I was not worthy to be in proximity to that woman. Something like that went through my head, I am embarrassed to admit. Mr. Edwards introduced me as his new friend and she awarded me with the warmest of smiles.

"How do you do, Alexis?" she said with this ethereal voice. "My name is Eileen". To me, James Bond could not have made a more dramatic entrance. As I told you, it would have been the same to me if she had come out and said, 'My name is Aphrodite. You know, Goddess of Beauty and Love'. It goes without saying that I just froze. In fact it took me like a week to actually manage to mumble something to her.

That name sounded so exotic to me. I know it's much the same as Helen is for us. And I also know that a lady bearing *that* name was so pretty a thousand ships were launched to go get her back, like our friend Stasinos told us. But this Eileen name, it was more remarkable to my ears. I tried to say it with the correct intonation, like Mr. Edwards did. Never to her face of course. Not once did I ever call her by her first name, always Mrs. Edwards.

She was so very kind from the start. When I worked outside in the yard she would bring me some cold sweet lemon juice and tell me to take a break. She noticed that my trousers, the ones Mr. Edwards gave me, were too long on me and that I was folding them inwards. So she grabbed a measuring tape and she had me stand on a kitchen chair while she adjusted and pinned the correct length. Then she ordered me to take them off in the bedroom next to the kitchen so she could fix them. I took them off, put them outside the door and quickly closed it. She came over and picked them up. I was really embarrassed standing there waiting, half naked. I didn't have any underwear yet! But I was also so moved that someone, that she, a regular deity, would bother with something as trivial as the length of my trousers.

She also made me throw away those precious shoes I told you about because she said I looked like Charlie Chaplin. Mr. Edwards' shoes were much closer to my size, so she gave me a pair of his. When he came home I saw that he noticed. Thankfully Mrs. Edwards told him immediately that she had given them to me. He smiled in response, a genuine smile but ever so slightly bemused. I think he hadn't been quite ready to part with those shoes!"

ABC

A - B - C - D - E - F - G
H - I - J - K - L - M - N - O - P
Q - R - S - T - U and V,
W - X - Y and Z
Now I know my A - B - C's
Tell me what you think of me?
(The Alphabet Song)

Soon after I started working for Mr. Edwards and his lovely wife Eileen I figured out what they could so obviously see from their enlightened standpoint: a poor uneducated shaggy peasant boy. I wasn't dumb but that's exactly what I was. My self-awareness was enhanced by their refined presence. Not that they made anything of it, it was simply obvious for anyone to see, even me. Their mannerisms, their 'please give me this' 'thank you for taking that' politeness, nobody had ever talked that way in my company before.

When I first started working for them I barely knew how to read or write. What I did understand, I had picked up by myself or through asking. And in any case, up to then, I did not really see the point of reading or writing, to be completely honest.

Mrs. Edwards was to figure out before long that I couldn't read nor write. One day she went through a lot of things she needed me to buy from the local *mbakalis* (grocer). Since the list had grown she decided to write them down for me so I wouldn't forget. I tried to memorize the list she had read out to me on the way to the shop. I kept repeating the items to myself, singing them or trying to put them into a poem, in rhythm with my steps. It worked pretty well until I got to the grocer's. Then, I blanked. Even the silly shop owner couldn't make out what she had written. How did he run that business?

I went back with a couple of items, tail between my legs. I had to confess my ignorance.

I guess I became her pet project. She became Mrs. Higgins, so to speak. But without the irony. I was a quick learner, we were both glad and surprised to find. Within six or seven months I could read, even write. And, given my teacher's nationality, I was picking up both the English and Greek languages fast. I don't exactly know when I broke the code of the Latin and then the Greek alphabet. But somehow I did, I can't pinpoint when. One day, to my surprise, I simply read out a road sign for an old man. Road signs and shop signs tended to be written in both languages, so I was quickly picking out the 'subtle' differences. For example I noticed that the second letter in the alphabet 'code', that 'B' squiggle was, well a 'b' in English, but it was a 'V' sound in Greek and so on.

Mrs. Edwards would pick books from their substantive home library and we would read them together. I still have all those books today. They have her name or her husband's name written on the inside cover together with a date. Those books are very precious to me. They took away the blindness I was living in without even knowing it was so. Mrs. Edwards, Eileen, had an English grammar book called '*A First Aid in English*'. That was good, but boring. I preferred another series of novels that she had about a rascally boy called *William.** At first, she would read them to me, editing them, I later found out, as she read along, to make them simpler. Later she made me read them myself, painstakingly, while she explained the strange English rules. Whoever said English is easier than Greek?

I got to teach her some Greek too. Cypriot style Greek that is! Actually we taught each other. I have to tell you, Greek seemed much simpler to me, though not to her. Mainly, you read what you saw. But English, oh my God! She was puzzled

* By Richmal Crompton.

as I read 'te-he-ro-ou-gu-hu' I tell you. How come 'through' was written that way? But when she figured out what I was trying to decipher she laughed till she cried. We both laughed our hearts out. Mind you I didn't quite know why.

I really liked Mrs. Edwards from the first day I laid eyes on her, as I think I told you, but the special attention she gave me those days was too much. It amounted to the final little push. I fell in love with her, head over heels. It hurt so much to be so close to her and not be able to express my feelings. She was married, after all... She cannot have been much older than me. She was as fresh as the petals of a soft pink rose... They must keep people in fridges back in England, I tell you! The sun is god here, but it is also harsh. It leaves its marks on us. Anyway, we were different, from other planets. I had no hopes.

So I channelled all my love for her into our common medium – books. Perhaps that is why I don't only love books. I am in love with them. I concentrated on the texture of the covers and pages, on the letters, the words, the stories. She took me along with her on so many wonderful trips through them. We went to exotic places. Back in time to Egypt and the Pharaohs, or to super-modern England, France and America, you name it. Just me and her. The stories were much sweeter when she read them out loud, even changing her tone for different characters, like one would read to a child. To this day, when I read a book, I sometimes hear her voice in my mind, with her English accent, not mine. I still read more English books than Greek so I can catch some of that magic.

Once I could read they - I don't know if it was he or she - came up with this idea for me to get a driving licence. Mrs. Edwards refused to learn how to drive no matter how much her husband begged her. She always said she would surely crash or run over someone on a bicycle and then he would never forgive himself. A strong argument.

So, I came in the picture.

I would drive Mr. Edwards to work in the morning and stay at the British Council myself, doing odd jobs or driving people and things here and there. But Mr. Edwards would also send me home during the day, to take Mrs. Edwards to various places or to help out at the house. In effect, I became a fulltime driver. Most people who knew me those days associated me with this MG here. It was so much fun to drive it around.

But I also liked it when I had to stay around the house. Mostly I would work outside, in the garden. Mrs. Edwards would turn the radio on and turn up the volume a bit. So that I could hear too, through the wide open windows, I think. It was permanently tuned to an English station. The BBC, it must have been. I often reminisce about those days: Sunshine, working up a sweat among the smell of the roses, Mrs. Edwards coming outside with some ice cold lemonade just for me. Elvis playing on the 'Crown' radio. 'Heartbreak Hotel'."

Now with the Magnette in my 'possession', I had become a bit of a big shot. I would drive all over Nicosia as if I owned the world. And the flashy car I was driving around in. I never realised what a silly car can do to a person's image. It made me a lot of friends. But enemies also.

One day, as I was driving around the old city Walls, minding my own business, I saw a missile, a stone, flying towards me. I swerved to avoid the impact but it was too late. The stone hit the car roof with a big thud. I screeched to a halt and immediately ran out toward where I thought the assault had come. Two or three kids scurried away faster than the rats disappear these days when I switch on the lights downstairs in my house. But I heard one of them shout loud and clear.

"Traitor!"

What? Who me? What traitor? Or rather, a traitor of what, of whom? I had no idea where that came from. I swore at them, challenged the little scoundrels to come out of their hiding holes. Remember, I was brought up on the streets, and I was a biggish lad, I'd been up against Count Dracula, I was ready to take anybody on then.

No one took my challenge. But that word echoed in my mind as I drove away still fuming: 'Traitor!' I did not like the sound of it, not one bit.

I got my answer a few days later. I was parked downtown, close to the British Council, enjoying my morning coffee at a kafenes. Do you know of the place I am talking about? Let's drive there, I will show you. It's still there, right below the

Venetian Walls at the CYTA roundabout. Of course, only the sign remains today. The owner is probably long gone. This kafenes' name was a stylish one in years gone by: '*Spitfire*'. Wow. A powerful little word. It tells you of muscle and audacity and rudeness in such a short and snappy way. The kafenes owner could have got the name from the English Triumph Spitfire, a neat little convertible sports car from the sixties... come to think of it, it can't have been. That coffee shop existed before that car...I still see a couple driven around, they still look good. That car's original name was 'the Bomb'! An explosive name also, but I personally prefer Spitfire. So, that kafenes' name is most likely derived from those funny little planes the Englezi had flying all over in World War II. Now that I think about it, I seem to recall that the Cypriot owner of the establishment was actually in the RAF in the war, he had flown in one. They made thousands of them, over twenty thousand in fact. Hundreds of them went down in the war, but they persisted in making them. I wonder how many actually survive today. One hundred? More or fewer than the old Magnettes kicking around? Where did that old British cutting edge high tech go to? Down with the empire, I dare say. Anyway, those little fighters were born over seventy years ago, even before yours truly, and the prototype only cost about £14,500 English pounds! Later, in the 1940's, with mass production, one would cost about £10,000. Not bad for a whole plane huh? I saw some of them here in Cyprus, we'd talk about them and admire them once in a while flying in the Cyprus skies.

But I am straying away from the subject, boring you with things that you don't care about and which have no bearing today. But they did matter then, you know? I guess like people would maybe talk about the Space Shuttle Discovery today, if they actually bother with such things these days. What was I saying? Ah, coffee at the 'Spitfire'. I was sitting outside by myself, enjoying the morning sunshine and my Turkish coffee, when I caught sight of one of my old friends, an ex-fellow street bum. I called him over, offered him to sit down with me and have a coffee on me. He too, it seemed, had gone up in the world. He was dressed fine, for those days, grey cashmere trousers and a clean white shirt. We recalled some difficult situations we'd shared, had a good laugh.

So, we sat in the sunshine, two 'successful' ex-tramps, talking about the 'good old days'. We remembered how we used to manage to sneak into the various city cinemas, theatres and football grounds. This was serious business back then, it was our 'quality time' we were talking about after all. It was dealt with accordingly, as seriously as if it was work. In our heads we had meticulous plans of all the entrances, back entrances, half-open windows, air vents, sturdy water pipes or cracks in walls we could use to climb, etcetera. We had acquainted ourselves with when the whatever place's personnel patrolled the area, who was more sloppy, any information that might help. We would 'present' a map of the surroundings to the prospective participants. Drawn with a stick on the ground. 'What if' issues were raised, discussed, resolved. I tell you, we were good. Every single vendor had a weak vulnerable point. All you had to do was find it. Our planning was so painstaking, we could have broken into the White House. Of course, for some of our group, not me I assure you, this was also their daytime job. Breaking into places, I mean. Anyway, we reminisced about such and other things.

Then I remembered and indignantly reiterated my recent experience when stones were thrown at me and how one had dented the poor Magnette. I also told him what one of them had shouted, the traitor label. I reasoned that probably they took me for someone else, there was no other explanation. He was grinning, annoyingly.

"You know what is your problem?" he asked. Now let me

advise you, Alexis, never respond to this question. It is pure entrapment, the reply and whatever else follows can only lead to sorrow and bad news.

"What's my problem," I said, falling into it.

"You are an ignorant villager, that's your problem," he replied immediately, no venom in his voice, matter of fact. That made it hurt even more. See? I told you. Of course, now, he proceeded to qualify his diagnosis.

"Here you are in your nice clothes driving around in a fancy car. What should these people think? What would you think if you were in their place? You are obviously collaborating with the enemy, that's what they think."

He squinted his eyes at me and he looked me up and down, like I really was a turncoat.

"Where did you get your fancy clothes anyway?" I turned it around on him, instead of explaining my circumstance. I wanted him to go away now.

"Power of the people, man!" he replied. "We don't need these imperialists to make it in this country. We can help each other. We Greeks are the greatest race to have lived. We have given civilisation and democracy to the world and this is what we get in return. We stick together, we'll do fine."

What kind of an answer is this, I thought to myself. I kept quiet till he went away."

Today, it was just me and Mr. Aris once again.

"Now where were we?" Mr. Aris wondered out loud, a couple of minutes after we started on our weekly drive.

"Your meeting with that friend of yours at the Spitfire," I reminded him.

"I thought I was done telling you about that person," he said. But he went on anyway.

"Anyway, I was soon to figure out the patriotic stuff he was ranting on about. A few days later I was caught in another stone throwing episode. Mostly a group of kids, dressed in their school uniforms, were involved in a demonstration against the police, it seemed. The policemen, who were all Cypriots, Greek and Turkish Cypriots, were on one side, the demonstrators on the other. Me, I found myself right in the middle, caught in the crossfire. A policeman made a charge toward me, so I was forced to pick sides fast, you might say. It wasn't all that hard anyway. I was used to policemen chasing us away from places and generally giving us a hard time, from the days I lived out on the streets. I instinctively went against them. So, I ran behind the firing line, but I hung around to see what the fuss was about. That is when I started to make sense of what the pupils were shouting about, in unison. They were calling the policemen traitors. They were shouting for '*Enosis*' (union) with 'mother Greece', 'freedom or death' and such like. The passion in their voices, the proud faces, the smiling faces, the angry faces, the raw emotion, all these things made my skin tingle, they stirred something in me, I admit. These people had a common cause and they were making their voices heard. The police were outnumbered. The police were scared! We street kids, all we would do is run like the wind at their sight. But these people, they were holding their ground. No, they were advancing on them!

I suddenly felt a tap on my shoulder.

"What are you doing here traitor?" It was my 'mate' from the Spitfire. "Shouldn't you be over there?" he pointed toward the policemen, who were now barely holding their lines. "Power of the people!" he shouted excitedly, showing me the crowd around us.

We stayed there for a while, observing the skirmishes. He then pointed toward the general direction of the kafenes. "Let's go, I'll buy you a coffee," he shouted over the general din.

"I thought you didn't want to talk about that man anymore, Mr. Aris."

"I don't, but the man is central to this little story you see."

So we sat at the exact same table again. He told me that the reason we Cypriots were so dirt poor and generally miserable was because throughout our history we were occupied by almost every country you could think of. In fact, he gave me my first history lesson that day. Now that I know a bit better, his narrative was full of exaggerations and inaccuracies, but to me he sounded like Herodotus* himself. He said that enough was enough. No more getting pushed around. No more Mr. Nice Guy friendly natives. No more imperialism. We wanted the freedom to take our fate in our own hands. And so on. Overall, not a bad pitch, given who was giving it, I should add. He was passionate and raw, and he meant every word he said. Pretty powerful ingredients for any speech, wouldn't you agree? I was intrigued.

---

* Not that Mr. Aris would know of Herodotos at that time! Ancient historian Herodotus is considered to be the 'father' of the science of History.

"While you have been sleeping with the enemy, many others have been organising themselves. Where have you been? Haven't you heard?" he asked.

He was right, actually. Things had happened so fast in my own life those days, Alexis, that I had failed to notice the bigger picture. It was true. I had only shown a vague interest in the recent events which were unfolding around us. Almost a year before that conversation at the Spitfire, the Cypriots' armed struggle against British occupation had been formally announced with a bang. A real bang, that is. A bomb had exploded at a police station or somewhere like that and various English projects and interests were consequently periodically attacked. Responsibility for these bombings was taken by EOKA.

You may be wondering how I could effectively miss such important events. But you have to step into my shoes, Alexis. And into the 'Middle Ages'. Above all my excuses, I was an illiterate boy. This meant that I stayed away from newspapers on instinct. There weren't all that many around in any case. Just one or two of them at coffee shops. Most people wouldn't waste good money on such luxuries. There was just one scratchy local radio station, the Cyprus Broadcasting Corporation (CYBC or RIK in its Greek acronym), which was launched only a couple of years back, in 1953. Although officially independent, it was essentially controlled by the government, the Englezi that is. I vaguely recall hearing a transmission or two, again at coffee shops. Most people had no radios at home. Having electricity was luxury enough. TV? There was no such thing... In truth, that same station I told you about, RIK, also launched a semblance of a TV station a year later, in 1957. So, you must understand Alexis, information and news did not spread like it does today. Mostly it was word of mouth: someone heard this from someone who heard it from another who heard it from another. You could rarely locate the origin of the source. It wasn't the most reliable way to get informed. To me, it all sounded like gossip. Which it probably was, more often than not. Tales would grow taller as they made their way down the line. If someone had given a police officer a dirty look it then became a talking back which grew into a swear word which developed into holding the policeman by the shoulders while shouting at him which blossomed into a slap and ended up as an outright hiding! It was a bit like that 'telephone' game, where one person whispers something to another who whispers what he heard to another. Did I tell you about this game before? In the end, what you get is quite different to the original."

"You were saying that you couldn't or wouldn't get much in the form of reliable news back then..." I reminded Mr. Aris after the Magnette engine turned over.

"Oh yes. But some news eventually filtered down through my thick skull. The country's ethnarch, Archbishop Makarios, was deemed a troublemaker by the Englezi authorities, so he was kicked out of the island. They sent him to Seychelles. The almighty British Empire was getting angry with the little islanders. People from EOKA, freedom fighters to us, terrorists to them, were stirring up all kinds of trouble. Those among the Organisation getting caught would be summarily tried and executed, by hanging. Kids no older than me weren't being spared either. The old divide and rule tactic was put to full use by the English. They enlisted more Turkish Cypriots than Greek in the police, directly pitting us against each other. The country's whimper of a demand for freedom was growing now. The English were actually feeding it through their actions. Something like what they and the Americans are doing in Afghanistan and Iraq and to the Arabs today. They are helping to breed generations of very upset youths.

Well, that's what happened to many among us young Cypriots. Nobody wants to be pushed around, not even if he comes from a tiny dusty corner of the Mediterranean. And not even if you can fit all this place's inhabitants in a London neighbourhood. Old glorious days were stirred up and remembered: when we - the Greeks! - ruled the world. When we were the Empire through your namesake's 'good work': The Alexander the Great days.

I caught the bug too. A little bit, mind you. Now that 'my

horizons had broadened' I also saw that the Brits had no business being here. They bought us like we were things, a couple of times! Now, and in Richard the Lionheart's time.

But I was no warrior. Pygmalion - that was my friend's EOKA pseudonym, I will not tell you his real name lest he is still alive- bumped into me quite a few times in the next few months. He introduced me to other freedom fighters. He confessed to me that he and the others had taken a secret oath, to give all they had, even their lives for freedom from the English and unification (*ENOSIS*) with the motherland, Greece.

Now, I was only a child, perhaps an 'old' seventeen year old but still a child. I'd had enough trouble in my young life without actually going out looking for more trouble. So when Pygmalion finally came out and said it -'*why don't you too join the Organisation*'- I politely declined, assuring him full heartedly at the same time that I was sympathetic and that I was supportive of the cause.

So I never actually joined the Organisation. I never actually gave an oath to anybody about anything. But I did get involved in some very minor actions, almost inadvertently.

One day Pygmalion bumped into me again- was it chance? It was becoming a common occurrence - outside the British Council. I was on my way out, to deliver some things for a couple of managers. He asked where I was heading and I told him. He said he too had to deliver something in the area I was going, so I offered him a ride. But he told me that he was in a hurry and could I do him a favour and deliver it at such and such address? He said it was just his car mechanic's address. I said no problem so he gave me a sealed envelope. I drove the Magnette to the address he had given me and indeed, a mechanic's shop was there. I asked for Mr. So and So. Apparently it was the owner and sole employee of the place. He invited me into the garage area for a coffee. In those days it was bad etiquette to refuse such an offer unless you had a very legitimate excuse. And there were very few of those! You see, life moved at such a leisurely pace that just about everything could wait. He said he could top up the water and oil of the car and he could check the tire pressure for me while I had my coffee, if I wanted. I said ok, why not, thanks… That was it."

"That was what, Mr. Aris?"

No reply.

It was one of those rare dreary winter days that people are really more acquainted with in northern Europe. The powerful Cyprus sun, for once, had lost out to heavy dark and dramatic clouds. They hung very low, close to the ground, threatening to burst into a million pieces at any minute. No rain yet, but that somehow made it even worse. Like the environmental forces - or God himself- were holding back. Like something was about to happen. Something bad.

It was cold too, bitingly so. One feels much colder in Cyprus. The country is not really equipped to deal with such weather. For most of the year people try to find ways to fight off the sun's heat, so when the cold comes it is always a bit of a surprise. When it rains for a little more than a couple of hours- it is usually an almighty downpour- the streets flood, they become rivers crisscrossing the city blocks.

I was not looking forward to going out in this weather. I had the central heating blazing at home, wastefully, in all the rooms. It was definitely stay-at-home kind of weather. I almost cancelled on Mr. Aris but then I remembered the last time I had seen him. I could not quite put my finger on it, but I felt that he had not been his usual sprightly self. Maybe it was just the weather that was getting him down, like the rest of us. Perhaps it was just a silly premonition on my part. I pulled on a thick jacket and went outside. I did not bother to call Maria. It seemed that Mr. Aris wanted only me these days. He never said so, I just sensed it.

Of course, there was no one sitting at the veranda. I knocked on the door, using the old-style bronze knocker. It felt very cold to my bare hand. No reply, so I waited for the old man to come to the door. When he did not come, I put my ear to the door. I could hear no movement. I could not make out any light inside. I felt a pang of anxiety. I knocked harder. Nothing. So I tried the doorknob. The door was unlocked. I walked in, calling out his name.

Mr. Aris was inside the house, sitting on his old couch, cowering in front of the fireplace, freezing. Kypros the cat was nowhere to be seen. He was staring right at a miserable excuse of a fire. I went outside and brought in some firewood. I came back loaded and made my way through the maze of books. I fed the fireplace until it was glowing. I switched on a light.

"What's wrong Mr. Aris? Why did you not answer the door?"

He looked up at me and smiled. A sad smile.

"You know, the usual. I am feeling under the weather. I am tired. I am getting old. I am thinking of the days gone by instead of thinking of days to come. I am regretting things I have done and I am regretting things I haven't done. Like I said, the usual."

He smiled again, bitterly.

"Let's get out of here, Mr. Aris," I suggested. "Let's go see if the Magnette can still do ninety." When in desperation break the law.

"Alexis, please, let's not. Just for this time. I have been meaning to talk to you about some things for quite a while now and I think now is the time… sit down, please. Would you like some tea?"

He made as if to get up out of his chair.

"I'll get it," I said. "And I'll make you one while I am at it."

Skeletons in the closet

The words came out slowly, with anguish.

"Now, how do I say this... Alexis, I need to exorcise some demons or spirits or whatever... I've been having this recurring dream for most of my adult life. There are slight variations, but the basics are always the same. At first I just ignored it, vaguely recalling it and getting this deja vu feeling that I'd seen it all before. But once it happens enough times, it sticks, you know? You wait for it to reappear and that only makes it worse of course... Your mind has lost the game, because it simply obliges. Sometimes the dream would quietly go away for a while, months even, to the point that I'd almost forget about it. Other times it would constantly disturb my sleep. Then it threatened to turn me into an insomniac, for I could not fall asleep again once it woke me up. These days, now, I am hardly sleeping. It's back, with a vengeance."

Mr. Aris went on to describe the dream, nightmare rather, which I have related at the start of this book. I could see that it had taken its toll on Mr. Aris' mental state. That is why he sometimes looked quite tired. It had probably chipped away for a long time. Now he had to confront it, full on. His voice wavered, from start to finish.

"You know me. I turn to books to find explanations. What does sleeping in one's dreams mean? I asked myself. What's this Bible stuff signify? You know I am not particularly religious so why the hassle? Who's at the door? If I know who it is while I am dreaming, why then don't I see a face when I wake up?

I know what dreams are. I've read up on them. I'm not so

silly to believe that they mean anything more than our brain doing a bit of an unrestrained run-around all by itself. It's just doing its own thing, without the rational controls and reigning in of our wakeful consciousness... But that is exactly the point. My mind is stuck on that chapter and it runs and reruns it. That's why I can't help but appreciate the significance. I can't help but pay attention, you know what I mean?

I've always wondered who was at the door. In my dream, I always have this sinking feeling: I know who is there. I just do. But then, when I wake up, I just can't put a name, a face, to that person. It's like I forget the most important part... I try to concentrate, when I wake up, to focus on that person, but I see nothing but a vague human outline and a bright light. Sometimes I think maybe it's my father. He has returned from another trip of his. But why the sinking feeling that possesses me? Is it because I know he will be leaving again just as soon as he dusts himself off and gives us the treasures he brought back from his travels? Then I think, no, it's my mother, that troubled soul who was born in the wrong place at the wrong time. But what does she want to tell me?"

"So it's this dream Mr. Aris? That's what's bothering you? Or are you thinking that maybe the wiring in your brain is getting all mixed up?" I joke. But I am concerned.

"I'm not worried about that because I know it's jumbled up," he smiled back. "I think I've read one too many books, that's it. But no, I feel it's more than that. Please, let me go on with this, Alexis..."

I realise he does not really want any interruptions.

"As I said, I have been trying to figure out who is behind that door. A strong candidate is my sister, Stella. I haven't been completely truthful with you Alexis, I must confess. When you asked me what happened with my family I dismissed your question too abruptly. I did find out what happened to everyone. One day, once I began driving the MG around, I took the short trip to the village. I wanted to show off, to show the people there how I had gone to town and made it 'big'. But above all, I wanted to find out what had become of the rest of my family, to see if my sister and father would still be there. I made my way to our little shack of a house. I smiled triumphantly to anyone who saw me, as I drove through the village's narrow main, and only, street. But I was in for a disappointment when I reached the location of our home. There was nothing there! Wild bushes had taken possession of the whole area. It took me a minute to figure out where our shack had been.

As I stood there, where my mother's grave should have been, an old man came up behind me. It was a shepherd from our village. I recognised him and told him who I was. I asked whether he knew about what had happened to my family. He said that he had heard that my brothers had emigrated to Australia and England. He had heard that my father had died in a work-related accident. He knew nothing about my sister.

I ran into her, years later. She wouldn't talk to me, even after I got over the initial blow. She was a middle aged woman, living and still working in Limassol, at the 'Heroes Square' area. Yes, Alexis, she had been practicing the oldest profession in the world, just like Lais and Rhodopis..."

I saw his sadness. "It wasn't your fault, Mr. Aris," I blurted, somewhat shocked at this piece of information.

"I know Alexis. Still, maybe if I'd stayed..."

We sat there, in silence. After a while, he went on.

"But I do understand her and I don't criticise her for anything. Who am I to judge anyone? Still, maybe it's Stella at the door, in my dream."

I said nothing.

"In any case, this is not really what I wanted to tell you. It's something else... I think I've talked about all this before," he continued. "For Stella, for me, it was all about staying alive. When survival is your goal, it becomes your only goal. Survival and selfishness go hand in hand. It is ingrained in the animal. It can turn you into a beast. You can think of nothing else. You wake up in the morning, you think survival. During the day and until you lay your head down to sleep, you think survival. All your thoughts, all your actions, are geared toward this one word. At night, while you sleep, your dreams and nightmares also revolve around that same subject. There is no relief.

At such times, there is no room in your brain for higher ideals. There is not even room for real friends. In truth, the street kids I associated with were more like companions in misery, what's the saying. In the name of survival they could and would double-cross you in a flash.

So it's a real relief when you manage to escape that vicious cycle. When your head finally surfaces above the water, above the swamp you were previously swimming in, day in day out. Drowning in, rather I should say. That is what extreme poverty feels like, in case you were wondering. Slow suffocation. What a glorious breath of fresh air that first breath is, when you come out of it all and put some clean oxygen in your lungs! What a rush! What a surprise!

Beyond the practical things, like clean clothes and food, it is so... 'nice' to feel the luxury of having noble values and ideals, of seeing the bigger picture, of intellectually analyzing society and its woes in general, instead of being trapped in your own individual fishbowl of a life. Now don't you think that I suddenly made it big or anything like that. Remember, I was just a lowly clerk. I've always been a poor man, still am.

But, I had a job and a roof -which I shared with a noisy

washing machine, granted- to sleep under. I didn't have to constantly live in that egotistically oriented 'survival mode' twenty four hours a day. I could finally broaden my horizons beyond the universe of my own miserable belly. This is the state of mind I was in, you see, when I got involved in the fringes of the freedom movement. Now don't get me wrong. I am not trying to excuse myself here. I was proud of my contribution. I just want you to fully understand the circumstances, to understand the person I was during those tumultuous years. During the '*Troubles*', as we all called them. The whole of the country was in upheaval. The movement for getting rid of the English occupation was gaining momentum. Guerrilla strikes -small time bombs mainly - had already begun. We, the Cypriot minions, seemed to finally be making some headway. After cowering to everyone for several thousand years. The little skinny man was standing up to the big bully. David and Goliath. And there was an actual 'organisation' behind all this: EOKA!

I believe that many people were going through what I was during those days. Just maybe from a different starting point. They too were waking up out of a slumber caused by hundreds of years of poverty and misery. You know the words:

"I shall always recognise you
By the dreadful sword you hold,
As the earth, with searching vision,
You survey, with spirit bold.
It was the Greeks of old whose dying
Brought to birth our spirit free.
Now, with ancient valour rising,
Let us hail you, oh Liberty!"*

---

* The National Anthem of Greece, in use since 1846. Words by Dionysios Solomos, music by Nicolaos Mantzaros. The same anthem has also been adopted by Cyprus.

Anyway. I became a courier for the Organisation, informally, without really asking for the job. That mechanic I told you about, the one I took the letter to, he was a key contact, apparently. Call me foolish. Call it risky. Back then I felt neither was the case. It felt like it was all a relatively risk-free, tiny contribution to the cause and to my country. To tell the truth, I felt a little proud of myself. For once in my life, my actions did not centre on yours truly alone. I was doing my bit for freedom and justice. At no real cost whatsoever, I believed. Should something have happened, should I have been caught, I would have told the whole truth: I knew nothing. Most of the time I really did not even know if I was carrying messages with the Magnette. You see, I didn't carry messages by hand, ever, apart from that very first time. The Magnette carried them, literally. I did not touch them myself. The mechanic and the other liaisons would hide them somewhere in the car. At first I didn't even know exactly where. Later I found out: there is a little secret compartment somewhere below the dashboard. I can show you the exact place sometime, Alexis, if you like. (*I know, Mr. Aris*)

That is as far as my involvement went. Directly, I really had nothing to do with the Organisation.

You are thinking, I know, did I not feel guilty toward my benefactors, the Edwards? The straightforward answer is no. This struggle was being waged against an empire, a country, a government, not against any people in particular.

I admit that I was the one to suggest that using old Cypriot writing was a good idea for transmitting secret messages. The kind I showed you on the backgammon board I gave you. I had found a book on Cyprus archaeology, together with the decoding page I gave you, in Mr. Edwards' library. I suggested to Pygmalion, indirectly, that one could easily conceal a message that way. As far as I know, his was the only 'cell' in the organisation to actually adopt this form of communication. It seemed ideal: strange enough for a regular English soldier to dismiss as gibberish if he found it and easy enough for an ordinary freedom fighter to decipher without using too much brain power.

The messages were transferred, as far as I could make out, mainly between three people: the mechanic, a car electrician and a petrol station owner. I would take the car for a 'service' to the mechanic. He would sometimes suggest that I take it to a particular electrician to check the electrical parts of the car and he in turn would suggest I take my car for fuel at a specific station because, he said, the petrol station owner would wash the car for free if I filled the tank. Each of them 'meddled' with the dashboard compartment. I turned a blind eye, literally looking away while they were at it.

This 'arrangement' went on for a little over a year. Although I could see that a fully fledged armed struggle was now being waged around me, like I said guerrilla-style with random targets, it had little impact on my personal life. I still went to work at the British Council, as usual. I continued to work at the British Council as a messenger and to do odd jobs at the Edwards's home. I persisted in learning how to read and write, with Mrs. Eileen's patient and committed contribution. We shared meals. They often took me on road trips in the Magnette. I cannot claim to have been their guide on those occasions. They usually knew more about Cyprus and its attractions than I did. I guess you could say that I served as an informal translator. I dare say I felt like a member of the family. Like an adopted stranded cousin. It never felt like charity, and even less like a 'let's-educate-this-native' Mr. Higgins project. They both had too much compassion and class for that.

I must get on with what I am really trying to tell you Alexis... One day, a Cypriot man I had never met before came to the British Council looking for me. He said he wanted to tell me something in private. So we went to the back of the building, where I always parked the Magnette. We sat in the car as he talked. He said that he had been sent to me by 'my good friend' Pygmalion. That he had been given some very important documents which absolutely needed to be delivered today. He was holding a faded brown leather briefcase, one like school teachers use. Battered and scratched. He held it up a little, discreetly, to indicate that the documents were inside there. I casually looked at the briefcase. It was locked.

I contemplated. This was not the way I did 'business' with the Organisation. Remember, I did not come into contact with any papers or people. That was the arrangement. And, I did not even know this person sitting next to me... I did not like this deal. It was too risky. So I told him to try and find someone else to take care of the matter.

"I can't do that Aris," he persisted. "You are the only one who can handle this thing. You see, you are going to be taking your boss to the prisons where our captured freedom fighters are being held*, later today. He will be helping to set up a small library up there, as I understand it. You know, to convert the hardened criminals," he added with an ironic smile.

I knew our schedule that day. Mr. Edwards had already told me early in the morning. But how did this man know? I did not like it. It all felt wrong. He answered the question I had not asked him.

"We have an insider there, a Cypriot policeman who supports the cause. It was he who informed us of this visit of your boss. Anyway, this is all you have to do: when you take your big shot boss there, after he sets off to see the director or whoever, you will go to sit with and have a coffee with the officers

* They still stand today, serving as Cypriot military barracks. They are situated in an area called Kokkinotrimithia a few kilometers outside Nicosia.

working there. What's more natural than that?" he added, to ease my visible anxiety. I did not even like the idea of being with this person in the back seat of the Magnette. Anyone could see us.

"It's the first office to the left, right across the parking lot. You can't miss it. There's only one main entrance, everybody goes through there. As you enter, you will see a small table and three or four wooden chairs inside that office. Sit down on the chair nearest to the officer's desk. That's our inside man's desk, he will be there waiting for you. He is the one who will ask you where you are from. Leave the bag exactly where you will sit, on the floor next to you, closer to the desk. Our man will take care of it from there. He will deliver its contents to a specific freedom fighter. It's really no big thing you see."

I believe that he saw that I was still not about to accept this 'little' assignment. He then appeared very frustrated. He suddenly changed his approach, abandoning the laid back 'it's no big deal' approach. He tensed and there was now flame and urgency in his eyes. In his new more intimidating strategy he appeared to decide to take me into his confidence.

"Look Aris," he said, leaning even closer toward me. I instinctively backed away a little, like to defend myself. "I will come clean. These documents in this here bag describe details of a prison break to be carried out tonight. Aris, listen to me man. It must be done today because otherwise two fellow fighters will be hanged early tomorrow morning. They were convicted a month ago and there is no more room left for legal appeals. There is no hope for a stay of execution. Their lives depend on you man! You have to do this, do you understand? None of us have a choice. You are their only chance!"

What was I to do, Alexis? What would you do? Before I had a chance to respond, he disappeared. I never saw that man ever again. Like the whole incident was just part of a bad dream. But it wasn't. He had left the bag in the car, right next to me. I remained in the MG, confused and trying to decide what to do.

Right at the time he had told me he would come, a few minutes before noon, Mr. Edwards opened the driver's door. He startled me. I was still sitting in the back seat, as I had been when I talked with that man. I had been lost in my thoughts and consequently I had not heard him approach. He asked for the keys, so that he could drive the car. In truth, he did not really need a driver. He quite liked driving his Magnette.

He noticed the leather bag in the back seat.

"What's this?" he asked.

"Oh it's mine Mr. Edwards," I answered quickly. "Books."

He frowned, and then he let it go. He trusted me after all.

We made it to the prisons in less than half an hour. Mr. Edwards was in really good spirits. He kept talking and talking. I was hardly listening.

The guard let us through the gate. We parked right across the building, no more than thirty feet away from the main entrance.

Nobody greeted us there. In fact, security seemed surprisingly lax for a prison*. Mr. Edwards disappeared inside to find whoever he was supposed to meet.

I got out of the car. I took the bag along with me. I went inside, to the first room of the building.

There was nobody in there. I saw the chairs and the officer's desk. I sat down and put the bag on the floor, next to me.

I waited for someone to come, sweating profusely. The fan on the ceiling was turning so slowly you could see the blades go round and round.

---

* Actually, it is well documented that quite a few inmates escaped from that prison during its brief existence.

After a few minutes a policeman came in. Now, what was he supposed to ask? I'd forgotten. But he just nodded hello and disappeared somewhere in the depths of the building.

I couldn't take it anymore. I got up and rushed outside. I needed some air.

I stood next to the Magnette, nervously smoking a cigarette and I waited for Mr. Edwards to come out. He was taking forever. He had said he would only be a few minutes. I kept my eyes on the door.

I saw Mr. Edwards come out.

He walked out toward me, a smile on his face.

He was holding the bag, Alexis!

I reflexively looked away with the explosion.

I *killed* him, Alexis, do you understand? I killed him."

Tears were streaming down his face.

Through unbearable pain and distress, he narrated the remaining details of this whole terrible episode to me. Like he could see it all unravel in front of him. Like it was happening right then, as he talked, right before his very eyes. I was apparently the first person to hear this man's confession since it had occurred, more than a half century ago. It was a story which had begun as an unselfish 'harmless' contribution toward the freedom of his country, a country he dearly loved, and which had ended in a very close to home human tragedy.

As he continued to speak, my head was spinning at the unexpected culmination of Mr. Aris' recounting of his past. I could see his mouth moving and I could hear his deeply distressed voice but I hardly understood what he was saying.

"*I killed him.*" Those three words kept ringing in my head, crowding my brain, chilling my mind and leaving little room for anything else that he was saying to really register.

Still, a few of the other things he said that night did manage to hammer their way through:

When Mr. Edwards came out that door with the leather bag and into the bright sunshine he had a broad friendly smile on his face, as if saying 'look what you left behind, you silly fool!' But then, in the split second before it was all over, he had just enough time to see the horror on Mr. Aris face.

"He saw it, Alexis... He knew that I had betrayed him. I will never be able to explain..." he told me, despair in his trembling voice. "To explain that I was forced to do it. That I had no idea it was a bomb."

Mr. Aris said about how he had run to Mr. Edwards who was lying motionless on the ground with a look of surprise frozen in his wide open eyes, how the Englishman was bloody all over his nice suit and crisp white shirt. How Mr. Aris had held him in his arms while he wept and wailed uncontrollably. How the guards had to eventually pry him away. Mr. Edwards had died instantly, of course, but it was not such a big bomb. It had gone off with a minor sound, almost like an implosion. Like a weak Easter firecracker. Perhaps the bomb was never meant to kill anybody or it had been crudely put together.

The killing of any English person, including soldiers, was bad enough from the point of view of the occupying force. But the murder of an English civilian working for a harmless government department was an outrage that could stir emotions and make the headlines of newspapers in Great Britain itself. The death of Mr. Edwards was front page news in all the major issues there and in Cyprus too.

The British led Cypriot police immediately released stern promises that the culprits would be caught, tried and summarily hang. But of course, that never happened. As far as Mr. Aris knew, the case remains open in local police files, unsolved, to this day.

Small A4 sized 'Wanted' posters were placed on walls all over Cyprus. Any information leading to an arrest carried a one thousand pound reward, a royal sum for those days. People were brought in for questioning and then released, one by one. Mr. Aris too was requested to come to the station for a statement, immediately after the incident. He was genuinely too grief-stricken and traumatised to open his mouth and say anything. To incriminate himself, to confess. He just sat on a chair and swayed his head and his whole body to and fro, over and over again*. It was probably this deep pain he was going through that saved his miserable hide, he said. They must have reasoned, how could a man who so obviously cared so deeply for the deceased man have anything to do with his death?

Still, the more Mr. Aris had thought about it later the more he was convinced that he had been an involuntary accomplice in a well-engineered cover up. Had really no one connected the bomb and the visit of that man who came to see Mr. Aris at the British Council on that fateful day? Had nobody seen the bag this same man was blatantly holding? Had no prison guards seen Mr. Aris himself take the bag out of the car and into the building?

Mr. Aris could only surmise a doubtful 'perhaps not' to these questions: that everyone in actual fact had missed the obvious. That he got 'lucky'. That the police really had been so inept. That they had assumed that the bag was already at the prison when Mr. Edwards and he arrived. That maybe no one had suspected that Mr. Edwards could have driven the bomb himself into the prison. All this could have happened. But it all seemed too coincidental. Some people must have kept their mouths shut, he had concluded.

The most heartbreaking part of Mr. Aris recounting of those events was when he had to face Eileen. When he saw her, the next morning, she had already been notified by the police. He parked the MG in front of the house and got out. He was a pitiful sight. Still wearing that bloody white shirt from the day before. With Mr. Edwards' blood all over it. Dishevelled from lack of sleep at the police station. Shattered inside. She had run to him as soon as he parked. She had hugged him tight and cried uncontrollably. He just stood there, motionless, eyes dry, arms limp. He had caused this much pain to the one person in the world whom he cared for the most. He had

* As he was doing now, alarmingly.

killed the man that had changed his life. Eventually, he found the strength to put his arms around her. This is how Judas must have felt when he kissed Jesus.

I was reeling. I needed some air. I got up and left him there in his misery.

I sat in my living room, my head in my hands. Some friend I had turned out to be. Running away like that, like a child. But, what does one say to him? It's ok that you murdered that man, the one who just happened to drag your miserable excuse for a life out of the gutter? You did not really mean to do it?

Did he think he had been playing a game, even when he was only delivering messages? Did he not realise that the stakes were so high?

I know who's at the door in your dreams, Mr. Aris. It's Mr. Edwards, that's who.

The messages, the pieces of paper in the Magnette. I had forgotten about them. What had they said? Rusty tomatoes or something silly like that? I brought them out once more.

'*Papose theka theka*' and '*Aiose tometiose mia enia*'. 'Papose ten ten' and 'Aiose tometiose one nine.'

"Come on man, think!" I urged myself, in a bad mood.

I centred my thoughts on the second document.

"Aiose tometiose... aiose tometiose... Ayios Dometios! That's it!" I shouted out.

'Ayios Dometios' is a Nicosia district. So, the second parchment was a rendezvous, a call to a meeting or something like that: at Ayios Dometios at one o'clock on the ninth (-month?). I turned my attention to the first photocopy:

"Papose... You are a place aren't you?" I asked the word. I removed the last 'e' once more. I recalled that my name had been read as 'Alexese' on the tavli board by Mr. Aris. Just then

I realised why the 'e' had to be there in ancient Cypriot script. Because it was a syllabic system, every consonant had to be accompanied by a vowel. The 'S', then, had to come with the 'e'.

So, Papos'. Where is that? Something occurred to me. I went to the decoding sheet. Just like I had thought: there was no 'f' symbol, no way of writing a 'ph' sound. What we had here was the birthplace of the goddess of love Aphrodite: Paphos! Another meeting, in Paphos, at 10 (am or pm?) on the tenth, that was the first message.

Then I did something I perhaps should not have. I telephoned Maria and asked her to come over.

I recounted Mr. Aris' whole story to her, an abridged version but including the worst part. I broke his confidence in me.

She listened, intently, without interrupting, just like I had done all those times when Mr. Aris had so vividly related his past to me. When I finished, almost tearful myself, she got up and went to the kitchen. She made herself a cup of coffee, unhurried, and slowly came back to her seat. I liked this about her. She had a sharp tongue, she could spontaneously blurt clever quips, but at other times, at the right times, she could be so protractedly thoughtful and reflective.

So it took her a good few minutes to say anything. She asked to see the photocopies.

"*Ayios Dometios* and *Paphos-gate* are police stations in Nicosia," she said in a matter of fact way. "I bet, if you look it up in some kind of archive, you'll find that these two police stations were attacked or bombed. The first one at one o'clock, probably in the morning of the ninth month -September- of whatever year. The second one at ten, maybe at night, in October. Same year. You could look it up. 1956, 57 or 58, I'll bet you."

I did not want to look it up. I did not want any more bets. To find what? More blood?

“But I think you are missing the point,” she continued. “You know what is very important to Mr. Aris right now? That you understand.”

“Understand what? That he unwittingly killed his benefactor?”

“Yes, exactly that, Alexis. Why do you think he painstakingly explained to you his entire background and the whole context of that time?”

“So ok, just like that, I justify what he did?”

“Not justify, understand. It’s quite different. Above all, understand that he was young. That he got caught up in a dangerous war. That he didn’t exactly realise then that that is what happens in wars. That they are messy things. That people die in wars, sometimes innocent people. Sometimes loved ones.”

“In love and war all is fair,” I commented offhandedly.

“No, that’s a silly expression. The two are so different, so opposite. Love *can* be fair, war never is. With love, there can be two winners, at least sometimes. In war, there never are. No one ever really wins a war. Both lose; it’s just that one of the two loses least.”

I didn’t exactly agree with her analysis but I went along with it.

“And the ‘least loser’ is the winner?”

“Right.”

Pause.

“You know, now that you know Mr. Aris’ little secret, you too are liable, if the case is really still open… Concealing information that could lead to an arrest, perverting the course of justice,” she toyed with me, half serious half joking.

“So now, if I don’t go and tell the police what I know I am considered a criminal?”

"No, don't panic Mr. Goody-Two-Shoes. I'm sure nobody cares any more. It's ancient history. Anyway, I too know the story so…"

We sat in silence. Minutes passed. A sign that by then she and I were relaxed with one another. That we did not need to fill every silence with just any words.

"Except there may be someone who cares," it suddenly occurred on me.

Quickly, I got up. I grabbed the car keys and sprinted to my car, Maria toiling along behind me. As I turned the ignition and the car came to life it dawned on me that Mr. Aris could do something rash. I sped away. I was already blaming myself for getting up and leaving him.

A plan

Even though more than a couple of hours had passed since we had had our last dramatic conversation, Mr. Aris was still sitting in the same place I had left him. He looked up, unsurprised, when I rushed in through the unlocked front door. He saw me - and Maria- behind me. He made no comment.

"Thank God you are ok!" I exclaimed, relieved.

He smiled, bitterly. "What, you thought I was going to kill myself or something?" he mocked. "You think I'd wait fifty years to do that? Believe me, the thought did occur to me a few times over all those years. Sorry I gave you a fright... Hi Maria, how are you?"

She nodded 'ok', closely scrutinizing him, too caught up in my panic to say anything.

"Look, Mr. Aris. You do know this: It really wasn't your fault. You just happened to be the wrong person at the wrong place, nothing more."

"Thanks for the words of encouragement Alexis," he said, matter of fact, noncommittally. Like he had heard it all before. He had probably told himself those exact words a million times.

"Actually, I am not quite done," I said. "I have a suggestion I would like you to think about."

He looked uninterested.

"Mr. Aris, do you know where Mrs. Eileen lives?"

He perked up a little at the sound of her name.

"Why do you ask?" he inquired, suspiciously.

"Do you know?"

"Of course I do," he replied. "Who do you think owns this house? Did you imagine that I bought it, somehow? Alexis, I am, always was, a poor man. I have told you, I was just a messenger in an office. Not what you would refer to as exactly a dazzling career... when Mr. Edwards died, a couple of weeks later, Mrs. Eileen packed up and left. She left almost everything behind. The furniture, the appliances... she even gave me Mr. Edwards clothes! I never wore them of course, how could I? It seemed perverted enough to stay at this house. The clothes are still hanging in the wardrobe where she left them."

"She *gave* you this house?" asked Maria.

"Not exactly. I pay rent. A nominal sum. You would laugh if I told you how much. And even so, in those days, I sometimes couldn't make the payment every month. But I always made it up later, mind you, with interest. I increase my own rent, you know, every couple of years. She never notified me herself for a raise, what was I to do?"

"*Have* you kept in touch?" I persisted.

"Well, to be honest, she has never actually communicated with me, not directly, ever since she left. I have a bank account number, that's where I send the money."

I remembered the car.

"So the Magnette is hers as well?"

"No, she did actually give me the MG... apparently she was -*is*?- quite a wealthy person. That's what she told me herself when she left Cyprus, over fifty years ago. When I retorted that I didn't want anything, that I could sell all her stuff for her if she didn't want to haul it back to England."

"You have never seen her since then?" asked Maria.

"No. As I said. As far as I know she has never been back here, and I have never been to England, so, yes, I haven't seen her."

"Anyway, Mr. Aris, you do at least have her home address?" I asked.

"Well, no, actually," he corrected himself now. "I only have that account number I told you about. Why?"

"Do you think you could find her address?" I asked him.

"I don't see why not," he replied. "It's not like she's been hiding or anything."

I wasn't too sure an English bank would be willing to divulge personal information, even a simple client's home address. But I persisted with my idea.

"Mr. Aris, this is what I think. You -we, me and you- must go to England. You must go see Mrs. Eileen. You have some things you need to tell her."

"What things... What good would that do?" he wondered. "Why do you think she'd want to dig up the painful past?"

"Mr. Aris, you need to tell her what you never had a chance to say to Mr. Edwards himself. You need to explain everything to her. To come clean. Tell her what you told me."

He did not immediately respond. He was thinking. Maria kept quiet, in the background.

"What if she didn't understand?" he eventually asked.

"Well that's a risk you'll just have to take."

"And a price I have to pay," he added.

"Mr. Aris, you've already paid the price, a hundred times over," I answered.

I did not tell him that I thought this whole affair had probably kept him away from people for half a century. That he maybe had buried himself in all those books in order to get rid of his ignorance but also to travel away from reality. That, possibly, he had never married for this same reason. That he had been beating himself up for all this time, exactly because he was such a decent man whose conscience kept pinning him down. He was too intelligent to be told all these things. I was sure he knew.

Again, he did not say anything. But you could see that the idea was beginning to appeal to him.

"If I am to confess to someone, why not go to the proper authorities? Why not go to a judge or to the police or someone like that?" he asked.

"Because they don't care anymore, that's why."

I did not add that, depending on whom he talked to, he could even be labelled a hero rather than a killer. One less colonialist. That kind of thing.

"You know, maybe you have a point," he said eventually. He was still contemplating.

I quickly took his hand and shook it as if he had already agreed and we had just made an important business deal.

He sat, thinking.

"I've never actually travelled before," he informed us both, apologetically. "Actually, I've never been out of Cyprus before, you know." He smiled, nervously.

He was visibly unsettled. Again, like his visit that time to the college lecture hall, he stood very close to me. He stared directly ahead at nothing in particular, eyes wide open. He kept shifting his weight from foot to foot. And he appeared to be too pale for my liking. Fact is he was making me nervous as well. Like we were standing in line preparing to attempt our first ski-jump or something. Or, as if we were going to parachute out of the thing.

But I empathised. He had left it too late to take his 'maiden flight'. The idea of being in midair in a two hundred ton steel bird for the first time, completely out of control of one's destiny, and on top of that at his age, must be a daunting prospect. Still, his jaw was firmly set. He was not backing out of this one I felt sure.

The queue was enormous. So much so that the line almost snaked outside of this 'provincial' airport. The Larnaca International Airport* had been initially built as a temporary construction, only until the rest of Cyprus would be freed, and it showed, despite the numerous tacky face lifts. The automatic doors kept opening and closing behind us, as they were being continuously triggered by people standing near the doorway. It was going to be a long wait, I informed Mr. Aris, but he was in no mood for small talk. He would just nod in reply to whatever I said. I searched with my eyes outside in the adjacent parking lot and I spotted the Magnette, patiently waiting for us to return from our voyage. I pointed it out to him and he was comforted to catch sight of it. We would be sitting back in it in less than a week.

* There is now a new airport (2009).

I asked him if he would prefer an aisle or window seat and he nodded yes, so I told the check-in lady to give him the aisle. Perhaps he would be needing to visit the toilet more often than me, I reasoned to myself.

It still amazed me. A man of such depth and he had never travelled, never been out of the tiny confines of Cyprus. Here was a worldly man with no world experience. He had done all his travelling through his books. We finally boarded the plane. I almost felt like holding his hand during take off, but I held myself back, preferring to pretend not to have noticed his mounting anxiety…

A bit over four hours later we were at Heathrow Airport.

A few Cypriot passengers started clapping when the plane landed and he joined in. I think that if he had not been strapped to his seat he would have given the pilot a standing ovation. He looked toward me, happy to be over the four hour ordeal: we had made it! I clapped too. What the heck, I thought. And anyway, it wasn't too shabby a landing was it? Show some appreciation.

I considered that taking the underground would have also made him apprehensive, but when I mentioned it that did not faze him at all. After all, he had just flown in a plane. This was nothing. We checked in at the hotel. I suggested we take a nap, or go see some sights, but he would hear none of that.

"Let's get it over with," he said.

So we went outside again, minutes after we had checked in. Of course, it was drizzling. Being from Cyprus, we did not have an umbrella handy with us. We walked on, slowly getting wet, in a 'civilised way', nothing like the way one would instantly be drenched to the bone in a rare but typical Cyprus downpour. We made our way by taxi to Barclay's Bank, Mrs. Eileen's branch, which was not too far from the city centre. We asked for the manager, a lady teller told us to wait. I looked around: cold, not welcoming. Not even a couple of chairs to sit on. The tellers were behind bullet-proof windows, condescendingly talking to customers through little holes. Where's the human touch? In a Cyprus bank, even a prospective robber might be offered a coffee. Mr. Aris did not seem to notice all this.

Ten minutes or so later, the bank manager, a young man, came to greet us. He ushered us through a door. His office was directly behind it. At least there were chairs in there. He asked us to sit down. I introduced myself and Mr. Aris, and told him that we had come all the way from Cyprus. I explained that Mr. Aris wanted to see his landlady whom he had not seen for half a century. For sentimental reasons. The young man hesitated. Not the usual day to day business he was used to. He excused himself. He came back with an older looking bank-type gentleman, a perfect replica of the younger guy in twenty years, who introduced *himself* as the bank manager. I had to reiterate our story. Mr. Aris sat next to me, I think pretending he did not understand a word.

"Why don't I ring this lady first, to see if it is all right with her to give you her address?" he decided. I said ok, no problem, he went to another place to apparently make the telephone call.

He eventually came back. "It would appear that this lady is not expecting you," he stated but then he smiled. "She was quite surprised to hear that you are presently in the UK and that you request to see her. But she said you are welcome to go visit her. Here is her address."

He gave us a bank printout. It only contained an address. We thanked him and got up to go. Before we reached the door it occurred to me to ask for directions. He took the paper back and read the address. He thought about it.

"You know, this address isn't too far away from here," he

commented. "It's probably only a five or ten minute walk, if you don't mind it. It's slightly uphill though. Alternatively you could take a bus which heads that way." He was about to give us bus directions.

"Let's just walk," said Mr. Aris, speaking out for the first time, his voice sounding rougher than usual, with a heavier accent. Perhaps I was comparing it with the bank man's refined Oxford English.

A few minutes later we were standing outside the house, a relatively large detached white three-floor building. We looked through the thick black gates, as it was partially concealed by a ten-foot high wall. The gates were almost equally high. Like Mr. Aris' house in Nicosia, this residence was also somewhat out of place in the middle of London. There was an electrical bell on the right side of the gates. Below it I noticed a fading plaque with the name 'James Hollingsworth' on it. This was perhaps the name of the original owner, or more likely, I contemplated, Mrs. Eileen's family name: her father's name. I rang the bell before Mr. Aris palpable nervousness would stop me. We heard a faint buzz somewhere inside the house. We waited. Nothing happened. Just when I was about to press the buzzer once more, the gates began to open, very slowly. I walked through the widening gap. Mr. Aris took a deep breath and he followed me into the yard. I noticed a posh older car parked in the driveway at the side of the building. Looked like a Jaguar. We walked to the front door. It too was painted glossy black, like the gates and the window sills up and down. Again, we waited. I nervously looked at my watch. As if we had somewhere else to go. A purely reflex action. I did not even notice the time. Just as I was preparing to lean over to knock on the door by using the brass doorknob, we heard the door unlock. An old lady appeared behind it. She looked like she was in her eighties. Still, despite her age, her skin appeared surprisingly smooth. She smiled at me and then, slowly looking toward Mr. Aris, she raised her hand for him to shake it.

"Welcome Aris," she said. "Last time I saw you, you were barely a man."

The greeting seemed too matter of fact. Barely a smile towards him, with little show of emotion. Mr. Aris introduced me as a good friend of his. She invited us into the house and she slowly led us into the large but cosy living room. I had enough time to look around me. Much like the large plain façade of the house, there was also nothing too fancy anywhere inside this house, but you could sense old wealth all over: the thick-framed painted portraits on the walls; the large white fireplace; the high ceilings. But above all, it was Ms. Edwards herself. Even at her age, perhaps more so because of it, she held herself with confident grace, like a queen.

Mr. Aris seemed to regress a little. He said nothing. He followed Ms. Edwards obediently and he sat, his demeanour like that of a good boy, in the old fashioned, slightly faded, soft red velvet chair she pointed out to him. She sat on a similar chair next to him. I sat across from them. She offered us tea, pointing out that unfortunately there was no 'help' around at the moment. We both declined the offer, lying that we had just had some.

Perhaps I had made a mistake bringing him here, I thought, nervously. Perhaps we should never have made this journey. Perhaps Mr. Aris had meant little to this well-off English lady.

She had brought out a photograph album for Mr. Aris and her to see. It was on the coffee table in front of them. Both their faces brightened as she turned the pages and they saw pictures that jogged their memories. I think, mainly because they saw themselves like they used to be: young, vivacious and beautiful.

She only wanted to show him pictures of Cyprus, the ones which included him, but he insisted on seeing them all. From the very start, a few going way back, with Mrs. Edwards as a little cute blonde child of no more than five or six. Once in a while he asked me to lean over and see but mainly they were slowly immersing themselves in their own world, the two of them riding a time machine on a nostalgic back-in-time trip.

"There you are!" she told him, pointing to a picture. "A dashing young man, you were."

"Look at my hair, so thick – and black," he commented, but he was more interested in her image.

"Just look at you, Mrs. Edwards-". She grabbed his hand, as swiftly as she could.

"Please, call me Eileen."

He nodded, but he did not say her name. He continued:

"-You are so beautiful. Aphrodite herself would have been envious," he dared to blurt, his voice trembling a little. He turned the album towards me.

I looked at the black and white picture. They all were black and white, of course. This particular one featured a house in the background - Mr. Aris' house- and a nice new shiny car: the Magnette. But even it had to take backstage to the person in the foreground. He had not exaggerated. Despite the relative dullness of the slightly overexposed picture- age, and the brightness of the morning Cyprus sun does that to photographs - and a blotch or two in a couple of places, you could see this dazzling young lady in a bright, breezy dress, her blond locks freely falling on her shoulders, with a happy smile on her face: Mrs. Edwards. A contrast to Cypriots whom, in pictures of those days, always faced the camera with a deadly serious stare.

"Wow. You really were extremely beautiful, Mrs. Edwards," I honestly agreed.

"Well, I'm just old now," she said good-humouredly, picking up on the fact that I had spoken in the past tense, unlike Mr. Aris.

She turned the pages. They reminisced. They smiled. The ice was breaking. Despite the years having rolled by, you could see there had been a strong bond between these two. There still was. I sat back, unobtrusively.

She closed the album.

"So, Aris, tell me about your last fifty years."

"There's nothing much to say, Mrs. Edwards. The years just flew by, you know? One day I was the young lad we saw in those pictures of yours, the next day I am an old man..."

"I know what you mean," she agreed. "But do tell me what you've been up to. I understand you are still staying at the house?"

"Yes, I am. We must raise the rent, Mrs. Ed-" She gave him a stern look.

"... Eileen." He said her name to her face, at last!

"It's a joke," he went on. "Rents in that area are now three-four times higher than what you are charging me. And I owe you money for the car, the other things you left behind..."

She did not answer immediately. She was looking away. Was she paying attention?

"Look Aris, I've been meaning to contact you for some time now," she eventually answered, speaking steadily, slowly. "I don't want to raise the rent... In fact, I don't want you to send any rent at all. I am an old lady. I really don't need the money, I promise you this. I am sorry I didn't get around to arranging it earlier, but I must tell you that I have already decided that you can keep the house. Arrange whatever papers are necessary and I will sign the house over to you. It's yours, all right? Don't send me any more money."

Of course, Mr. Aris would have none of that.

"Listen, I am never going back to Cyprus, Aris," she insisted, stubbornly and a bit bitterly. "You've lived there all your life, you own it."

The matter would remain unresolved, I could tell.

She changed the subject.

"So, did you marry? Children? Grand-children?" she asked, cheerfully.

He hesitated.

"No, Mrs. - Eileen," he replied, apologetically. "I guess I missed that bus, is all I can say... I always thought there was plenty of time for all that. Now I know that there wasn't...."

She was looking at him intently, trying to gauge his deeper emotions.

"I've had a good life," he assured her, seeing her concerned expression. "It's just that I never got round to it. I lost my sense of time a little. Like, for a couple of decades! (*we smiled*) When I was in my twenties I was too young. In my thirties I was having fun. In my forties, I was too fussy. From my fifties on, well I was too old!"

We sat silently. I reflected about what he had said. I had been around that particular block one time, and a bumpy ride it was too. But, did I want to get on 'that bus' again? If so, perhaps I should hurry a little. My sense of time wasn't all that Phileas Fogg either.

She changed the subject:

"Do you still do your 'homework'? Have you continued to

read books like you promised before I left?" She was wagging her finger at him, like a caring school teacher.

Once more he hesitated. I could not help but smile. Has he ever? If only she could see the state of her house right now. He darted me a sharp look, as if this was a dirty little secret.

"Yes, I've been reading, here and there," he replied.

To me that could be classified as a big fat lie. Here and there? Everywhere was the answer he should have given.

Silence ensued. I could see he was readying himself. Steadying the ship.

"Mrs. Edwards, Eileen, I don't know if you have figured this out... we, I, came to England just to see you."

"For the silly rent?" she asked, a bit surprised.

"No, I need to tell you something I've been meaning to for a long time-"

She cut him off: "-It's really too late for all that Aris. Don't you see?"

He was halted in his tracks. He did not know whether to plough on, or retreat. Maybe he was a bit relieved: an opportunity to let it all go. But then he looked at me, in desperation. He really was at a loss about what to do next.

It suddenly dawned on me that Mrs. Edwards had gotten the wrong signal: she thought that Mr. Aris was about to make a very belated love confession. Of course she thought it was too late! So I suggested, firmly,

"Tell her anyway, Mr. Aris. Do you want me to leave the room?"

He did not.

He told her the whole story in one uninterrupted take. His voice was rock steady this time. Only the tears streaming down his face betrayed his emotions. He did not bother to wipe them or conceal them. He looked straight at her, their eyes locked. He only looked down once, when he told her about when he held Mr. Edwards' dead body in his arms. She just listened. She did not butt in, not even once. Like him she wept, quietly, but in an odd unblinking way. Perhaps time makes all kind of events appear more trivial and inconsequential, including the loss of life of a loved one. Perhaps time does heal everything. When he finished his narration she continued to look at him, straight in his eyes. But those eyes told nothing. The silence in the room was deafening. I waited -hoped- for her to speak...

"Why are you telling me all this?" she asked finally.

He hesitated.

"I- I'm not sure, Mrs. Edwards," he stuttered. He wanted to tell her, it wasn't my fault, but he did not.

"You're asking for absolution or something? Aris I'm not a priest or a god. What happened back then, well it happened. Nobody can undo what was done."

The words were cold, but not her tone.

He had nothing to say. Clearly, he agreed.

"Aris, I knew all along," she continued slowly.

His eyes opened wide.

She went on: "I knew it the minute I laid eyes on you, the day after. Maybe you didn't say anything, but everything else in your manner was obvious. The minute I saw you, you looked a ghost of the man I knew. I was aware, even then, that the death of a cherished one can cause immense harm to a person, but a guilty conscience and loss of self-respect can do worse. Much bigger damage, enough to break a person in two. That was you, at that moment when I saw you. You would not hold me, console me. You would not even look at me... then and there, straight away, I knew you had something to do with it. I didn't know why what and how, but I knew."

He just stared at her. He himself had been like his favourite past time all along: an open book. To the one person who mattered, there had been no secret all these years.

"But… why did you not tell me something? Why then did you not notify the authorities?" he wondered out loud.

"Because I knew in my heart that you could not intentionally harm a single living thing, not even an ant. I knew you were a good man, Aris. And by giving you to them, by handing you over, I would have lost both the men I loved in one go. I couldn't do that."

At that moment the big door flew open. One, two, three, four little children rushed in along with a gush of cool fresh air.

"Hello Grandma!"

They went to her, oblivious of the guests. They hugged her, all at once, like playful kittens. She warmly returned their embrace, glad to see them. Behind the children came in through the same door a smiling young woman. Beautiful beyond description: Eileen, like she was in the album's photographs.

When the minor commotion was over we introduced one another. Mrs. Edwards introduced Mr. Aris as a very dear friend from a hundred years ago. The young lady was, of course, Mrs. Edwards' daughter. Her children, four girls who looked like dolls, all with wavy blonde hair, were only five, four and three years old. Apparently the two youngest ones were twins, although they all looked remarkably alike, especially since they were wearing similar little dresses. All four of them had flower names.

We stayed a while, talking pleasantly about the weather and other trivialities. When we got up to leave the ladies suggested we stay for tea, but we politely declined. At the door, Eileen hugged Aris warmly. She looked into his eyes.

"Don't forget to arrange the documents for the house. And take care of yourself," she told him.

"I just wish-"

She placed her fingers on his mouth, gently silencing him.

"You are a good man, Aris... Goodbye now."

Now I think we both knew who had been at the door in Mr Aris' dreams. Perhaps it was Mrs. Edwards, Eileen. Anyway, maybe all that would be over now.

In retrospect, we could have done much worse. I was not sure how to comment about the meeting and Mr. Aris was not giving anything away. He was lost in his own thoughts. I felt the need to fill the gap. With the 'business' end taken care of we had a couple of days remaining before heading back home. I suggested we do the tourism thing.

"Ok, let us go see this empire," he replied, not uninterested. So we took in the usual sights. He enjoyed them and he was even happier to see the cultural venues: the National Gallery, the British Museum, the Natural History Museum.

He found, to his delight, that if he looked hard enough he could find a touch of Cyprus in nooks and crannies in all of London. For one, he heard people, here and there, talking in Greek, in the characteristic Cypriot dialect. In fact, these emigrants, he was delighted to note, spoke older Cypriot than their countrymen who had actually remained in Cyprus. While the language had progressed, refined itself, there in London it had stayed undiluted. Anything he spotted which related to Cyprus made him supremely proud, even if the item got there through dubious means. He would look around him like he wanted to tell tourists next to him:

"Look, ladies and gentlemen, this is '*The Birth of Venus*', 1632, by Peter Paul Rubens, the German Baroque-style painter. You know Venus? Aphrodite? Here she is, stepping off her shell and on to Cyprus. You know Cyprus? You do? I'm from Cyprus!"

The Natural History Museum featured the skull of a Pygmy Hippo in the Dinosaurs and Extinct species collection. From what we read it became a dwarf through insular dwarfism, a limited gene pool. Laymen call it in-breeding.

"That happened to some of my relatives," joked Mr. Aris.

We 'uncovered' lots of 'Cypriot' fish (*as if they have passports*) in the fish specimen collection, a bunch of Cypriot insects and we were both especially excited to see a map of Cyprus and the stuff he told me about – ophiolite –, at the Departments of Palaeontology and Mineralogy.

When we went back to the hotel we were both exhausted.

On the way back to Cyprus he behaved like a frequent flyer. He looked out the window. He walked up and down the aisles. He chatted with the stewardesses. Before we knew it we were flying over Cyprus. I pointed it out to him.

"Are you sure this is Cyprus?" he exclaimed rather incredulously. "It looks like a desert!"

It does, from above. But we know better. Up close, it is an oasis. It is home.

The trek

'To explore strange new worlds.
To seek out new life and new civilisations.
To boldly go where no man has gone before.
(Theme from Star Trek)

Lately, I have been thinking a lot about Mr. Aris.

I have come to the conclusion that Mr. Aris was a historian in the genuine sense. He searched into the past and he picked up little rough gems and brought them to life. He also spotted mistakes we humans have made and worried whether we would make them again.

A few years later, after Mr. Aris had passed away, it came to me, appropriately, while I was driving '*The Vehicle*', the catalyst that had originally brought us together, the trusty Magnette. With that eternal symbol on its bonnet.

It came to me suddenly. What this entire journey in an antique car had been about. Why Mr. Aris had told me all he knew, why he had related his experiences and shared his deepest thoughts. He had given me hints all along: his fury at the destruction of the great Alexandria library; his sorrow at the way humanity destroyed or collectively forgot about little things like traditional games in its quest to relentlessly move on. How he had it against God for bringing upon us destruction again and again and making us start all over from scratch.

It was about immortality. Not of the soul, he was too much of a pragmatist for such metaphysical illusions. Not even of the gene pool. After all, he had no kids of his own.

There was something a lot more important than those: wisdom. The collective wisdom of mankind. Yes, it could survive through his beloved books, but that was its dormant state. In order for knowledge and information to be truly alive, it must travel through people's minds, it has to dance around in their heads and in the ensuing shuffle to produce new ideas.

The vessel for this voyage, the car that drives us, is our collective mind. It can take us beyond even our wildest dreams. '*To boldly go where no man has gone before*' as the movie says.

I related all this to Maria. She said maybe Mr. Aris just wanted a friend.

I do not want to dwell on the latter years in case that impression of Mr. Aris lingers longer in your mind. So I will be brief:

A year or so after we came back from England, Mr. Aris' health suddenly and rapidly deteriorated. His sight grew dimmer, his mind even more. He was, of course, way passed reading. He became quite forgetful. He would repeat the same stories again and again. He would set off on long walks and lose his way back home. Once, hours later, I found him sitting in the dark on a sandbag at the barricaded 'Spitfire' coffee shop. Another time I got a phone call from someone at the now defunct ex-British Council library. Thankfully, I had placed a piece of paper with my phone number in his pocket. He had had the sense to show it to them.

Towards the end he would forget my name. He once called me 'Pygmalion'. On another occasion, Mr. Edwards. Maria he often called Mrs. Eileen.

He passed away, fittingly, in the Magnette. I was taking him for a ride, something he still enjoyed. I thought he had been taking a nap. I cried as I drove to the hospital.

I have kept the MG for myself. What happened to all his books? They are still there where he left them at his house. I had the entire house fixed up although it still looks quite out of place in that neighbourhood. His home is now a public library. If you would like to visit, look up '*Aristotelia Bibliotheke*' in Nicosia. The 'Cyprus Books' section is quite popular. If you are ever there, make yourself a free cup of coffee* and have a seat on the sunny front porch with a good book.

* 'though donations are welcome!'

Maria and I got married a couple of years ago. We have a child now, a son. His name? Well, it is Aris. I like to think that he will turn out to be a little like the god of war, more like the philosopher. But I would love it if he turned out to be much like Mr. Aris.

the end

Author's Note

Mr. Aris is not an alias. It is the man's real name. I hope he would not mind me using it, I saw no reason to change it now that he is gone. I hope that if he could have read this he would have been able to see my deepest respect towards him. Also, that he was a very special person who had paid for one incident for the rest of his life. He had served his time, many times over, I believe. I wish Mr. Aris himself could read this story. He loved books so much and in this one alone he is the star. But, of course, I could only publish this after his passing away lest I inadvertently got him into trouble with the law.

Winter mountain landscape from Troodos mountains in Cyprus

An Alternative Cyprus Itinerary

Day 1: Nicosia

Make your way around the capital city's Venetian Wall

This medieval wall was designed by Venetian military engineer Julio Savorgnano and built in 1570. It encircles the older part of Nicosia and has a circumference of about three miles. The Venetians boasted that the wall could endure a two year siege but it lasted less than two months of onslaught by the Ottomans in the same year it was completed. Over twenty thousand people were subsequently killed. Thus came Venetian rule to an end. In order to circumvent the walls you will need to cross over to the Turkish occupied territory (see Day 6).

Day 2: Take to the Nicosia-Limassol highway

The first modern dual carriageway of Cyprus, linking the country's two largest cities. It was completed in 1984 at a cost of fifteen million Cyprus pounds. Speed-limit 100km/h.

A road trip of approximately an hour or so to get from the capital to the coastal city, it took about three days for Mr. Aris to cover the distance in 1956 (but not on the highway and not in a car!)

Day 3: The Troodos Mountains

The Troodos mountain range is known worldwide for its amazing geology and the presence of intact specimens of ophiolite, a rock formed from the earth's magma. Troodos rose from the sea due to the impact of the European and African tectonic plates, resulting in the formation of the island of Cyprus. Its highest peak is Mount Olympus at almost 2000 metres.

Hala Sultan Tekke at Larnaca - Cyprus

Paphos Castle at Paphos Harbour

Day 4: Larnaca

Known as Citium in biblical times, the city was founded by the Phoenicians. Famous citizens include philosopher Zenon (founder of the Stoics: if you want to lead a simple life and be content, you may be a Stoic!) and Lazarus who famously rose from the dead when Jesus commanded him to come out of his grave. Lazarus stayed (permanently) in his final grave, in Larnaca. It is under the altar of a beautiful, well-preserved church. It bore the legend 'Lazarus, friend of Jesus'. It is worth attending Cataclysm-associated festivities in spring and viewing flamingos on the city's sparkling salt lake. Famed Hala Sultan Tekke is on that lake's shores.

Day 5: Paphos

On your way to Paphos, make sure you stop for a rest at 'Hassanpulia' rock, a hideout for the notorious turn-of-the-century bandits. Another rock worth visiting on the way is 'Petra tu Romiou', the supposed exact place where Aphrodite, the beautiful Goddess of Love, rose from the sea. Once in the city, visit Paphos castle, built by the Byzantines and successively 'renovated' by the Franks, the Venetians, the Ottomans and the current municipality. The ancient mosaics, nearby, are a must-see. Paphos has been declared a world heritage site by UNESCO.

Day 6: Occupied territory

You will need to show a passport and buy separate car insurance in order to cross over to the Turkish-occupied territory of Cyprus, at the island's north. The so-called 'green line' separates the country's capital city into two halves, thus rendering Nicosia the last divided city in Europe. Both Lapithos and Sihari, Mr.Aris parents' birthplaces, are minutes away from Nicosia. Unfortunately, these ancient names have been changed by the occupying forces.

Day 1: Engomi

This ancient settlement used to be known as Alasia. As such, it was the capital of Cyprus for half a millennium (1600-1050 BC). Although there's not much to see there today due to a series of earthquakes and other disasters, archaeologists have periodically dug up interesting artefacts, including a 3000 plus year old backgammon board. This is what Mr. Aris had in mind.

Day 1: Salamis

Teucer, son of the king of Salamis in Greece, founded this city of the same name in Cyprus upon his victorious return from the Trojan War. It too became the capital of Cyprus following the literal collapse of Engomi. Although it was also destroyed by a great earthquake in 76 AD, it was reconstructed by the Romans. Salamis still features a 140 seat amphitheatre of eighteen rows (it originally had fifty rows). The gymnasium and its steam bath are still discernable. Its latrines could accommodate forty four people! Some references to human sacrifice in Salamis have been found, apparently to honour Zeus 'Splachnotomos' (literally, entrails-cutter!)

Day 2: Lapithos

According to historian Strabo, Lapithos was founded by the Spartans after the Trojan War, although there is evidence that this settlement may be even older. Because the king of this city aided Alexander the Great in defeating the Phoenicians at Tyre, the island was declared free from the Persians. Mr. Aris' ancestry, from his mother's side, may be Spartan!

Day 2: Sihari

Mr. Aris spent his early years at this village on the slopes of the Kyrenia mountain range (known as Pantadaktylos). Its name is probably derived from Sihar (Palestine) from which the first settlers came. The village used to be one of the capital city's main water sources.

Day 3: Ayia Napa

The name derivation, as Mr. Aris explains it, is controversial. The town was walled at one time and evidence of an ancient aqueduct can still be seen. However, it is hard to look for historical evidence at this modern day hotel and club infested party town!

Day 3: Atlantis (Cyprus)

Robert Sarmast's 2003 book 'Discovery of Atlantis' (Origin Press) placed the legendary city on the coast of Cyprus. According to the author, Plato's description of the 'mythical' city is basically a depiction of Cyprus. Unfortunately, the theory has fizzled out in the last few years, as have all previous attempts to locate this elusive great kingdom. So if you head out off the Larnaca coast don't expect to see much. But do use your imagination!

Day 4: Shillourokambos

On the way to Limassol, this ancient settlement has clear evidence of cat domestication: two adjacent graves of a man and his cat.

Day 4: St. Paul's Pillar

In front of Agia Kyriaki Church, in Kato Paphos, is the place where it all began. Where Christianity had its first overseas success and where St. Paul was lashed 39 times before he could convince the locals to abandon their beloved and beautiful Aphrodite for Jesus.

ARMIDA PUBLICATIONS LTD
(member of the Association of Cypriot Book Publishers - SEKYVI)
(member of Independent Publishers Guild - UK)
office | 36a valesta str, 2370 ayios dhometios, nicosia, cyprus
mailing address | p.o.box 27717, 2432 engomi, nicosia, cyprus
tel: +357 22 35 80 28 | fax: +357 22 35 11 16
email: info@armidapublications.com
www.armidapublications.com